Flurries
A Zapstone New Voices Holiday Collection

Ryl Regehr

More Zapstone Books

Mystery
Cathy Wiley
Dead to Writes (Cassandra Ellis Mysteries 1)
Two Wrongs Don't Make a Right (Cassandra Ellis Mysteries 2)
Write of Passage (Cassandra Ellis Mysteries 3)

Science Fiction/Action
T. M. Roy
Convergence – Journey to Nyorfias, Book 1 (available now)
Gravity – Journey to Nyorfias, Book 2 (Coming Soon!)
Stratagem – Journey to Nyorfias, Book 3 (TBA)

~~~~

T.M. Roy and Sara V. Olds
Casualties of Treachery – The Ukasir's Own, Unit One
(check website for details)

~~~~

Sff-Romance
T.M. Roy
Discovery – A Far Out Romance (available now)

~~~~

Children
Sara V. Olds
Anna – A Farewell to Juarez (available now)

~~~~

Check our website for the most current news on available and upcoming books.

A Zapstone New Voices Holiday Collection

Flurries

Five tales of holiday romance and romantic suspense

Claire Taylor Allen
Mary Compton
Lelani Dixon
Ryl Regehr
Ronda Russell

Edited by
Cathy Wiley

Dare to be Entertained.

Zapstone productions LLC

Unique voices in fiction.

FLURRIES

A Zapstone Production
Printing History : Trade Paperback/November 2010

ISBN 13 978-0-9826419-2-7
ISBN 10 0-98264192-3
Library of Congress Catalog Number (LCCN): 2010941242

First Trade Paperback Edition
Published by Zapstone Productions LLC

Contents

Foreword

I am proud to present Zapstone Productions LLC's first "New Voices" Anthology. As a recently published author, I remember the thrill and joy of seeing my book in print. This is one reason Zapstone chose to create a venue for unpublished authors with our New Voices program.

It's also a great opportunity for you to read these promising new authors with their debut stories.

These stories feature characters at different stages in their lives and loves: from college students turning a childhood friendship into something more serious; to strangers meeting by chance in a busy airport; to a married couple experiencing being away from the rest of their family during the holidays. They may be set in various locations, from Winnipeg, Manitoba, in Canada to Nags Head, North Carolina in the United States, but they are united by common themes. There are strong female characters, powerful emotions, intriguing plots, and, of course, the holidays.

This time of year is always a time to dream and to make wishes. What better way than to curl by the fire and spend time with these five authors?

I know it will be a pleasure for readers to enjoy their creativity, hard work, and effort.

Cathy Wiley
Editor

MARY COMPTON

Once Upon a Flight Delay

Melanie hated Chicago.

Well, not the city of Chicago, with its gorgeous skyline and sense of something always just about to happen. She just hated the airport, especially now. She was stuck with a gazillion other harried would-be passengers, all of them waiting for a break in the weather. It was the day before Thanksgiving, and the light morning snow had turned heavy unexpectedly.

All around her, she heard the sound of people complaining, of fretful babies, of the general chaos that can only be a major metropolitan airport during the holiday season. She longed for the quiet of her condo in Bethesda, Maryland.

O'Hare Airport, always busy at any time of the year, was positively groaning. To kill time—and avoid the urge to kill any of her fellow travelers—she found herself playing her old favorite game and made up stories about the people around her. It wasn't hard for her to imagine that the scowling young woman to her right who was clutching a briefcase to her chest was actually carrying secret documents back from a recent clandestine meeting with a fellow spy. And that the information secreted away in her briefcase

9

needed to be in her superior's hands, making the flight delay a matter of life or death.

Or that the emo-looking young man nearby who was muttering into his cellphone while constantly pushing the hair out of his eyes was actually begging his girlfriend to give him just one more chance. That he hadn't meant to burn down her house, it was just an accident.

Whereas the airline personnel didn't have any hidden agendas. They all had the same tight-smile expression that clearly said, "I can't wait for this freakin' day to be over with" as they dealt with harried people all demanding what was going to happen if they weren't able to make their flight.

Melanie wondered how many of them wanted to reply, "Unless you think I have magical powers and can stop the snow from falling, why don't you get out of my freakin' face?"

Her cell phone chimed, indicating an incoming text message, and she groaned when she saw yet another gate change for her flight.

She'd already been at two other gates.

"What, do they think that if they keep changing our gates we won't notice that the time goes by without us ever getting on a plane?" she wondered to herself.

Every year when she flew back to California for Thanksgiving, she asked herself the same thing—*why am I putting myself through the agony of holiday travel?*

The answer was always the same: her family would be crushed if she didn't join them on turkey day. Ergo, she joined them.

Her family had already been disappointed when, rather than attend college in her home state of California, she'd elected to travel across the country to attend George Washington University in Washington, D.C. to pursue a degree in special events planning. As somebody who loved to plan and organize, when she discovered she could actually make a living doing so, she'd been over the moon.

She'd thrived in the program and graduated at the top of her class. Her friends loved to tell her that by being so anal, she had an unfair advantage over everybody else.

Could she help it if her love of planning extended to all areas of her life...even her love life?

A good plan, she had long ago decided, was all anybody needed to have a life worth living. Her meetings and parties were always huge successes because she took the time to make contingency plans. She wholeheartedly approved of the Boy Scouts' motto, *"Be prepared."*

It was her motto as well. For everything. But O'Hare Airport refused to follow her rules.

Her family had been even more dismayed when she discovered how much she loved the D.C. area and never left.

It had taken all of them, Melanie included, time to adjust to the separation. So when it came to the big holidays, she made every effort to fly home to be with them.

After all, she loved her family and had no desire to disappoint them, so every year she found herself buying airfare at such a jacked-up rate that she couldn't help thinking about the trip she probably could have taken for the same amount.

Never mind the fact that within moments of her arrival, she would probably be asked the dreaded question, "So, are you seeing anybody?"

Or her own personal favorite, "When are you going to get married again?"

As if once wasn't enough.

She knew her family loved her, and that they were genuinely concerned about her, but the question grated at best, and stung at worst.

She had observed there was something about a single woman in her early thirties that had some people wondering what was wrong with her. Take her family, for instance. She knew that they were proud of the independent woman she was, and yet she still got the drill every time she went home.

She knew she was lucky to have a family to go home to, but sometimes, she couldn't help wondering when her family would realize she was an adult and capable of taking care of herself. Even without a husband.

Her mother had already called twice, wanting to know when she'd be landing.

By the looks of things, it wasn't going to be any time soon.

She'd just arrived outside of her new gate area, puffing slightly from the weight of her carry-on, when she saw the departure time change yet again on the information board at the counter. The flight was pushed back another two hours, and she wanted to scream.

"Ugh, sometimes it takes all the running in the world just to stay in one place," she muttered out loud, then blew a stream of air up into her bangs.

"And any minute now, the March Hare is going to appear, late, of course," a voice behind her said.

Startled, she turned to find a man talking to her, a smile quirking the corner of his mouth. He was dressed in a charcoal gray suit with a pale blue silk tie and a white shirt, and it was such a contrast to the people around her in their jeans and sweaters that she couldn't stop herself from staring.

"I must say, you don't look anything like Alice," the man continued, and Melanie detected the faint British accent in his voice.

With her shoulder-length black hair and dark brown eyes, she supposed that was true enough. She felt the hated blush begin to heat her cheeks. "Are you an English professor?" she asked, simultaneously thinking that he didn't look like any English teacher she had ever seen and also cringing at how lame her question sounded. But even with the somewhat recent movie, she couldn't imagine some guy recognizing quotes from *Alice in Wonderland* like this man had done. She wondered if he, too, thought the movie was unnecessarily over-the-top and that Johnny Depp made the creepiest Mad Hatter ever.

"International foods, actually," he corrected. "You?"

"Me?" she replied. Oh, brilliant. That 1480 she'd scored on her SAT, back in the day, was certainly coming in handy now. She thought she detected a crisp whiff of his cologne and wondered if that was what was making her a little dizzy.

"Are you a teacher of the literary arts?"

"Uh…no. I just like to read." With dazzling conversation skills like this, how was it, she wondered, that she wasn't an inspirational speaker? It was certainly a puzzle for the ages. She wondered if Mr. International Foods could stand such brilliance.

But Mr. International Foods hung in there. "Bit of a madhouse, yes? I can usually avoid traveling at this time of the year since I don't celebrate Thanksgiving myself, but not this time, alas."

Every seat in the adjoining gates' waiting area was full, with several people sitting on the floor, laptops in front of them. A baby was shrieking so loudly that Melanie figured every dog in a fifty-mile radius of the airport had to be howling.

"It sure is," she agreed. "It's amazing what some people will go through just to eat some turkey, stuffing, and pumpkin pie."

"And something called green bean casserole, yes?"

She made a face as she gave her opinion of the dish that her mother always insisted on including in the family Thanksgiving dinner. She stood with him outside of two adjoining gate areas, and as their conversation continued, she found herself doing something she didn't think was possible under the circumstances. She started to enjoy herself.

She was more than a little attracted by the man's obvious intelligence, and she was shallow enough to admit to herself that the fact that he was cute as hell didn't hurt either.

He was tall, something that Melanie appreciated. His hair, a light chestnut brown, curled appealingly over his eyes, which were an unusually intense shade of green.

She realized she was staring and forced her gaze downward, where they landed on his sleek carry-on bag. His luggage tag faced upwards, and she noted a Chicago address written in a very precise hand. Too bad.

He smiled, and she thought, damn. There's nothing quite like being caught snooping.

"Look, my flight has been pushed back for another few hours. Would you like to have a coffee? Perhaps we can continue this conversation whilst we wait someplace a little more comfortable."

Against her will, she found herself charmed by the wording of the request, which sounded very British to her. "Sure, why not?" she surprised herself by saying.

14

Uh oh. What was she doing? Hadn't she recently decided to focus almost exclusively on her career? At least, that was her plan.

But what did it matter? He lived in Chicago, she lived in Maryland. It wasn't like even a few dates were very likely. She was surprised by the sudden pang she felt, but chalked it up to being tired. It had been a long day, and it wasn't ending anytime soon. She could use a diversion.

"Let's do it," she said. "There's bound to be a Starbucks here. There's probably one on Pluto, even though it isn't even a planet anymore."

He smiled at her joke and held out a hand. "I'm Graham Harrison."

"Melanie Cadman." They shook hands.

By some miracle, she found them a table just as another couple was leaving. She let her mind wander while Graham stood in line for their drinks.

Lately, she'd found herself questioning her beloved planning. For while a detailed plan was necessary when planning somebody's wedding, for example, it wouldn't do much good with regards to the actual marriage. There were simply too many variables.

She, of all people, knew that.

An unwelcome image of her ex-husband Ryan flitted through her consciousness, and she rubbed her eyes as if trying to rub away the image of the man she'd thought she would spend the rest of her life with.

Variables. They could be a real bitch sometimes, no doubt about it.

But on the other hand, what would happen to her if she simply abandoned all of her plans and let the chips fall where they may?

The thought was simultaneously exhilarating and frightening.

Her reverie was broken by Graham's return with their drinks.

"It's like its own little world in here, isn't it?" he said, placing a frothy cappuccino in front of her.

"In the Starbucks?" She firmly put her ex-husband out of her mind and turned her attention to the man sitting in front of her.

"The airport in general," he replied, setting a large coffee down and sitting across from her. "You get the whole spectrum. So many people and every single one of them has his own complicated life."

She found herself wondering if he was talking about his own life and snuck a glance at the ring finger on his left hand. Bare. But that didn't always mean anything. She gave a mental shake. Now why the hell did she care whether or not he was available?

Still, she wanted to have fun. But would he play? She tilted her head towards a stocky man standing a few feet away from them. His hair was stone gray except for two streaks of white at the sides, and he wore a shiny track suit. He pulled out his cell phone and frowned at it.

"I bet he's supposed to pick up a fellow wiseguy for a very special job, but the flight's been diverted," she said in a low tone before taking a sip of her drink.

He smiled, and it lit up the gold flecks in his eyes. "It all fits—he must have pull to be in the gated area."

"Or maybe he's trying to get to New York, but they keep changing his gate and delaying his flight. If he doesn't get there in time, there's going to be a hit on the wrong guy."

"Maybe his name is Paulo Peanuts."

At that, she started laughing so hard she almost choked on her coffee.

The Starbucks was situated at the intersection of two busy walkways, and the time flew as they invented lives for the people walking by. It was different and fun, and a far cry from the kind of dates she usually found herself on. It seemed like those dates either ended up with someone who wouldn't shut up about themselves, or someone so shy they wouldn't say a word and she'd have to hold the conversation by herself. She often ended up fantasizing about escaping out of a bathroom window.

But it wasn't just the entertainment factor. Melanie couldn't remember a time she had felt so instantly comfortable with someone. It stirred up longings inside of her that she thought had simply switched off inside of her long ago.

"What would somebody come up with for the two of us, I wonder?" she wondered aloud.

He regarded her for a long moment. "I wonder," he said, staring straight into her eyes. It seemed as if he wasn't just looking at her, but *learning* her and she felt her face grow warm.

Danger, Will Robinson!

"I should get back to my gate," she stammered, glancing at her cell phone in order to break the contact. Suddenly, the phone beeped. "Oh, no," she murmured.

"Problem?" he inquired, with an expression of concern that made her heart give a sudden flutter. She wondered if he could tell that he was having an effect on her, and found she was hoping equally that he could and that he couldn't.

Damn it, her ex-husband had initially charmed her, too. But then again, her ex would never invent a story in which a complete stranger in an airport was actually a member of the Sopranos, either. It would never occur to him.

Clearly, Graham was a different kind of charming. A much more fun one.

Just what was going on with her? It had to be the weather. And the holiday. Traveling at Thanksgiving—she had to be nuts to put herself through this every year.

"It's probably another gate change. Or flight delay. Or both," she explained. "I'm afraid to look." She opened the phone and shook her head as she read the newest text message. "Oh, boy. Another two-hour delay."

But the thing of it was, she didn't really care anymore. Not if it meant more time talking to this man who had appeared out of nowhere.

"I'm sorry. Where are you off to, if you don't mind me asking?" he asked. He wiped a fleck of foam off of his upper lip with his napkin.

"Home," she replied simply. "San Jose."

"Is everything okay?" she asked when he nodded and looked away for a moment.

Graham's cell phone suddenly buzzed.

"Ruh Roh," she said, giving him a look of sympathy.

He flipped open his phone and gave a shrug. "Three hours for me."

"Damn snow." But Melanie was thrilled; she could actually feel her stomach fill up with butterflies, just like back in the seventh grade when Mark Stofer smiled at her once in Algebra class.

Graham appeared lost in thought for a moment. "Yes, I suppose it is," he said. He loosened his tie and then spoke. "You're delayed, I'm delayed…how about we have dinner?"

She gave herself an internal shake. It was simply ridiculous how her heart was going like a jackrabbit's. After today, she would never see this man again. But hey, she may not have any options with Graham—not that she really wanted any, she sternly reminded herself—but didn't she have this moment? And was there anything wrong with enjoying this moment for all it was worth? She'd soak it up like honeyed sunshine.

She smiled at the handsome man across from her. "Aw, our first date. I accept."

A slow smile spread across Graham's face. "I guess there's nothing like cutting to the chase, is there?" He plucked a rather sorry-looking plastic flower from the vase on their table that had no doubt been added to provide some atmosphere. "In honor of our first date, I present thee with a flower." He rose and held out his hand.

She accepted his gesture and placed her hand in his, letting him help her rise gracefully from the small café table. As they strolled to a nearby eatery, she couldn't help mentally checking off *"first date"*, *"holding hands"*, and even *"flowers"*.

Stop that! she chided herself.

"Stop what?" Graham asked.

They reached the restaurant, where in true airport fashion, the decor reached for classy, but slipped and landed firmly in the land of tacky thanks to the paper tablecloths and plastic plants. She longed to dust off the plants. They found a table, and she decided the hell with it and told him the truth.

"I was checking stuff off from a mental relationship list. It's silly. Don't mind me."

He picked up a menu and nodded. "I see. And it's not so silly. I do that kind of thing all the time. I have certain criteria, and when I meet a woman, I can't seem to stop myself from measuring her against it."

She raised her eyebrows. "Criteria, huh? Like what?" She waited for his sure to be superficial answers. He'd probably say, *"great body, blond, makes other people envious."*

"Oh, you know. Important stuff, like does she like Nirvana? Does she order a side salad as if she doesn't have any kind of appetite at all? That kind of thing."

Graham's reply made her smile and she found herself wishing that Scotty could really beam people wherever they wanted to go in a heartbeat, making physical distances between people meaningless.

The universe could really be a tricky bastard at times.

"Good stuff, that," she finally said. Damn it.

The waitress approached them for their order. "I'll have a double cheeseburger with bacon, fries, and a chocolate shake," Melanie ordered. She gave Graham what she hoped was a saucy smirk.

He laughed aloud. "I'll have the same," he told the waitress.

"You do realize that Nirvana was an American band," she said after their waitress had left their table. "You're not faking that British accent of yours, wot wot?"

"Wot? Hey. Just because I was born in England doesn't mean I can't appreciate a little grunge. I like a flannel shirt and torn jeans just as much as the next man."

And she bet he'd look amazing in them, too. The snow fell in fat flakes outside of the window, and she felt as if she and Graham existed in a bubble created just for them. Maybe it was hormones.

"What brought you here?" she almost whispered.

He looked as if he understood she meant more broadly, and not in the literal sense, in this airport, in this restaurant, with her. He cleared his throat. "Ah, my parents were killed, you see, whilst I was still a boy. I had, have, an aunt here in Chicago who took me in. I've been in the States every since."

"I'm so sorry."

"Well, hardly a day doesn't go by when I don't think of them, but my aunt made a good life for me here."

"She must have. You're still here."

He nodded. "Yes, I suppose you're right. Although I make frequent trips back to England for my business."

"Is that where you are headed now?"

"No, not this trip. I'm visiting a few stores in the Seattle area. I was supposed to be meeting with a distributor this afternoon, but I'm afraid that's out." He gave her a long look. "I can't say I'm terribly disappointed."

There was a moment of awkward silence then he continued, "My friends are always setting me up on these awful blind dates."

She laughed. "Mine, too. They're married, and it's inconceivable to them that anybody could want anything else."

He grimaced. "That must be it. At any rate, thank you. Because this is the most fun I've had in ages on a date. But perhaps it's because I know that, eventually, you'll get on your plane, and I'll get on mine. And that will be that."

She nodded. "That will be that." It was true. She knew, and obviously, so did he. So why did she suddenly feel like arguing her case and getting him to change his mind?

He took a long sip of water. "You know, I travel quite a bit for work. Maybe, we…"

Her heart fluttered for a moment, and then sank as she thought about her Ryan. About six months after their wedding, he'd been sent to Iraq. While she had remained lonely at home, he had apparently decided that marriage vows were null and void when one of the parties was in a foreign country.

When she'd found out about his cheating and filed for divorce, she added *"no long distance relationships"* to her checklist. They were difficult and lonely at best, and devastating at worst. She thought about changing her mind on that subject and felt the panic fill her.

"I don't think so. To be honest, I've tried the long distance thing before," she finally said.

He nodded. "I have as well," he admitted.

"Didn't work for you either, huh?"

He didn't need to reply. His glum expression told her everything she needed to know.

She had to put the longing that had sprung up in her away. That was all. She read the message from the universe loud and clear: *this one is not for you.*

Begging the question, why did she care? Wasn't she done with all of this? Hadn't she decided to do just the opposite in her updated plan for her life?

She suddenly felt just as trapped as she had years ago when she'd first found out about Ryan and realized that she didn't really know the man she had sworn to spend eternity with.

Somehow, she had unknowingly boxed herself in again, but this time, instead of living outside of the box, she had just made a different box, mistaking it for freedom.

But it all boiled down to the same thing—she was following a plan and not her heart.

"It stinks, doesn't it?"

His voice brought her back to the present and she found that she didn't care that her eyes were filling up with tears. She picked up her napkin and unashamedly wiped them away. "It does. It really does."

"The whole boy-girl thing has always been a bit tricky for me. I've always felt a bit of an outsider, you see," he said.

"But you're so smart, cute, and funny!" she exclaimed, grinning a bit when an unmistakable blush swept across his cheeks. "Aw, look at you. You're blushing."

He smiled. "Yet another one of my curses. But, thank you. It wasn't easy being the new kid, let alone the new British kid. It also didn't help that I was so skinny the wind could have easily blown me away, and I had a rather unfortunate case of spots when I was a teenager. I wasn't filled with the confidence and charm you see before you now."

"It's hard to imagine, actually."

He tilted his head in wordless thanks. "And later, it took all of my time to get my business off of the ground. It was hard to find the time to do much more than casually date once in awhile. It always seemed like it came so easily for the people I knew. Like my friend Ted, for example. He met his wife by literally bumping into her at a club, causing her to spill her drink all over the place. They were pretty much inseparable after that night, and they got married a year later."

The waitress appeared at their table at that moment, and set down their food. "Anything else I can get you?"

"No, this looks just fine," he replied.

"From England, huh?" she asked, giving Graham a smile that had Melanie wanting to punch her.

"No, Alabama," he replied.

Melanie choked back a snort as the waitress gave him a puzzled look. "Oh. Well. Let me know if you need anything." She left.

"It's the drawl. It's unmistakable," he said, his voice sounding impeccably British. He made a show of tucking his napkin into his shirt front before picking up his fork. She knew he was trying for redneck, but somehow, on him, it looked elegant.

"It shore is." She picked up a fry and popped it into her mouth, wishing she never had to get on the plane at all, but could just fly off into the sunset with Graham, just like in the ending of some incredibly corny movie. She knew it was stupid, but it was true.

"Ted wants to save me, I think." He gave a rueful smile. "He thinks I'm too picky. But really, I don't think spending the evening with a woman who spends the entire time telling you why every single thing on the menu is bad for her diet is an improvement over staying at home and reading a good book."

"I don't think you can be picky enough," she said

"You're very beautiful," he said abruptly, surprising her. "Ah, excellent. You're a blusher as well."

She stuck out her tongue. "I am. And thank you."

"But right now, I don't want to be at home reading a book. I don't even feel like getting on my plane, if you want to know the truth."

"Me either," Melanie admitted.

"I wish I could see you again. I know it probably isn't practical. I don't know how, or where, or when, but I do." Graham leaned forward and laid his hand over hers.

She felt a warmth go down to her very toes and suddenly knew that she had been right that she needed to stop thinking about her life in terms of plans, or anti-plans. It was if doors that had been locked inside of her suddenly flew open, and even though she knew it was likely that she wouldn't see him after today, she would always be grateful to him for showing her that shutting out possibility was no way to live.

To her complete surprise, he stood up, walked around the table and bent down, brushing a soft kiss onto her mouth before she had a chance to think what she was about. "There. Got our first kiss out of the way." He sat back down and didn't seem affected by the grins coming their way from the next table.

"You're a real charmer, aren't you?" she murmured.

"Not really. Just tired of letting life pass me by without me making an effort. My Aunt Charlie is always telling me that this isn't a dress rehearsal, this is life, and you don't get another one, so, make it count."

"Seems like I've heard that one before."

"Yes, but did you believe it?"

She was suddenly annoyed. "I like my life, you know. I'm not miserable."

"I didn't say you were, but I'm getting the feeling that you don't even want to try to see where this could go." Graham broke off and ran a hand through his hair.

"I know where it will go. We'll see each other a few times, and it may even be great. But you have your life, I have mine, and what is the old saying? Never the twain shall meet?" It took a huge effort, but she managed to keep her voice low, aware of the other diners around her.

"You don't think they can meet." It was not a question.

"I don't see how."

"Are you always this stubborn?" he asked.

She was about to make a retort when she stopped. Although she didn't know this man all that well, she could perfectly read the combination of annoyance, frustration, and, to her sudden happiness, affection that filled his face. Here was a man who wasn't closed off, who didn't, or couldn't, hide his feelings all that well. She had to laugh.

"What?"

"I think we just had our first fight."

He looked at her for a moment, and then a reluctant smile quirked at the corners of his mouth. "Can't you see how we're already progressing? Whether you like it or not, we're already a couple."

"This is the damndest relationship I've ever been in." She shook her head and took a bite of her hamburger.

"Me, too. I'd ask you where you've been all my life, but I think the cliché police would arrest me."

"They would. They definitely would."

"So, who won, you or me?" he asked, stealing one of her fries even though he still had some of his own.

"Hmmm. I'd say that one was a tie."

He nodded. "I think you're right."

They finished their meal and after he insisted on dragging her carry-on bag as well, in spite of her protests that it would be awkward for him, they slowly made their way back to their adjoining gate area. They decided, along the way, that the woman leaning against the wall with the long black hair and nose ring was on her way to New York City to form a new punk band called Magic Bullet Theory, who would then single-handedly revive the punk movement.

"If I had the chance, I'd take you somewhere we could dance, so I could hold you in my arms properly," he said.

26

She allowed herself to imagine the moment. The music would be big band, but soft, with a hint of longing. Ella Fitzgerald would be singing. And it would be dark, but with just enough glow of light to see the curve of his jaw and the way he looked at her as if there wasn't anybody else in the world but her.

Yep, it was official. She was a sap, no doubt about it.

But damn. It would be wonderful. *Saps of the world unite.* If she was going to be honest with herself, and at this point, why the hell not, that cynical coat she'd been wearing for awhile never had fit properly. It was tight across the shoulders. The color did nothing for her.

Plus, it itched.

"Hey, do you hear what I hear?" he said. Before she could answer, he leaned their carry-on bags against the nearest wall, put his arm around her waist, and pulled her close in the classic ballroom dance pose.

And then she heard it. Music. Romantic music, as it happened, coming from the airport sound system.

It wasn't Ella, it wasn't anybody she recognized, but it worked. Oh, did it work.

People continued to walk by, and around them. Some of them smiled, some of them laughed, and some of them made snide remarks about blocking the aisle, but she didn't pay them any mind. As she put her left hand on his shoulder and began to sway along with him, she simply forgot about her fellow travelers, and the weather delay, and how her worried mother was probably wondering if she'd make it in time for their planned family dinner. She even forgot how she was usually embarrassed about drawing any kind of attention to herself and simply floated, fitting in Graham's arms as if she'd always belonged in them. It was sappy and clichéd, and damned wonderful.

The song ended, and without a word, they headed back to their adjoining gates. They found a piece of relatively clean floor that said home to them, and Melanie found herself telling Graham about her short-lived marriage. Other than her best friend Lucie and her family, she had never really talked about Ryan with anyone, and she marveled at how easy it was to share this part of her life with the man sitting next to her.

"You know, after I confronted my husband about his extra-curricular love life, he told me that I shouldn't be so upset about it, that it was just casual sex. As if that made it okay."

"He was a wanker."

She had to smile. "Yes, he was. I told him that I doubted the women he was meeting felt the same way, and he said that any woman expecting something more than a casual fling in that situation was stupid. That how could any woman expect more from somebody they don't really know? Who they're basically just meeting, and under such trying circumstances like war?" She broke off and looked at him for a moment. "It would be like me expecting you to want more than, well, what you could possibly be expected to want."

He shook his head. "No, it wouldn't. Because, guess what? Your ex-husband was a selfish ass who was using that line of reasoning to justify what he was doing. And yes, I suppose there are a lot of men who think, and act, that way. But it isn't fair to lump me into that category. It's a little like being tried for a crime that somebody else has committed."

He was right. It was unfair. But it was scary to risk that kind of trust again. It had only led her down paths of pain and confusion.

"You're right. I'm sorry."

Graham put an arm around her and rubbed her shoulder. "I'm sorry you had to go through that. It must have been awful."

"It was. But I really think our marriage was doomed from the start. It was like we were both playing a part that was written for somebody else. We looked good on paper, but it just wasn't enough to make it work. To make us work. I'm not excusing his actions, and agree completely with your assessment of him, but I can't say I'm sorry that we ended up going our separate ways."

A couple near them rose from their chairs and headed towards the nearby restrooms. As if one body, Melanie and Graham both rose and dove for the chairs, earning them a few dirty looks from some nearby carpet dwellers.

"Hey, you snooze, you lose." Melanie said, settling into her chair with a sigh.

He slid an arm around her. "That you do," he said.

She felt the weariness settle deep into her skin. It was as if her neck was suddenly boneless, and her head sank naturally, sweetly, down onto Graham's shoulder. She didn't know how it was possible to feel so close to somebody she had just met, but she did know that she no longer had the energy to fight it, or to care if it was the right thing to do. At that moment, she felt that there was no right and no wrong.

There just was.

And as his hand rubbed small, gentle circles over her arm, she drifted off.

Melanie was flying.

There was a part of her that knew it was only a dream, but in the way of dreams, she knew that she could beat back reality for a little while and live in this moment. She soared through puffy white clouds through a sky so sweet that she could not only smell the freshness that surrounded her, she could taste it as well.

It tasted like summertime.

She wondered why she bothered with walking, and cars, and especially airplanes and airports when this was so peaceful, so easy, and so right. She tilted her head back, her hair streaming behind her as she rose ever higher through the blue, endless depths.

She stirred as she felt Graham's lips brush against her temple.

"Hey, sleeping beauty."

She slowly opened her eyes and straightened. Her mouth felt gummy. "What?" she murmured, giving her neck a quick rub. She blinked against the harsh florescent lighting in the terminal. Then she smiled. "Does this mean we've now slept together?"

"Well, you slept. I pretty much just watched you sleep." He smiled at her, and he looked so sweet and so serious that she wanted to cry. "It seems they've moved up my flight and they're announcing the last call. I'm afraid I can't put it off any longer. I must be off."

"Oh," she said, and her voice sounded so small that she was embarrassed again. She straightened a little. "God, you don't want to miss it. Anyway. Well. Hey. It was nice to..." She broke off and tried to smile. "It was amazing meeting you."

He took her hands in his. "It was amazing to meet you too, Melanie. I wish things could be different, but I guess they aren't, are they?"

"I guess not."

He leaned forward and gently kissed her. "Our first goodbye kiss."

Before she could reply, he strode to his gate and joined the few stragglers who were boarding, and she watched until, with a final wave, he disappeared into the jetway.

She leaned forward, her elbows on her knees, and took in a long, slow breath, and then another. "And the last," she murmured aloud. Her cheeks felt unusually warm, and yet the rest of her was chilled, as if a warm blanket that had been covering her was suddenly whisked away.

She knew that part of what she was experiencing was sadness, but there was something else tickling against her senses as well. Whatever it was, it mystified her and caused her heart to speed up.

"Ladies and gentlemen, at this time we would like to begin boarding on flight one-two-seven four, with non-stop service to San Jose, California. If you are seated in Zone One, you are welcome to board."

As a huge cheer went up in the waiting area, it came to her.

She felt alive.

* * *

Melanie thought about Graham often over the next few days, even as she listened to her family, nodding and smiling at all of the right moments, and contributing to the conversation when needed.

She wondered what he was doing, how his business trip went, and, of course, if he was thinking about her, too.

It was Thanksgiving Day, and from her spot in the kitchen she could hear her grandmother out in the living room, watching football with her brother and father. Every year, Melanie's brother begged their grandmother to watch the game with them, and every year she happily accepted, never suspecting that Melanie's mother was grateful for the peace in her kitchen.

Melanie, alas, did not escape kitchen detail, but considering how much she hated football, she couldn't really complain. She smiled when she heard her grandmother yell out a particularly inventive curse involving the referee, his mother, and a donkey.

"Sweetie, you haven't looked so relaxed in a long time. It's nice to see you smiling," her mother said as Melanie peeled potatoes for her in the kitchen that hadn't changed much since she was a little girl. The walls were still yellow, albeit a fresh coat, and copper pots still hung in a neat row over the stove.

"Mom, what are you talking about? I smile," Melanie said, tossing a freshly peeled potato into the large pot on the stove and picking up another one.

"I just meant that the last time you were here, you seemed a bit frazzled. That's all." Her mother put the last of the cut up vegetables onto a large crystal platter she always referred to as "the relish tray" and set it on the kitchen table. She wore a large apron over her wine-colored dress, and her hair was swept into an old-fashioned, but flattering, updo. Per Margery Cadman's edict, there were no jeans allowed during the Cadman family Thanksgiving.

"I was just really busy at the time," Melanie protested, scraping the peel off her potato in neat strips. She, too, wore an apron over her long black skirt and lavender silk blouse, and it felt a little strange to be cooking. More often than not, her job kept her so busy that she found herself eating a lot of frozen dinners and takeout.

They worked in silence for a while. Once the potatoes were boiling on the stove, she excused herself to check her email. She sat in the family's cozy den, filled with pictures ranging from herself on the first day of kindergarten to one of her parents taken earlier that month at a party, and let her mind wander once more to the man she had met at the airport. Then she logged into her email account and looked eagerly for an email from him before remembering that, duh, they hadn't exchanged email addresses. She shook her head at her foolishness.

She couldn't resist the temptation to type Graham's full name into Google and immediately found an article about his company and their annual food drive to benefit The Safe Haven Foundation in Chicago. Her eyes misted slightly as she read the piece, especially the quote given by Graham that talked about the importance of giving back to a community that everybody was a part of, and how everybody was connected.

The words rang especially true for her. She had felt connected, incredibly connected, to Graham, in spite of the fact they had only known each other for a few hours.

"Okay. Enough of this," she said aloud. She logged off of the computer and made herself return to the kitchen, knowing that the only way to move past was to move through. And there was no better way to do that than to immerse herself into the life she had with her family.

"The potatoes are ready," her mother said, nodding towards the large, steaming pot on the stove.

Melanie drained the potatoes into the large colander her mother had already placed in the sink for that purpose and shook them back and forth until she was satisfied that all of the water had drained out. She looked forward to what promised to be an amazing meal, and wondered if Graham, too, would eat turkey today, despite it being a holiday he said he didn't celebrate. And thinking about him made her smile again in spite of herself.

"You get laid right before you left, or what?" Her younger brother had wandered into the kitchen to snatch an artichoke heart from the relish tray, and now he leered at her.

Melanie was irritated to feel her face growing warm.

"Robert!" their mother protested, while she gave him a good, older sister smack and told him to mind his own business.

"Robert, why don't you make yourself useful and fetch your father. The turkey needs to come out of the oven so it can rest for awhile." After he left the room, she wasn't surprised when her mom pounced. "That is it, isn't it? You're seeing somebody! And when were you going to tell your mother about this, I'd like to know? If you have to keep something a secret from your own family, it means it's probably not a situation that's good for you."

"Mom!" She wanted to sigh and laugh at the same time. "Mom, look. Maybe I'm smiling because I'm happy to be with my family again. Okay? Or maybe I'm smiling because I'm on vacation." *Or maybe I'm smiling because I can't stop thinking about the sexiest man I've ever met, even though I'm never going to see him again.* She poured the potatoes back into the pot and added milk and butter to them.

"Leave the girl alone, Margery." Her father's voice was mild, with a hint of amusement as he walked into the kitchen. He patted his wife's bottom on the way to the oven.

"I just want to know what's going on with my only daughter," she replied, but she was smiling, and to Melanie's relief, the subject was dropped.

Or so she thought. Over dinner, the family sat around the old mahogany table draped with the same cream, gold, and burgundy tablecloth they used every Thanksgiving, candles prettily lit in their ceramic turkey holders. After grace, bowls of food were immediately passed around, and as Melanie put a large spoonful of stuffing on her plate, her mother gave an odd little throat clearing and looked her way. She immediately tensed.

"Melanie, dear, you haven't told us much about what's going on with you," her mother began.

"Mom, I told you all about the two New Year's Eve parties I'm planning, and the Smythe wedding that's just about to kill me, and the huge annual meeting that isn't taking place for nine months, but is already taking up a lot of my time. Enough about me. What's going on with you?" Melanie could hear the perkiness oozing out of her mouth and could hardly believe that she actually thought this would work on her mother.

"That's all very fascinating dear, but I want to hear about *you*. Are you seeing anybody?"

Well, there it was. The question. The question that was thrown her way every time she visited. But this time, it felt different. Melanie was surprised to find that it didn't really bother her. Somehow, instead of feeling like an accusation, as it had in the past, it amused her.

"Actually…"

Melanie could see her mother's eyes practically pop out of her head, and it made her even more devilish.

"Yes? Go on!"

"I met a really hot guy in the airport yesterday," she said in a deliberately breathy voice.

"Wow, you did it in an airport?" Robert asked.

"Now this I want to hear about!" her grandmother said, pausing in the middle of buttering a roll. "And don't spare any details."

"Really, Mother!" her mother said, aghast. Her shock turned into a withering glare as she turned to Robert. "I'm quite sure that Melanie didn't…that is to say, she wouldn't…"

Melanie grinned even as she elbowed her younger brother. "No, we did not know each other in the biblical sense. But we had a really nice relationship." She enjoyed the thought even as her mother gave her one of her patented skeptical looks.

"I wasn't referring to a man you just met, Melanie." There was a pause. "But are you going to see him again?"

She shook her head. "He lives in Chicago, Mom. No more long-distance relationships for this girl. Remember?" She took a long sip of the good Napa Valley wine her family always served at holiday dinners and let the buttery chardonnay momentarily soothe her senses.

Her mother gave her a look filled with love and understanding. "Well, you know what's best, sweetheart."

Melanie set down her glass and smacked her forehead with the back of her hand. "Mom! You can't be serious! You can't mean that *I* know best!"

"Of course she's not serious. Your mother's known what's best for this family for over thirty years." Melanie's father put down his fork and smiled at his wife.

"And it's a good thing, too," her mother retorted without missing a beat.

The subject was finally dropped for good, and Melanie, after one last thought of Graham, put him away and focused on the here and now. She was lucky, damned lucky, to have a family who loved her. It could be enough.

It was time to let it be.

It was nearing the end of the weekend, and she and her father were taking their old walk on Silver Creek Valley Trail at the nearby park. It had rained the day before, but today was sunny with just the merest hint of chill in the air. The air was fresh and clean, and the sunlight hitting the green leaves of the surrounding trees made her feel as if she was walking in a little piece of heaven on earth.

It was at times like this that she especially wondered why she had moved to the East Coast, with its persnickety weather and brown trees once the weather got cold, although she was very happy with her job.

"You look happy, kitten. I'm glad to see it," her father remarked after they had walked in contented silence for several minutes.

"Did I look so bad before?" she asked. She leaned her head back slightly and drank in the sunshine that warmed her face. She simply felt too relaxed to be annoyed with her father, who she knew meant well. She breathed in the smell of the Aqua Velva he still insisted on using despite several attempts on the part of her mother to make him try other brands. Melanie was glad he wouldn't change. He smelled like home.

Her father took her hand and gave it a brief squeeze. "Of course not. But you did look a bit tired and stressed. Frazzled, as your mother put it."

"You heard that, huh?"

He grinned. "Of course I did."

37

She shrugged. "Well, that's life on the East Coast for you. Everybody's a Type A personality out there, and it rubs off on you after awhile."

But her father was shaking his head. "No, that's not what I mean. I just wasn't convinced that you were in the right place for you."

She gave her father a wry smile as they passed by the playground. "You just want me to move back here."

Her father grinned, unrepentant. "Of course I do. I miss you."

"I miss you, too." She could hear the sound of the dirt trail scuffling underfoot and the whispery sound of the breeze blowing through the trees, and she wished she could somehow record those sounds to play back at times when she was stressed and lonely.

"It just seemed like you were trying too hard to convince all of us that everything was just great and wonderful, and it made me think you weren't too sure about it yourself and needed to be talked into it."

She nodded. "Well, yeah. I guess there is some truth in that. But I've been doing some thinking, and I'm just, I don't know, I'm not going to feel like I have to make this happen, or that happen. Or not happen. I'm not going to do that anymore. I'm going to enjoy my life, just the way it is, and be thankful for it."

Her father nodded at her. "Good. It's a waste of time anyway. You know the old Yiddish saying, right? *'Mentsch tracht, Gott lacht.'*"

"Why wouldn't I, Dad? After all, we're just one, big Jewish family, right?" She laughed. The Cadmans were as Anglican as they came.

"Smartass. Don't you ever find the time to read anymore? Anyway, it means 'Man plans, God laughs.'"

Melanie let out another laugh. "Yep, that pretty much sums it up."

He put an arm around her and gave her an affectionate squeeze. "Of course, if you want to start planning your return to California, that's an entirely different matter."

"Oh, of course it is."

Her father gave her another hug. "I just love you, honey. What can I say? I miss you."

"I love you, too, Dad. And trust me I miss you, too."

California's beauty and her affectionate family didn't stop her from looking forward to getting back to the life she had made for herself. When the day came for her to leave, she hugged each of her parents extra tightly and promised them that yes, of course she would be back.

"Don't I always come back?" she said.

During the long return flight, she found her mind wandering from the book she was trying to read until she put it aside and simply looked out at the clouds. It was a scary thought, living life without lists, without rules, and even without anti-rules. But it was exciting, too, and she could hardly wait to begin.

As usual, she had made sure to score a seat on the left side of the plane just in case they approached National Airport from the north, and she smiled as she spotted the Washington Monument, the Capitol Building, and the Lincoln Memorial as the plane descended.

She found a good spot near her baggage carousel and watched as several large black suitcases, all looking the same, circled by. She was glad she not only had a red luggage set, but had also thought to tie a scarf to the handle.

39

She was finally rewarded by the sight of her familiar bag and swung it down, depressing the button so she that could pull up the handle.

As she turned to head to the taxi stand, she got the shock of her life.

For there, at the baggage carousel right next to hers, she spotted a familiar figure, wearing a blue button down shirt, a tie loosely knotted around his neck, and khaki pants. It was in rather sharp contrast to the black leggings and black turtleneck sweater she was wearing, but she couldn't stand anything with buttons or zippers when she flew.

She could only stand there, unable to move, as Graham easily swung the mate to his carry-on bag off and onto the ground. Like her, he pulled the handle up and turned.

And like her, his mouth dropped open as his eyes met hers.

They both moved towards each other, and Melanie's entire body trembled.

"What are you doing here?" they both said at the same time as they met in the middle.

"I live here," they replied, also simultaneously.

He put down his smaller bag and held up his hand. "That's enough stereo. I don't think my brain can handle anymore. It's obviously not functioning because I thought I just heard you say that you live here."

She doubted that a crane would be able to remove the smile from her face. "I did say that. I do. Well, not right here, obviously. This is an airport. People don't live in the airport." She could hear herself babbling, but didn't really give a damn. "I live in Bethesda."

"Bethesda," Graham said, slowly.

"Yes."

"But you said you were going home when I asked you where you were going."

"I was. Oh!" She covered her mouth for a moment before letting her arm drop limply at her side. "I meant my childhood home. I still think of San Jose as home, even though I haven't lived there in years. Stupid, huh?"

"Yes. I mean, no! Bethesda," he repeated.

"And I thought you lived in Chicago!" she exclaimed. She wondered why Graham seemed a little blurry, and then she realized it was because she was starting to cry. "Your luggage tag said 'Chicago'," she finished. "And, well, I googled you and found an article all about your company. In Chicago," she admitted.

"Oh, God. I did live in Chicago, for many years. But I've been living in Washington, D.C. for several months now. I guess I never got around to changing the tag. And the article you read was from last year." He moved closer and wiped under her eyes with his thumbs.

A voice started yelling inside of her head. Would he want to start seeing her? Did they have a future together? Should she ask him? And then she remembered the dream she had in the airport, when she let the air currents take her where they wanted, and she willed the voice to be still.

She glanced up at him to find he was looking down at her with a boyish smile.

And decided it was time to let what would be, be.

"Would you like to have a coffee? Then we can continue this conversation someplace a little more comfortable."

He smiled broadly. "That sounds familiar. And wonderful."

As they left the baggage claim area, she discreetly gestured towards a man who was wearing torn jeans, a white

T-shirt, and, inexplicably, a top hat. "He's a magician who has to go into the Witness Protection Program."

Graham whispered back. "He used to make dead bodies disappear in exchange for having his gambling debts erased, but he got greedy and wanted more until one day, he was caught dealing H and was forced to cut a deal with the authorities."

"That's quite a story," Melanie said.

They reached the automated glass doors that led to the outside world, and exited the airport into their own story.

The End

About Mary Compton

Mary Compton is an East Coast transplant who grew up in Northern California. She earned her Creative Writing degree from San Francisco State University and was previously published in *Fresh Hot Bread*. She is a meeting and conference planner and currently lives in the Washington, D.C. metro area with her boyfriend, three cats, and a guinea pig.

Her inspiration for the story came from a long layover spent in O'Hare Airport in Chicago. As the hours passed and her frustration mounted, she started feeling as if she had spent her entire life in that airport. The idea for the story grew from that thought, and bloomed into "Once Upon a Flight Delay".

Snowbound

Friday, December 23

Rainey Brookfield stared out the window of her room in the South Residence Hall of Simmons College, watching as the fluffy white flakes of snow fell, thicker and thicker as the day wore on. It was late afternoon, and the gray sky showed no signs of clearing. Every bit of the magic that snow usually held for her had been wiped away when she awakened to the news that a major winter storm had all roads leading out of Boston closed to nonessential traffic.

"So much for being the hub of the solar system," Rainey grumbled, thinking of Boston's famous nickname. "The hub of the solar system should have a better plan for snow emergencies."

Her roommate had left the previous day, but Rainey's last exam hadn't taken place until the end of the last day of the semester. She had been too tired to face the south and west-bound traffic last night, after the draining week of finals. Now she was almost alone. The only other student left on her floor was her friend Ellen Carlton, whose cross-country flight had been canceled by the storm.

"I was going to drive back home today," she said to the framed photograph which held a place of pride on top of her bookshelf. "In two more days it'll be Christmas, and I'm going to be stuck here in Boston. No time with family, no catching up with Jill and Laura. All the gifts I've made for everyone at home…I won't be able to give them out on Christmas Day."

Taking the picture, she sank down onto her bed and studied it. Three faces stared back at her, smiling, tanned, and happy. It was the most recent group picture of her and her two best friends together, taken at the end of the summer during a picnic at the Brookfields' lake. A tear of self-pity escaped and rolled down her cheek.

"Everyone's gone home except me—well, me and Ellen. And she's visiting her boyfriend's family today." Rainey placed the picture face-down onto the desk and busied herself straightening the bedspread. She scanned the room for stray bits of paper or other oddments that needed to be discarded or put away, and checked that her suitcase latch was carefully secured. She tended to overfill suitcases, and more than once clothes had gone tumbling as the suitcase popped open. So now she always doublechecked.

Then she picked up the picture again.

"At least I have a place to stay," she said to the smiling faces. The same news program that announced the road closings had also announced that college dormitories, normally closed to students at the end of finals week, would remain open until the roads were passable again. With the holiday weekend approaching, authorities cautioned that it was unlikely road conditions would be favorable for interstate travel before the twenty-sixth.

"Everyone's gone except me," she repeated, slouching into her desk chair. Suddenly she sprang up, wiping her tears. "Me...and Kevin."

Kevin Shelton was the older brother of her best friend Jill. He was midway through his fourth year at Harvard Medical School and also held a part-time job at Children's Hospital in Boston. As a result, Rainey rarely saw him, although they were both in the same city and, in fact, didn't live a great distance from each other.

Kevin worked as a phlebotomist at Children's Hospital three days a week, and according to Jill, spent nearly all of his free time studying or preparing for residency interviews.

Rainey had been busy as well that semester, and she hadn't had the spare time to look up her best friend's brother. Besides, although she had always had a slight crush on the handsome, dark-haired Kevin, he treated her as another kid sister. Sure, he was her next-door neighbor at home, and a good friend of her older brother Drew. Still, he was just far enough ahead of her in school that he had always seemed terribly old.

Both Kevin and Drew were so focused on their education and career goals that they had never spent a lot of time with their sisters at home. She and Jill had almost lived at each other's homes, but they were more interested in socializing with their own group of friends, while Drew and Kevin concentrated on their studies.

Now, however, she wondered what his schedule was for the next few days.

"I'm almost sure Jill said he was working the weekend of Christmas," she muttered as she pulled out her address book to find his phone number. "He needs to work as much as he can, and with no classes over the holidays, I bet he's going to be here."

She located Kevin's information and flipped open her cell phone. Staring at its glowing screen, she hesitated in a sudden, unexpected burst of shyness, and almost folded it closed again before she could key in the number.

After a few seconds of vacillation, she finally punched in Kevin's number, only to be rewarded with the monotonous sound of his phone ringing over and over.

Just as she was certain her call was going to voicemail, there was a click on the line and a breathless voice said, "Hello! Kevin Shelton here."

"Kevin! This is Rainey—Rainey Brookfield," she said, suddenly feeling shy again.

"Well, since I only know one Rainey, I guessed it was you." Kevin chuckled. "How are you doing, Rainey? Where are you?"

"Snowbound," she grumbled.

"You're in Boston? I figured you'd have left by now," he said, sounding puzzled.

"No. I'm right here in my dorm at Simmons," she said.

"What are you doing still in town?" he asked. "I thought you would have skedaddled yesterday."

"I couldn't leave before today because I had a late final yesterday. So now I'm stuck in the snow, right here." She tried to laugh, but the laugh ended in a sigh. Taking a deep breath, she started to speak again. "So, what are you doing this weekend?"

"Well, I just got off work," Kevin answered. "I've got to spend the evening studying tonight, because I start my pediatric medicine rotation a week from Monday. The chair of medicine has each student do a presentation during the first week of rotation, and I've been assigned infectious diseases."

"Is that a good thing or a bad thing?"

"Good, I guess. Better than some of the other topics, like removal of swallowed objects from the GI tract. But I'm nervous since Children's Hospital is one of my top choices for residency, and I want to make a good impression on the attending. And of course, I'm working three to eleven tomorrow and Sunday at the hospital, because I needed the money, and holidays are always a good time to pick up extra shifts."

Kevin chuckled, but Rainey thought she detected something wistful in his voice. He'll be missing his family on Christmas, too, she thought.

"Well, um, if you have any free time in there, I was just thinking. I won't be able to leave before the twenty-sixth, probably. Would you like to get together for lunch…or dinner …tomorrow?" She scrunched her eyes closed as the words tumbled from her lips. She had never, ever invited herself to dinner with a guy.

He hesitated for a moment before answering, and she was sure she'd been too aggressive. "The hospital cafeteria serves a special dinner for employees who have to work on Christmas Eve, as well as on Christmas Day," he finally said. "So if you wouldn't mind meeting me at the hospital, I'd be honored to have dinner with you."

"Okay, then!" Rainey tried to sound matter-of-fact, although inside she felt as quivery as a bowlful of jelly. "What time shall I come to the hospital? And where shall I meet you?"

He gave her directions for reaching the laboratory at Children's Hospital, and explained that he usually took his supper break at about five-thirty. "But maybe I can take it at five tomorrow. I hate to think of you walking back to your dorm after dark." He sounded worried.

"I'll come at five," she said. "But it's no problem to eat a little later. I'll have my whistle and my Mace with me, and I doubt if anyone will bother me."

"All right, then. I'll meet you at the lab tomorrow afternoon, at four-fifty," Kevin agreed.

Rainey rolled her eyes. As always, Kevin was precise. There were many times she couldn't believe he was related to her best friend. Jill was anything but precise, but that was part of her appeal.

✳ ❄ ✳

Kevin hung up the phone and ran a hand through his hair. Rainey's call had surprised him. Not only because he had expected her to be back in Croton by now, but also because she had never called him before, even though they'd both lived in Boston for three and a half years. He wondered what had caused her to take the initiative. It wasn't that Rainey was shy—she had always seemed perfectly poised and easy around him, as she was around all of his family.

She spends so much time at our house, she's always seemed like practically another little sister, he mused.

But at Thanksgiving, things felt a little different. He had managed to get off work and had gone home to help with his parents' annual Thanksgiving buffet for all their friends and neighbors. Rainey had been in and out at their home all weekend, just as usual.

But this time, he had found himself noticing for the first time how grown-up she was. In the past, he had always thought of Jill and her friends as being a lot younger than himself, part of another world. In addition, Rainey's family

49

was much wealthier than his. While they lived in the same neighborhood, their families' social standings were far apart. He frowned. That had never bothered him when he thought of her simply as Jill's friend.

And it wasn't as if their age difference was that great—just four years. Rainey was a beautiful, intelligent girl—no, make that woman, he corrected himself—then shook his head. What was he thinking? She was his sister's friend and off limits. And she probably wasn't attracted to him anyway.

"This is not a date," he said aloud, feeling stupid for even thinking of the possibility. Shaking his head, he sat down at the desk—one of the few pieces of furniture in his sparsely furnished apartment—and opened a heavy textbook on pediatric infectious diseases and their diagnosis and treatment.

Two hours later, he stood and stretched before going to the tiny kitchen to prepare a meager supper of canned soup and a grilled cheese sandwich. He couldn't stop thinking about Rainey and their plans for dinner in the hospital cafeteria tomorrow. He decided he'd better check to make sure he had something decent to wear—something besides his usual faded scrubs.

The life of a medical student and part-time lab tech was not conducive to regular laundry schedules, and Kevin was dismayed, but not surprised, to find that none of his better clothes were clean. He bundled a couple of oxford-cloth shirts, several pairs of khaki pants, and a half-dozen pairs of underwear and socks into a pillowcase and headed for the all-night Laundromat down the street from his apartment.

He whistled "Have Yourself a Merry Little Christmas" as he walked in the bracing air, swinging his improvised laundry bag in one hand and his textbook in the other. Minutes later, his brisk stride had slowed. Even with boots, he was slogging through the snow-covered sidewalk. He began to wish he had brought his snowshoes from home, especially when he spied a group of laughing students swishing their way toward him. The group spanned the width of the street, and all wore either snowshoes or cross-country skis.

"Hey, Shelton!" One of the figures detached himself from the group. "What's up?"

Kevin recognized one of his fellow med students and a neighbor in the apartment building. "Emergency laundry time, Carlisle," he answered with a grin, swinging his pillowcase.

"Hey, I'm going inside," the other man said. "Got a stack of residency applications to work on. You can use my snowshoes if you want. Otherwise you'll be half the night covering the next block."

"You're right, I'll save some time with those," he agreed.

His friend quickly removed the snowshoes and Kevin strapped them onto his feet. In a few minutes he was making much better time, and for the first time he felt a moment of gratitude that he hadn't been able to drive home today.

All up and down the narrow street, cars were nearly buried under drifts of snow, and he had heard news reports that numerous vehicles had been abandoned on the expressways when the snow overcame the city's ability to clear it. The peaceful scene held a luminous glow, and from time to time he caught sight of a lighted Christmas tree behind a window, or heard a snatch of Christmas music. For the first time in months, he felt himself relax.

The previous semester had been intense—less because of a heavy course load than because of the pressure of choosing, applying, and scheduling interviews with the residency programs that would best fit his own plans and interests. Now, with only one semester left, he was looking forward to graduating from med school and beginning his residency training in pediatrics.

He had completed applications to programs at several of the finest children's hospitals on the East Coast, in Chicago, and in an unusual burst of spontaneity, to one in San Francisco. Choosing his top three was going to be difficult, but he was sure that his first choice would be Children's Hospital of Boston, where he was currently employed. Boston wasn't excessively far from home, and the hospital itself was partnered with Harvard Medical School, so he would know the attending physicians—which might or might not prove to be a positive point.

Reaching the Laundromat, which was quiet on this evening of Christmas Eve's eve, Kevin quickly loaded his clothes into a washing machine. He added a precisely measured amount of detergent and fed several coins into the coin slot.

As the washer filled, he noticed how warm it was in the small space. An idea began to percolate in his brain, and just before the machine began to agitate, he yanked off his shirt, jeans, and socks, stuffing them into the tub.

Dressed only in T-shirt and boxers, he began whistling again and pulled a semi-comfortable chair close to the folding table. He returned to his place in the textbook and began to transfer the most important information in the chapter to index cards. But as the washer sloshed and spun, his mind kept flashing back to Rainey's phone call. He imagined how she must have looked during the call: her eager face, her sparkling green eyes, and her long, shiny, dark brown hair.

He visualized her wearing jeans, neatly ironed, and a green sweater that was a favorite of his.

By the time the washer finished its cycle, his thoughts had completely abandoned pediatric infectious diseases, and Rainey's face and voice had taken over. He could picture her pacing back and forth in her tiny dorm room, lonely and frustrated at being stranded.

He was tempted to slam the book down—anything to create a disturbance in the quiet Laundromat. No one else was around to complain. But the prospect of breaking the spine of a very expensive textbook stopped him. He'd need the standard reference book not only for the coming semester, but for several years into the future. Instead, he marked his place with an index card and moved his clothes from the washer into the dryer.

Forty minutes later, Kevin was once again fully dressed. He had folded each shirt and pair of khakis neatly and stacked them on top of his book. The socks were balled together in pairs and dropped into the pillowcase, although, with that perverse habit particular to socks, one of them had disappeared.

He shrugged, gathered up his things, and was soon again whistling "Have Yourself a Merry Little Christmas" as he retraced his route back to his apartment.

Saturday, December 24

Rainey stood next to her bed, gazing down into her opened suitcase. All of the clothes that were returning home with her for the Christmas holiday had been laundered and neatly packed before the snowstorm. Now she had to choose something to wear to the hospital to eat dinner with Kevin.

In her mind, she had already tried and discarded five possible outfits. *Nothing too dressy...he'll think I think it's a date. And it's not a date, it's just two old friends eating together. But not too scruffy...I want him to think I took a little bit of trouble to look nice—just in case he ever thought about asking me on a date.*

Sighing, she began to pull sweaters and slacks out of the suitcase. Kevin had seen her in the sage green sweater a dozen times or more. *It's my favorite sweater, that's why! Not that he's probably ever noticed,* she acknowledged to herself. *Why do I even have this blue sweater...blue isn't a good color for me.*

The blue sweater went back into her drawer. The brown sweater was too boring, the pumpkin-orange one was too Thanksgiving-y, the black-and-white houndstooth was too loud.

"Why do I even own any of these clothes?" she moaned, plopping down on the bed and burying her head in her hands.

Dejected, she sat for a few moments without moving, doing a mental rundown of the names of friends she might call for advice. About to give up, she had a sudden thought and pulled her phone from her pocket. Quickly, she pressed the number for Brookfield Haven into the keypad. *Please, Mother, be home,* she silently begged.

"Brookfield Haven, Evelyn Gordon speaking." The familiar and beloved voice of the Brookfield housekeeper lifted Rainey's spirits.

"Miss Gordon! It's Rainey," she blurted out. "How are you?"

"I'm doing well, Rainey," Miss Gordon answered. "We're all so sorry that your trip home has been delayed.

Drew arrived late yesterday, and your parents got in last night from Florida. Do you know yet when you'll be able to travel?"

"If it wasn't Christmas Eve, I'd say the roads would be cleared later today. But with the two-day holiday weekend, I'm figuring it'll be Monday," Rainey said, trying to keep her tone cheerful. "Miss Gordon, is my mother available? There's something I need to ask her."

"Yes, dear. She's in her office. I'll let her know you're on the phone." Rainey could hear Miss Gordon's voice speaking into the intercom. "Mrs. Brookfield, Rainey's on the phone for you."

Her mother's lovely, modulated voice came on the line, and Rainey heard a quiet click as Miss Gordon hung up her extension.

"Rainey, darling! Hello, how is everything in the hub of the solar system?" Jacqueline Brookfield asked teasingly. "I'm so sorry the storm has delayed you," she continued in a more serious tone.

"Oh, Mother, I'm sorry too," Rainey answered. "Everything here is fine, it's just annoying to have to wait when I want to see everyone so badly. I doubt if the roads will be cleared before Monday, but as soon as they are, I'll be on my way."

"Darling, just be safe," her mother pleaded. "Don't take any chances. Dad and I aren't going away again until we see you. And Drew will be here until January eleventh. Now, do you need anything?"

"Mother, actually I wanted to ask your advice," Rainey began. "You know that Kevin Shelton is here in Boston, and he works near my dorm." She hesitated, worrying her lower lip with her teeth.

"Yes, dear. His mother told me he's either in class or at work at least six days a week. Have you seen him?"

"No, I haven't seen him, not since Thanksgiving, I mean. I mean, of course I saw him at Thanksgiving but we don't really run into each other, but since he's here I thought he might be stuck like me. So I called him yesterday and he's working today and tomorrow, but he invited me to eat dinner with him at the hospital tonight."

Rainey took a deep breath. "It's not a date, you understand. Just two old neighbors keeping each other company since we're both stuck here." She stopped, realizing that she was protesting too much.

"That's very nice, darling. I'm glad you'll have some company tonight."

"Well, I do have one problem." Rainey tried once more to raise the subject she wanted to discuss. "I was going through my clothes, and nothing seems like the right color or style. I was hoping you'd have a suggestion."

"Don't you have a red or cranberry-colored sweater?" her mother asked. "Most men like red, it's seasonal, and it's a very good color for you. I think that would be lovely."

The smile was so apparent in her mother's voice Rainey had to smile in return. "You're a genius!" she exclaimed. "Why didn't I think of that? I do have a pretty cranberry-red sweater I was saving to wear at home. Now, since it'll be after Christmas before I can get home, I'll just wear it tonight," she continued. "Thank you. You're the best!"

"I'm glad I could help, darling. And I'm glad you have some plans for tonight. I was feeling sad because you wouldn't be with us, and sad because you would be alone. Now that I know you'll be with a friend, I'll feel much better," her mother said.

"I was down in the dumps, too. And now I find myself looking forward to the dinner, even if it's hospital cafeteria food." She smiled in spite of herself. She was suddenly looking forward to eating hospital cafeteria food with great anticipation. "I'd better hang up now. I've got to repack my suitcase and get ready. I'm walking over to the hospital—it's so close and the streets are still almost impassable."

"Good-bye, dear. Have a wonderful time."

She waited for her mother to hang up before ending the connection on her own phone. She stepped back across the small room and once more reached into her suitcase. Pulling out a vibrant, deep red tunic sweater with a cowl neck, she shook it out and laid it on the bed. Then she pulled out her newest flared jeans and a pair of knee socks that matched her sweater.

Carefully, Rainey repacked her suitcase and checked the items she planned to wear, making sure they wouldn't need ironing. She didn't care that her friends made fun of her for ironing jeans, she liked the sharp crease. Next, she selected a fine gold chain and tiny gold earrings shaped like Christmas trees.

At four-fifteen, Rainey locked the door of her room behind her. Swinging her shoulder bag by its strap, she made her way briskly down the steps to the front lobby and signed herself out until six-thirty.

"I'm so sorry you have to work, when you were expecting to be home with your family today," she told the gray-haired dorm matron.

"That's all right, dear," the woman replied. "I'll be going to my daughter's after work today. One good thing about working is that it gets me off the hook for cooking." She winked at Rainey, who grinned back.

Outside, dusk was already settling. The sidewalks were still covered with a thick coating of packed snow, but Rainey had no trouble maneuvering in her high-heeled black leather boots, and she was warm in her wool coat and red gloves decorated with snowflakes. A matching scarf was tied loosely around her neck.

The few people she met looked happy. Despite the weather, it was a beautiful scene, and Brookline Avenue looked lovely in its winter dress.

Rainey smiled at young couple pulling a sturdy sled with a backrest, with a toddler perched in the seat. Between the child's legs rested a gallon jug of milk and a loaf of bread. The child and his parents waved a greeting to her as they passed.

She hummed "Have Yourself a Merry Little Christmas" as she strode along. The plaintive melody was one of her favorites; she enjoyed the old movie *Meet Me in St. Louis* just for the sake of hearing it, and always tried to find a broadcast of it at Christmas time. Last year, she had asked for a copy of the movie for her own.

Soon she had reached the intersection of Brookline and Longwood Avenues. She waited for the light and crossed the street, still humming the wistful Christmas song. Turning left on Longwood, Rainey noted the wreaths that hung from the streetlights, and the outdoor Christmas trees, twinkling with clear lights that peeked from beneath their blankets of snow. Some of them were festooned with treats for the birds that perched in their branches.

It was a short walk, only a couple of blocks, to the Children's Hospital of Boston, and she arrived at the front lobby of the hospital sooner than she expected. Once inside, she consulted the directions Kevin had given her for locating the laboratory, and soon she was knocking on the door of his workplace.

An older woman wearing a white lab coat and reading glasses perched far down on her nose opened the door. "May I help you?"

"Hi, my name is Lorraine Brookfield, and I'm supposed to be meeting Kevin Shelton," Rainey said with a friendly smile.

"Ah, yes. Kevin's friend, Rainey." The woman's face relaxed and she returned the smile. "Kevin asked me to watch for you. Come on in and hang up your coat while you wait. He's up on the floor collecting a few specimens, but should be back soon."

She waved toward a tiny lounge which held a small table and a couple of chairs, as well as a coffeemaker and a plate of Christmas cookies. "Help yourself to a cookie, Rainey," she said. "Oh, and by the way, my name is Karen. We really like Kevin. He's a hard worker and very kind to the patients."

"He's always loved anything to do with medicine, and he enjoys helping people," Rainey agreed.

Karen bustled about, checking on various machines and tearing off a printout. Rainey nibbled on a dainty, crumbly pecan cookie coated with powdered sugar, and sipped the coffee Karen had urged on her. She hoped she didn't look as nervous as she felt.

"So, how long have you and Kevin been dating?" Karen asked, sitting down in the other chair.

Rainey choked on the coffee she had just started to swallow. She coughed, then jumped up to grab a paper towel to catch the wet cookie crumbs that escaped from her mouth. Once she finally had her breathing under control again, she was horrified to discover a wet spot on the front of her sweater, and wet a wad of paper towels to dab at it and get the coffee smell out.

Her face was flaming, but when she finally answered, she tried to sound casual. "Oh, we're not dating—not that I don't like him, but we're just friends. His sister has been my best friend for over eight years, and I've known him for most of that time. We're next-door neighbors at home, and both of us were going to be stuck here over Christmas, so we decided to eat dinner together today. That's all." She stopped abruptly, and checked her watch as soon as Karen turned her head. *Come on, Kevin.*

A buzzer sounded, and Karen stood up, walking over to one of the machines. Rainey went to the sink in the lounge and tried ineffectually to blot the wet spot dry with paper towels. Sighing, she stopped when she saw that she was only stretching the knit garment out of shape.

She was adjusting the cowl neck of her sweater to try to cover the still-wet area when the door opened and Kevin walked in, carrying a tray full of blood-filled test tubes. Standing by the sink in the tiny lounge, she was out of his direct vision, but she was able to see that he wore a blue oxford cloth shirt and a red tie under his long white lab coat. Khaki pants were neatly creased over a polished pair of Bass Weejuns. Kevin's dark hair was a bit longer than she was used to seeing it, and the length had allowed it to curl, although it was still not as curly as his sister's russet locks.

"Hi, Karen," he said. "Has Rainey arrived yet?" His handsome face wore a smile and a dimple creased his right cheek as he spoke. Rainey felt herself melting inside.

"She was right in the lounge, there," Karen said, waving in Rainey's general direction. "I'm afraid I embarrassed her.

She seems like a very nice girl, and I can't believe the two of you have never dated."

Rainey knew she should come out and greet Kevin, but this whole conversation was so embarrassing that she hesitated. She could see that Kevin's face had flushed.

"She's a very nice girl," he answered. "But it's hardly fair for a med student to ask a girl out when he can't offer her anything but his company. Besides, when do I have time to date—to date anyone?"

Deciding she had held back long enough and that Karen would hopefully stop her intrusive questioning if she reappeared, Rainey picked up her purse and stepped out into the lab from the lounge. "Hi, Kevin," she greeted her old friend. "I'm ready to eat whenever you are."

"Let me wash my hands," Kevin said, suiting his action to the words. In moments, the two were walking briskly along a labyrinthine maze of hospital corridors.

"I'm sorry if Karen embarrassed you," Kevin apologized. "She means well, and she must have liked you, because she's been trying to fix me up with her daughter."

"It's okay," Rainey assured him. "I was just surprised, since we've never thought of each other that way." *Well, he's probably never thought of me that way,* she thought to herself.

They walked in silence for a dozen yards, until Kevin broke the silence.

"I guess you have a boyfriend here," he said. "Any guy would be lucky to date you."

"It's not like I haven't been out with anyone since I've been at Simmons," Rainey admitted. "But right now there really is no one." She worried that her last comment might sound a bit desperate, and added, "Of course, I don't really have that much time for dating either."

The aroma of prime rib wafted out to greet them as they neared the cafeteria. They entered the line and each took a tray. Rainey gasped and looked up at Kevin in amazement. "Is your cafeteria always this fancy?" she asked.

"Oh, no. I've never seen it like this," he answered. "Normally it's a plain-Jane cafeteria."

Rainey gazed around the space, taking in every detail. The dining room looked like an elegant restaurant, with dim lighting, snowy white cloths on the tables, and candle centerpiece decorations. The cooks at the steam tables each wore a white toque and there was a decorated Christmas tree in front of the cashier's station.

They received their filled plates and Kevin led the way to a table where two young men were already seated. Both of them stood as Rainey approached, and Kevin introduced them.

"These are a couple of my classmates," he said. "Matt Carlisle." He pointed to a slightly built, dark-haired young man with straight brown hair and tortoise-shell glasses, wearing a white uniform. "And Phil O'Reilly." He indicated a stocky fellow in rumpled green scrubs and a white lab coat. "Matt's an orderly and Phil is a scrub tech in the O.R. Guys, this is Rainey Brookfield, a friend of mine from back home. She's stuck in town for the next couple of days, so we thought we'd get together for dinner today."

"It's nice to meet you, Rainey." Phil reached out to shake hands with her and enveloped her hand in a beefy paw.

She smiled and extended her hand to Matt as soon as Phil released it. "It's nice to meet both of you, too. Really, Kevin took pity on me when he invited me to eat with him. I hope it's not a problem for me to be here."

"It's no problem, Rainey. I called and asked about it yesterday," Kevin said. "The dinner is free to employees, but anyone who gave twenty-four hours' notice could bring one guest. It's the hospital's gift to us."

"Besides that, we get an hour for dinner today, compared to a half-hour normally," Phil said.

Rainey and her new friends began to eat a delicious meal of prime rib au jus, garlic mashed potatoes, steamed broccoli, and tossed salad.

"Hey, Shelton, you've been holding out on us," Matt said as he cleared his plate. "You never told us you had a girlfriend." He moved a saucer of Italian cream cake onto his empty dinner plate, and attacked the sweet treat.

"Rainey's a good friend, guys. That's all," Kevin said firmly. "Hey, this food's delicious," he added, apparently trying to change the subject.

"Whatever you say, Kev. But you're crazy if you don't try to go out with her," Phil insisted. He winked at Rainey. "Kevin's a great guy, but he's too serious. He needs a woman to help him lighten up."

For the second time that afternoon, Rainey's face was flaming. "Really, we're just friends," she managed to say. Trying to deflect the conversation in another direction, she asked Kevin's friends about themselves. "Phil, Kevin said you work in the operating room. Do they really schedule surgery on Christmas Eve?" She cut a dainty bite of prime rib and popped it into her mouth, savoring the succulent morsel.

"No, but it never fails that an emergency or two happens," Phil responded. "Right, Matt?" He took a forkful of Red Velvet cake, the expression on his face becoming beatific as he chewed and swallowed.

"That's right," agreed Matt. "Kids fall, break a leg; they get appendicitis or cut themselves on new pocketknives. They swallow something and have to get it removed from their stomachs. It's always something."

"Hey, Shelton, are you coming to the Christmas party at the Home of the Innocents tomorrow?" Phil asked. "I'm going to play Santa this year." He pushed himself away from the table and stretched.

"Yes, I promised Sister Cabrini that I'd help until I have to go to work at three," Kevin said. "I'm to help with some of the kids at lunch and then help Santa distribute the gifts."

"What's this?" asked Rainey. "Isn't the Home of the Innocents where kids live whose families can't care for them? How awful to have to spend Christmas in an institution." She had just started on her own serving of Italian cream cake, but suddenly it felt like sawdust in her mouth.

"Yes, it's really too bad, but every year the administrators have a big party for the kids who are living there, with Santa Claus, gifts, everything," explained Matt. "Some of the kids are there temporarily because of a family situation; some have complex medical needs and their families aren't able to care for them. Those kids can be there permanently. Some kids have been in the foster care system and the foster families can't handle their needs."

"All of them have a lot of challenges," agreed Kevin. "When I started volunteering there, I really began to appreciate my own good health and my family."

"I hate to admit I've been so close to their building and have never been there," Rainey exclaimed. "Do you think it would be all right if I came along and helped, too? Since I'll be here anyway, I may as well be doing something for someone else."

"Obviously you haven't been around nuns much," said Phil with a grin. "They'll take anyone who volunteers." His voice took on a more serious tone. "But if you're not used to being around handicapped kids, you might be in for a shock. Some of the kids are deaf, blind, in wheelchairs, or scarred from burns or abuse. If you can't cope with that, you probably shouldn't come."

"I'm sure I'll be able to cope with it," she told him, her chin lifting in determination. "And if I find out I can't take it, I'll leave or do something else to help. If anyone needs a Christmas, it's got to be those kids."

"Let me drop by your dorm around eleven-thirty tomorrow; we'll walk over together," offered Kevin. "Right now, would you like a quick tour of the hospital? We've got another twenty minutes and I can show you around a bit of it."

"I'd like that," she replied. She stood, causing the two young men to jump up from their seats as well. "It was so nice to meet you, Matt and Phil. I'm looking forward to seeing you tomorrow." With a smile for Kevin's two classmates, she moved aside so he could push her chair into place, and took her tray.

"See you tomorrow, guys," said Kevin. His friends returned the farewells and he steered her toward the tray return.

Fifteen minutes later, they waited in the lobby for a taxi to take her back to the Simmons residential campus. After a very quick tour of the state-of-the-art pediatric emergency department and the children's playroom, they had returned to the lab so she could retrieve her coat and purse. Karen had put her foot down over the idea of Rainey walking back to the dorm alone.

"Kevin Shelton!" Karen's gray hair was vibrating in indignation. "No way are you going to let that girl walk back to Simmons alone! This neighborhood is not that safe. I'll give her money for a taxi myself if you don't have it."

"Please! I have enough for cab fare," Rainey hastened to say. "If cabs are running, I'll just call one. Thank you just the same, Karen."

Kevin had insisted on covering the cab fare, and since he didn't have any scheduled blood draws for another hour, Karen told him to wait with Rainey until she was safely ensconced in the cab.

"Kevin, I've really had a lovely time," she began, turning to him with a smile. "Thanks for letting me eat with you and your friends. It helps to keep my mind off of what I'm missing at home."

Against her will, her eyes filled with tears as she thought of her parents and brother relaxing around a crackling fire, and of her two best girlfriends getting together without her. Everyone in their old crowd would be home, too. She dug in her pocket for a tissue, and pretended she had gotten something in her eye.

Kevin watched for the lights of an approaching cab. He had enjoyed Rainey's company, and appreciated the attractive picture she made, in her cranberry-colored sweater, stylish designer jeans, and boots. Her gold-flecked green eyes had glowed with interest when he explained his work.

"I'm glad you could come," he told her. "I enjoyed myself." Noticing that she was dabbing her eye with a tissue, he asked in concern, "Are you all right? Do you have something in your eye?"

"Yes, I'm fine. That is, I did have something in my eye but it's gone now." Turning back to him, she smiled, and if the smile was a bit watery, he pretended not to notice. "I had a great time, and I'm looking forward to tomorrow."

"Here's your cab," he said, opening the door for her.

He walked her out to the curb, checking to make sure the cab had chains on its tires. The driver followed the direction of Kevin's glance and scowled. "I should be off duty, but when I get a call from the hospital, I try to help out. So, do you have a problem with my car, buddy?"

"Oh, no," Kevin hastened to assure him. "I was just surprised to see any taxis running tonight."

"Like I said, I'm only out because it was a hospital call. I've had a sick kid myself before." The cabbie jerked his head in Rainey's direction. "But this doesn't look like a sick kid."

"No, she's not," Kevin agreed. "She's just a good friend who is stranded here for Christmas. I'm on duty or I'd walk her home." He handed the cabbie a bill. "Good night, Rainey," he said. "I'll call you tomorrow before I come over."

"Good night, Kevin," she answered. "I really had a good time. Thank you for showing me around." This time, her smile was incandescent.

Returning to the lab, Kevin felt as if the hospital had suddenly grown a bit colder and darker.

Karen was bustling around, checking the printer for new requisitions and wiping down the counters.

"Go on to supper, Karen," he suggested. "Everything is delicious. Take your time."

"So, you got your little friend into a cab?" she asked. When he nodded, she shook her finger at him. "You'd better ask her out, Kevin. That little girl is perfectly perfect for you."

Hearing Rainey's favorite accolade coming from Karen's mouth caused his jaw to drop in astonishment. "You just said 'perfectly perfect'. Why in the world did you say that?"

Karen's brow creased in thought. "I don't really know," she admitted. "It's not something I usually say. That still doesn't change the fact that I think you two would be great together."

He laughed. "Go on to supper. Enjoy the hospital's treat."

While Karen was gone, he continued the housekeeping chores she had begun. Emptying the trash, calibrating the machines for the next twenty-four hours of testing, and putting the tiny lounge in order, he moved about the laboratory performing the routine tasks.

Most required minimal attention and concentration, which was fortunate because he kept seeing Rainey's shiny hair, her sparkling eyes, and her slender figure, set off by the vibrant red sweater. He could hear her musical laughter and feel the touch of her graceful, slim fingers on his arm.

Stop it, Shelton, he lectured himself. *You told Karen you didn't have time for dating, and you were right. Rainey belongs to another world, no matter how good a friend she is. Forget about dating her.* His thoughts were still in turmoil when Phil showed up at the lab window.

"Hey, Shelton!" His friend slouched at the window, leaning on his elbows. "What are you doing after work?"

"Going home and hitting the sack," Kevin replied. "What did you have in mind?"

"My uncle is the pastor of a historic church over in Roxbury, and I'm going there for Midnight Mass after work, meeting the rest of my family there," Phil said. "I just thought maybe you and your girlfriend might like to go. The church is beautiful, and the service is…well, it's inspiring. It puts you into the spirit of Christmas, even if you weren't there already. Anyway, I thought your little girlfriend seemed sad that she was stranded here."

"Roxbury?" Kevin wasn't sure. The area was not known as one of Boston's safest. "I guess we could take the T," he ventured. "The storm hasn't shut it down."

"That settles it." Phil sounded as if the discussion was over. "Call her and see if she's interested. I'll check back with you after I finish my smoke."

"You need to make quitting smoking your New Year's resolution," Kevin said with a grimace. "Think of what a good example you'd be for your patients."

"I know, I know. One of these days." Phil waved and moved away from the window.

"I'll call her. But she's not my girlfriend," Kevin protested to Phil's speedily retreating back.

Hesitantly, he began dialing Rainey's number.

✳ ❄ ❄

After arriving back at her dorm, Rainey curled up on her bed and opened the latest book by one of her favorite mystery writers. Engrossed in the heroine's adventures in a sprawling English country estate, she jumped at the sound of the ringing phone. Who in the world could be calling her? She had spoken to Jill and Laura before going to meet Kevin, and had called her parents and Drew just after coming in from her dinner with him.

The paperback novel flipped shut as she dropped it and dug into her purse for her phone. Seeing the readout, she took a deep breath before saying "Hello" in a voice that—she hoped—sounded casual.

"Rainey? It's Kevin." His voice hesitated for the space of several heartbeats.

"Hi, Kevin. What's up?" For no explainable reason, she felt a prickle of worry as she waited for him to speak. "Is everyone all right at home?"

"Oh, nothing's wrong." He laughed, and although he still sounded unlike himself, Rainey relaxed. "Um, are you busy right now?" he asked.

"No, not really," she said.

"I was just wondering…would you like to go to Midnight Mass with me after I get off work tonight?" The words came out in a rush, and it took her a second to process the question.

"Midnight Mass? Are you thinking about becoming a Catholic?" Rainey was puzzled.

"No! I mean, no, it's just that Phil's meeting his family for Midnight Mass after work, and he says the church is really beautiful and historic, and it will put you into the real spirit of Christmas. I thought I'd go, since I'm stuck here. It's better than sitting in my apartment wishing I was home."

"Hey, I'm not doing anything else tonight," she reassured him. "Do you want me to meet you somewhere?"

"The church is in Roxbury, so it's not really that far as the crow flies," Kevin explained. "But it's a pretty good hike, especially at night. And Phil says we'd better be there by eleven-thirty if we want to sit down. One of the ambulance crews from the Roxbury station will be here at eleven, and they'll take us out there. We can get back on the T, as long as you don't mind walking a bit more. It's a ten-minute hike each way from the church to the closest T-stop, and from the Longwood stop to your dorm."

"I don't mind walking." She smiled. It might be magical to walk outside in the snow with Kevin at one-o'clock in the morning under the full moon.

"We'll stop for you at the Brookline gatehouse—don't walk back to the hospital alone," he cautioned.

"I'll be waiting for you at the gatehouse at eleven," she promised. "I'm looking forward to it." Her book was forgotten as she began to rummage thorough her suitcase again, seeking a warmer pair of socks to wear under her boots—and a dressier pair of slacks to wear to church. Minutes later, she stood in front of her mirror, refreshing her makeup.

✳ ✳ ✳

Normally, Kevin walked or rode the T for the majority of his destinations in the city, saving his car for trips home. However, the T-stop distances would make it almost impossible for him to reach the church in Roxbury from the hospital in the available time—even in good weather. He thanked his lucky stars for the chance that had led to his ride with the ambulance crew. While drawing blood on a patient in the emergency department, he had asked one of the nurses about the best way to get to Mission Church. One of the EMTs had overheard, and made the offer of a ride.

"We're back and forth all the time, and it's only a ten-minute ride out there. You can bum a ride with us," the young man had promised. "But you'll have to get back on your own."

Sitting in the back of the ambulance, Kevin couldn't see out the front windows, and although the Simmons gatehouse was only a few blocks away, the journey seemed endless. He was surprised at his sudden impatience to be with Rainey again. *She's not my girlfriend,* he reminded himself. *I'm just trying to look out for her—like I would for any friend.*

71

Then he shook his head. He wasn't being honest with himself. His family prided themselves on their honesty, although his sister Jill occasionally took it too far, stumbling into tactlessness.

But he was attracted to Rainey, and not just as a friend. Still, there was no way she'd be interested in him. She probably had tons of rich guys asking her out, taking her to shows and fancy dinners. How could he compete with that? Taking her to church? A children's home? Buying her dinner at a hospital cafeteria?

He shook his head again. He didn't stand a chance.

The ambulance stopped in front of South Hall and he jumped out when the side door was opened, walking as quickly as possible on the snowy sidewalk. Rainey darted out from the gatehouse entrance just as he reached it.

He offered his arm to assist her to the waiting vehicle, which reversed in the drive and headed back up Brookline. Normally, the trip took ten minutes, but tonight the piles of plowed snow narrowed the streets and a thin coating of ice made the pavement treacherous, so despite the vehicle's studded tires, the driver had to use extreme caution.

Kevin worried that they might have to stand during what he feared would be a lengthy service, and checked his watch for the fourth time. Beside him on the bench seat, Rainey was quiet. She seemed to be studying the layout of the ambulance, with its array of emergency equipment. He wondered what she was thinking.

"What do you know about the church, Kevin?" she asked suddenly.

Used to both her and his sister's random *non sequiturs*, he barely blinked before answering. "Its official name is the Basilica of Our Lady of Perpetual Help, but most people

72

call it Mission Church—I don't know why. It's over a hundred years old. I got Phil to tell me a bit more about it, and he says it's enormous. Very ornate, lots of paintings inside." Kevin shrugged. "Other than that, I don't know anything."

Finally, the ambulance pulled up in front of a huge, double-towered edifice, set back from the street on a wide plaza. He craned his neck to see the gigantic rose window set in the front wall above the door and between the two spires. Illuminated from within, its colors were jewel-bright against the dark stone façade.

Bells pealed from both towers, welcoming the throngs of people heading into the church. He leaned over the driver's seat and thanked the EMT as the driver's partner opened the side door. Kevin jumped out and extended a hand to Rainey, who stepped down gracefully onto the snow-covered pavement.

The two of them joined the crowd entering by the central doors, and were enveloped in the warmth inside. Kevin blinked as his eyes adjusted to the dim, flickering light emanating from a row of candles above the ornate carved altar that backed up to the rear wall of the sanctuary.

Inside, a choir was singing the closing notes of "O Little Town of Bethlehem" accompanied by organ, violin, and flute.

Kevin felt as if the vibrations from the music were penetrating his whole body. Banks of red poinsettias flanked the altar and created bright splashes of color in the window wells. An usher greeted them and led them to a seat on the aisle, more than two-thirds of the way toward the front.

"We're not Catholic," he whispered to the man. "Shouldn't we be sitting in the back?"

"There's room for you here," replied the usher with a warm smile. "And you'll be able to see better. Welcome to Mission Church."

Kevin gave up and stepped into the pew after Rainey. Copying those around him, he knelt for a few seconds and then sat on the hard wooden pew, absorbing the details of the elegantly decorated interior of the church. Double columns of marble ran the length of the nave, and ribbed vaulting accentuated the arched, domed ceiling far above. The area was so dimly lit that he couldn't make out any details about the sumptuous artwork that was supposed to decorate the interior.

He glanced at Rainey and saw that she was also looking around with interest. He took the opportunity to admire her glowing skin and the long, dark lashes that touched her cheek each time she blinked. When she reached up to brush a strand of hair away from her face, he took note of her graceful, ringless fingers with their neat, short nails. He'd somehow expected her to wear nail polish and a ring or two. The simple bareness of her fingers was surprisingly alluring.

✳ ✳ ✳

Rainey felt Kevin's gaze on her and turned to him. "It's beautiful," she murmured. "Thank you for asking me." Her eye was caught by a large, elaborate Nativity scene set up on the left side of the church, behind the old communion railing. The stable was flanked by several Christmas trees, but she couldn't tell if they were real or not.

At the signal from the choir director, a boy who appeared to be about twelve years of age detached himself from the rest of the young choir massed on the right side of the sanctuary and carried a figure of the baby Jesus over to the stable tableau. Carefully, he placed it into the manger and returned to his place.

Several traditional carols, including Rainey's favorite, "The Little Drummer Boy," were beautifully sung by a choir before midnight began to strike. At that time, church bells went silent and the organ began to play a joyful processional.

As the priest walked up the center aisle, he swung a censer and Rainey inhaled the fragrant incense as she listened to the singing.

The music and the singing began at a rather subdued level, but the volume rose with each line, until the triumphant final lines burst forth, ending with a trumpet fanfare. As the music increased in volume and the procession neared the altar, the lights were also brought up, until the interior was as bright as it might be during the morning. It felt singularly appropriate when the priest began the first reading from Isaiah.

"The people who walked in darkness have seen a great light; upon those who dwelt in the land of gloom a light has shone."

Rainey had attended church services many times. During her boarding school years, it was required, and her parents held a membership with the Episcopal Cathedral of St. John the Divine in New York City. But her family's churchgoing was sporadic, and she was not in the habit, especially since she had lived in Boston. The Catholic service felt strangely familiar, yet somehow different from the Episcopal services she had attended in the past. Still, the ritual was comforting as well as joyful.

She watched others around her in order to stand, sit and kneel at the right times. She could tell Kevin was affected by the service, just as she was.

After Communion, the boy who had placed the figure of Jesus in the manger stepped up to a microphone as the rest of the choir sat. As the boy sang "O Holy Night" in a clear, sweet voice, Rainey felt shivers run up and down her spine when he reached the high notes.

As the Mass ended, the choir was joined by the congregation in a rousing rendition of "Joy to the World." Kevin and Rainey waited until the church was mostly emptied, and walked up to the front to take a closer look at the crèche.

"I'm glad we came, Rainey," Kevin said, as they gazed at the gentle scene. "I was feeling kind of sorry for myself since I'm working tomorrow as well as today. But now I'm getting into the real Christmas spirit."

"I know what you mean," she replied softly. "I was so upset because I couldn't go home when I wanted to. But if I'd been able to do that, I'd have missed all this. There will be other Christmases when we can be at home, but this one will be special."

Kevin took her hand and clasped it firmly. "Absolutely special." He smiled at her. "And now, we'd better get outside and head for the nearest T-stop, so we can make it home in time to get some sleep before the Home of the Innocents party."

Sunday, December 25

Rainey knew she'd never forget the Christmas party at the Home of the Innocents. Its residents were twenty-four children, from toddlers to age twelve, who had no one else to care for them.

Gathered in the cafeteria, they were a diverse group. Several were in wheelchairs or used braces and crutches to get around. Others wore tight stretchy masks over faces and hands, to inhibit scarring from severe burns. Some of the children breathed with the assistance of ventilators; some had facial or vocal tics or twisted their hair compulsively. Many needed help to eat. Rainey was seated between a dark-haired boy of about twelve, who seemed somehow familiar, and a little girl who appeared to be around six years old and was in a wheelchair, attended by a staff worker.

Although it was hard to speak above the buzz of conversation that permeated the cafeteria, Rainey felt that she should try to socialize with the quiet boy next to her.

"Hi, my name's Rainey," she said in a friendly voice. He stared at her but did not speak. When she moved to touch his arm, he scooted away, although he kept staring at her as if she fascinated him.

"This is Daniel," said one of the staff workers. "He's autistic and doesn't talk much. He was recently returned to us when a family that wanted to adopt him became overwhelmed with his need for rigid routines. We're trying to show him that it's okay to trust people, but his past experiences haven't done that. By the way, I'm Jenny."

"Hi, Jenny, I'm Rainey." She turned back to Daniel. "I'm sorry. I won't touch you if you don't want me to."

Daniel didn't reply, but brushed his arm repeatedly. "Hands carry germs," he finally said.

"Daniel loves to sing," Jenny added, "and he promised to sing after Santa visits." She added, "Daniel, eat some more of your turkey. It's your favorite."

Daniel stopped brushing his arm, and began to eat his dinner again, methodically cutting each bit to precisely the same size.

Rainey suddenly realized why Daniel seemed familiar. "Did he sing at the Mission Church last night?" she asked. "I couldn't see him well, but there was a young boy there who sang 'O Holy Night' beautifully."

"Yes, he did," the worker confirmed. "He's one of a group of our children who sings in the Mission Church Youth choir. Most of them are younger, though, and couldn't stay up that late."

"Daniel, I really enjoyed your singing last night," Rainey said, careful not to touch the boy again. "Your voice is beautiful, and I can't wait to hear you sing today." She smiled warmly at Daniel, and after a long minute, he smiled back at her.

One of the nuns who administered the Home moved around as the children ate, checking to make sure every one was being attended to. Rainey had met her when she and Kevin arrived, and immediately felt attracted by the woman's serene expression and the quiet strength in her voice and handshake.

Kevin was feeding a small boy named Jon, whose head lolled against a neck rest built into his specially adapted wheelchair-stroller. She wasn't surprised to see how gentle Kevin was, and how carefully he adjusted his motions to accommodate the boy. She remembered how patient he had always been with the younger children in their neighborhood.

"He's going to be a good doctor," Jenny said, apparently noticing the direction of Rainey's gaze. "And Jon is really a champ. In spite of all of his challenges, he has a sweet personality and never gives up. He's a hero."

"Yes, a real hero," agreed Rainey. "And you're right, Kevin will be a very good doctor." He really was a great guy in general, she realized. Too bad he wasn't attracted to her.

Although he had been treating her differently that day, not so much like a kid sister. Was there a new warmth in his eyes when he glanced at her?

Before she had time to analyze it further, it was time to clean up. More quickly than she would have believed possible, the tables were cleared and wiped, and Santa Claus entered with a great jingling of bells and a jolly "Ho, ho, ho." He carried a great bag on his back, obviously bulging with toys. An elf, several inches shorter than Santa and much thinner, followed, dragging his own bag of toys.

The children responded, many of the younger ones jumping, waving, or wriggling in their excitement. Cries of "Hi, Santa" and "Where's Rudolph?" mingled.

After walking among the children for a few moments, Santa sat down in a large armchair at the front of the room and pulled a roll of paper from his bag. Peering through a pair of rimless glasses, he seemed to be reading it.

After a few seconds of study, he announced, "Now, boys and girls, I've got my list and I've checked it twice. It has the names of everyone who's been naughty or nice." He glanced around the room at the assembled children. "Ho, ho, ho, I hope everyone here has been nice. I've got gifts for all of the nice boys and girls."

A few of the children looked worried, Rainey noticed with a smile. However, as Santa began to read off the names of children who were to receive a gift, it became obvious that every one of them was going to get a toy, a book, or a game. Santa's elf trotted back and forth from the chair to the children as each name was called. Kevin was helping some of the children open their gifts, and gathering the discarded wrappings and bows into an empty box.

"Well, well, well. I see that everyone here has been good this year," Santa announced after giving out the last gift. "You're a great bunch of kids, and I'm glad I had the chance to come here today. Now remember, you've got to be just as good next year. Ho, ho, ho." With that, Santa laid a finger aside of his nose, but instead of exiting via a chimney, he and his elf simply walked back out the door by which they had entered.

On a signal from Jenny, Daniel stood and walked to the spot Santa had vacated. Sister Cabrini moved a microphone in front of him, and another nun took a seat at the upright piano which had been moved away from the wall. Daniel stood up tall and straight, and waited for his cue. Rainey expected a repeat of "O Holy Night" and was surprised when, instead, she heard the opening notes of "Have Yourself a Merry Little Christmas". His pure alto voice held each note perfectly.

She clapped with great enthusiasm as Daniel finished the last verse. With the end of the musical performance, the party began to break up. The staff began to collect the children to return to their rooms.

Rainey joined Kevin, who had turned Jon over to an attendant. "You seemed so comfortable with Jon," she remarked. "You must have been coming here for a long time."

"Yes, Phil and Matt got me involved here when I first started working at the hospital," he said. "I was nervous at first. It's a lot different reading and learning about kids' conditions and health needs than dealing with them directly. Volunteering has made me more familiar with situations I'll see in practice. It's given me a lot more respect for the parents and others who care for handicapped kids. And made me realize how lucky I really am."

"Yes, I know," she agreed as she watched the children heading back to their rooms. "How do you keep coming back, though? Some of the situations are so sad—I'm afraid it might get depressing after a while." Unexpectedly, her eyes filled with tears and she dug in her pocket for a tissue.

Kevin put his arm around her slim shoulders and gave an encouraging squeeze. "That's one reason I don't want to work exclusively with handicapped kids, because I think I'd be too sad. Hopefully as a physician, I can make a difference in the lives of kids, help to find effective treatments and cures for their physical problems."

"But Kevin, the problems of the kids here are too complicated for one doctor to take on," Rainey protested. "How can you really help them?"

"As part of a team. I want to make a difference in their lives from an emotional and mental health standpoint, too," Kevin explained. "Nurses, social workers, therapists, and aides—so many people bring different skills to the table, and all of them are important. And I hope I'll be able to educate parents. Maybe I won't be able to help these kids and their parents, but my own patients...those are the people I want to help. And I think I can help them."

Kevin's eyes blazed with enthusiasm as he spoke, and Rainey realized that he had more of his sister Jill's stubborn determination than she had ever thought.

Phil walked back into the cafeteria, where Kevin and Rainey were still standing. In each hand, he carried a large shopping bag from Filene's department store. Inside one, Rainey could glimpse a bit of red velvet and a strip of white fur; the other held a fluffy pillow.

"Old Santa outdid himself this year, didn't he?" Phil asked with a grin.

"Great job, you jolly old elf," Kevin agreed, clapping his friend on the back. He fetched Rainey's coat and held it while she slipped her arms into the sleeves. While she tied her scarf and pulled on her gloves, Kevin donned his own outerwear and checked his watch again. "Now, where's Carlisle? We'd better hotfoot it to the hospital if we don't want to be late for work."

"Here I am," announced Matt, jogging into the cafeteria.

He also carried a Filene's bag, Rainey noticed, but it hardly appeared to contain anything. The green elf costume wasn't nearly as bulky as a Santa suit, she supposed. As she was about to greet him, she looked at his face and did a double take. Matt's ears were long and pointed at the top, and his nose was a bit longer and redder than seemed natural, too. Her jaw dropped and before she could compose her features, she heard Phil and Kevin guffawing. Matt's face went crimson—except for his nose and ears!

"Yeah, laugh all you want, guys—I forgot my cold cream," Matt said, beginning to laugh himself. "I use cold cream to get the fake nose and ears off," he explained to Rainey. "Well, the patients will get lucky today—one of Santa's elves will be helping to take care of them!"

She joined in the laughter, and they all walked outside, heading back toward the hospital, only a block away. Rainey took deep breaths of the crisp, cold air, and watched it come out in puffs of white vapor. The deep snow that blanketed the ground glittered in the sunlight; it had not lost its freshness yet.

She held Kevin's arm to balance herself, although she wasn't really worried about falling. Kevin was solid and steady next to her, but she had seen the passion in his face when he spoke of his ambitions just a little while ago, and she was filled with a desire to help him realize his dreams. There was much more to him than "Boring Kevin", as he sometimes—scornfully—referred to himself.

The walk didn't take as long as they had expected, and as the group reached the front of the hospital, Kevin said, "I'm going to walk Rainey back to her dorm. Can you guys let Karen know I may be a few minutes late? I'll be there as soon as I can."

"I don't believe my ears," exclaimed Matt. "Kevin the punctual might be a few minutes late!"

"Go on," said Phil. "It's only two-fifteen. Don't sweat it, I know Karen won't mind." He gave Kevin a slight push. "Get going, Shelton. Have yourself a merry Christmas!"

"Thanks, guys!" Kevin grinned and turned to her. "I guess I've got my orders," he quipped.

"Bye, Matt! Bye, Phil! Merry Christmas!" Rainey cried. "I had a wonderful time." She turned, took Kevin's arm again, and the pair strode briskly toward the entrance to the gated residence campus. They began to catch each other up on their career plans as they walked. Rainey told Kevin about her internship at a design studio that was to start in January.

"At first I worried that design was something really… um, shallow…to be studying," she admitted. "But it's fascinating to learn ways to adapt design to make people's lives easier and more convenient, and still have beautiful lines and colors."

"I think you'll be able to help plenty of people that way," Kevin said.

She glanced quickly at his face and was encouraged by the glow in his eyes as he looked back at her. "That's important work. And if the adaptations can be attractive as well as useful, well, it's not shallow at all."

"I'm excited about it," she agreed. "What about you? Jill said you've been busy applying to residency programs. When will you know what you're doing next year?"

"I should start hearing back from the programs I've applied to in January," Kevin said. "Then I'll schedule interviews at the top three programs that accept me, so I'll have a better feel for my fit to them, as well as them deciding if I'd fit in there."

"Sounds complicated," she said. "But I'm sure your top three will all want you."

"I hope so—but that might make the decision harder!" He chuckled for a moment, and then sighed. "I can't remember when I didn't want to be a doctor," he continued. "Med school has been really hard, and there were a few times when I wondered why I ever thought I could do it. But I can't wait to put the things I've learned in the classroom into practice. Working as a lowly phlebotomist has helped keep me humble, too." He laughed, a deep, warm laugh that settled into Rainey's heart.

"Speaking of work…" He checked the time. "I should be able to make it on time if I hurry. We're almost back to your dorm now."

Sure enough, the gatehouse was only a few yards away. Rainey fished her student ID from her jeans pocket, and showed it to the security guard, who pushed the button that unlocked the gate. They walked as briskly as possible up the last few yards of sidewalk, still covered in trampled snow. At the top of the steps to the dorm, she turned to Kevin.

"Good-bye, Kevin," she said. "Thank you for inviting me to the Home of the Innocents party. In fact, thanks for everything you've done to keep me from being lonely. I was wallowing in self-pity, and I hate wallowing, but you've helped me to find the real spirit of Christmas."

"Me too, honestly. I didn't realize I had been wallowing a little too. But it was great to be able to spend time with you in the past couple of days." Kevin took her hand. "Seeing how much you've grown up. Maybe we can get together again soon. Like, out to dinner or something? What do you think?"

"What do I think?" Rainey couldn't believe her ears. "I think it would be perfectly perfect."

Impulsively, she threw her arms around Kevin's neck and kissed him. After an instant of shocked stillness, she felt Kevin return her kiss, and he wrapped his own arms around her. A current of electricity flared between them, and the kiss became more urgent as their mouths ground against each other. Kevin's tongue teased Rainey's lips apart, and time seemed to stand still.

"Get a room!" a voice called.

Rainey pulled away from Kevin. She noted he was breathing as hard as she was. Her face flamed as she looked for the source of the voice. It was Ellen, the other girl on her floor who had been stranded by the storm. Ellen waved and grinned. She had passed them and was headed for the gatehouse.

"Just kidding, although the dorm has plenty of empty rooms right now! Merry Christmas, Rainey! Merry Christmas, Tall, Dark and Handsome."

"Merry Christmas, Ellen!" Rainey waved back. Beside her, Kevin sputtered with laughter before calling out a "Merry Christmas" to Ellen as well.

She turned back to face him. "So, I probably won't see you before next weekend."

"Probably not," he agreed. "Be careful, and tell the folks I'll see them next weekend—if it doesn't snow again!" He was looking at her in a totally new way, and it made Rainey feel all tingly inside.

The sky's blue had dulled, and a few flakes of snow were falling. "I hope we won't get any more accumulation," Kevin commented. "I'd hate for you to be delayed again in leaving."

Rainey nodded. "Me, too. I mean, me neither. I mean, I hope I can leave tomorrow!" She wondered if that last statement was really true…now. "Hey, you'd better get going. I don't want you to get fired." She gave him a little push.

Kevin pulled her to him again, returning his lips to hers in another electrifying kiss. Rainey found herself growing dizzy with the sensations he created, and it was all she could do to push him away again. "Remember, you don't want to be in trouble," she said, her lips still tingling.

"I'm claiming a raincheck, though," Kevin protested. "We weren't really finished here." After a final peck on her cheek, he released her and began to retrace his steps. Rainey could hear him whistling as he walked away, and her heart lifted as she recognized the familiar melody.

Now this is what I call a merry little Christmas, she thought, slowly climbing the steps to her room.

The End

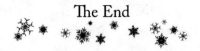

About Claire Taylor Allen

An Army brat, Claire Taylor Allen lived in many different places while growing up. Although she loved the frequent changes of scene and meeting new people, she also found a sense of stability in the imaginary worlds she entered through reading. In the past few years, she has begun to write as well as read.

She was inspired to write "Snowbound" when she read about the great blizzard of 1979 that brought Boston to a standstill. She wondered how two people who knew each other slightly would cope with being away from their families at Christmas.

Claire enjoys reading (particularly mysteries), walking, cooking, and making webpages. She is married and has three grown daughters. She has worked as a registered nurse for over thirty years, and in her spare time she enjoys listing and selling books online.

RYL REGEHR

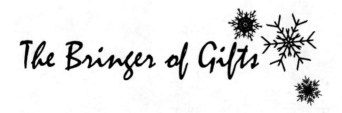

The Bringer of Gifts

It wasn't until she was almost to the front of the line that Carol Merton realized that she'd forgotten toilet paper. Again. Her shoulders slumped as she weighed her options. She could stay in line, head home, and hope that there was enough Kleenex in the house to cover any emergencies, or she could brave the crowded aisles and stand in line for another twenty minutes.

While she was still biting her bottom lip and trying to remember the exact thickness of the current and last roll of toilet paper hanging in her bathroom, she heard someone behind her clear his throat. She turned around and saw a man about her own age with casually messy light brown hair standing two people behind her.

"Forget something?" he asked, a friendly smile on his face.

Carol eyed him warily, visions of psychopathic murderers dancing in her head. Wasn't this how some of them lured their victims? By being friendly in normal, everyday settings?

"Maybe."

Realizing that the man was probably harmless, and that she sounded ungracious, she added, "Same item the last three trips. I think I have a mental block."

The man laughed. "Well, that doesn't sound healthy. I'll save your place if you want to go back for it."

She stared at him, still undecided if it would be worth the frantic rush. The Christmas crowds were cut-throat, especially at Superstore.

"I'm completely trustworthy," he assured her, his blue eyes crinkling with amusement. "Scout's honour. And you can leave your cart with me."

"You really know how to sweeten a deal." She laughed, shoving aside all thoughts of mass murderers. "Thank you! I'll be right back." Her industrial-size black catch-all bag firmly tucked under her arm, she set off toward the paper aisle at a brisk speed-walk. Her deep red wool coat swung against her knees as she hurried, determined not to lose her place in line or inconvenience the other customers. She returned to the check-out, clutching a jumbo package of Royale toilet paper. The kind stranger had, indeed, saved her spot, and there was only one customer ahead of them.

"You sure that will be enough?" the man teased, laughing at the pack of twenty-four double rolls.

She blushed and shoved the offending item in her cart. "I'm not running out again any time soon," she explained. "And I always wanted a cat," she added, staring at the fluffy white kittens on the packaging. She clapped a hand over her mouth. Where had that come from? Five minutes in the presence of a virtual stranger, and she was babbling like a ninny.

"Cats are good," the man agreed, his lips twitching.

Carol pushed her cart forward and loaded her items onto the conveyor belt. Out of the corner of her eye, she watched as her spot-saver unloaded a jug of windshield wiper fluid and a can of automotive oil from his basket.

"Well, it was nice meeting you," she said awkwardly when she had paid for her purchases.

"My pleasure," the man insisted, holding out his hand.

She hesitated for only a second and then shook his offered hand. Because really, the odds that he was a maniacal axe-wielding butcher of helpless females were pretty slim. Probably.

Upon making contact with him, however, her opinion changed. Her eyes widened as a strong, calming heat spread through her, starting at the fingertips. Even more strange was the sudden, distinct aroma of peppermint. Who was this man?

Her eyes flew to his, and she noted that he seemed almost as surprised as she was.

"My name is Nick," he said abruptly, removing his hand from hers. He shifted away from her, although his eyes remained locked with hers.

"Carol," she stammered before she could stop herself. Great, she inwardly cursed. You've given your name to a complete stranger. Why not just take out an ad in the paper inviting people to stalk you?

But Nick didn't appear to be using her slip against her. In fact, it seemed as if he were trying to get away from her as he jammed his change in the pocket of his navy pea coat and swept up his purchases.

"Drive safely," he called over his shoulder as he strode away, his bag of car maintenance items dangling from his hand. He was gone before she could blink.

Shaking her head at the bizarre encounter, Carol pushed her laden cart into the parking lot. After fighting her way over the snow and slush-covered surface, she loaded the groceries into her ten-year-old Toyota and settled into the driver seat. After only minimal coaxing, the car sprang to life despite the frigid temperature. Ten minutes later, she was hauling everything up the two flights of stairs to her apartment.

"Carol! You shouldn't be carrying all those heavy bags," Mr. Braun scolded as she neared her apartment.

Carol smiled at her elderly neighbour. "I didn't want to make two trips," she said, pausing to stamp more snow off her shoes.

Mr. Braun shook his head and made tsking sounds. "What you need is a man to help you. I have a very nice nephew…" he said, referring to his nephew living two provinces to the west in the city of Calgary.

After several years of practice, she was able to refrain from rolling her eyes. Mr. Braun had archaic attitudes in some respects, but since he was as kind as he was vocal, she tried not to take him too seriously.

"I'm perfectly capable of carrying my own groceries," she said, setting them down to dig her keys out of her pocket.

He only shook his head, obviously unconvinced. "But a nice girl like you shouldn't have to. Why don't you let me call my nephew and put in a good word for you? I never see you with any young men."

She laughed, having had this conversation with him many times before. The lines changed only slightly, and both enjoyed the verbal sparring. "But then I might have to share my remote control. Nope. Not going to happen." She pushed open her door and dropped the bags of groceries just inside her apartment. "Have a good night, Mr. Braun," she called, closing and locking the door behind her.

A good night was exactly what she planned to have, herself. After everything was put away, she could enjoy her dinner, pop in a movie, and ignore the work she had brought home with her. Well, not precisely work, she reminded herself. More like party planning. She shuddered. As the legal assistant with the most experience at her firm, she had been roped into planning the annual Christmas party. Once again, she cursed her friend Marge for quitting the previous summer and leaving her with all sorts of extra responsibilities.

Well, the party planning could wait for another day. It was almost complete, anyway. The only task left was decorating the bonus envelopes.

The thought of a bonus cheered her immensely, and she rummaged through her cupboards and fridge with new interest in supper. Though she was tempted to skip supper and go straight to the microwave popcorn and movie, she forced herself to open a pre-packaged bag of stir-fry meat and vegetables. Turning up the volume on her over-played and much-loved Boney M Christmas CD, she sang along as the wok sizzled. Her stellar performance, though, was interrupted by a knock at her door. With a sigh, she turned down the volume of the stereo and temperature of the wok.

"Mr. Braun?" she called, heading for the door. Since no one had buzzed to be let in, she knew it was probably a fellow tenant at her door. "I'm sorry about the music—"

She stopped abruptly as she peeked through the peep hole. Her mouth dropped open, and she stood, frozen.

The knock sounded again.

It was the man from Superstore. Carol felt the first licks of panic. It had happened. It had really happened. He had followed her home, and he was going to kill her. Her hands began to shake.

She couldn't even try to pretend that she wasn't home—he must have heard her music, and heard her call to Mr. Braun. But he couldn't force her to open the door. She just wouldn't open the door, and everything would be fine. He'd leave, and she could go back to making supper and watching a movie.

"Mr. Braun?" Nick called. "Are you okay?"

Mr. Braun? He must have read the tenant roster in the foyer, she decided. Just because he knew her neighbour's name was no reason for her to open her door.

"Mr. Braun, I'm the man you just buzzed in. I have the package from your nephew here. Would you like me to leave it outside?"

She edged away from the door as quietly as she could. Hoping that she was doing the right thing, she picked up her cordless phone and dialled her next door neighbour.

"Mr. Braun?" she whispered. "There's a man at my apartment door asking for you. Did you buzz him up? Do you know who he is?"

A hearty laugh answered her questions, and she sighed with relief.

"Yes, I'm expecting him," her neighbour said. "You just go back to your singing, Carol. I like that CD."

Carol blushed and hung up the phone. Seconds later, she heard Mr. Braun greeting Nick, and she turned back to her supper. One look in the wok told her that she'd left the vegetables too long, so she scraped the soggy, over-cooked mess into the garbage with a frustrated sigh. Apparently she would be having that popcorn sooner, rather than later.

Before she could even get the package unwrapped, there was another knock at the door.

This time when she glanced through the peep hole, she saw both Nick and Mr. Braun.

"Open up, Carol," Mr. Braun called. "There's someone I'd like you to meet."

Carol winced as "Matchmaker" from *Fiddler on the Roof* played in her head. Somehow though, she didn't recall the Matchmaker being dressed in a cardigan and pants that were hitched to the armpits.

"Coming," she called. For half a second she wished that she hadn't changed out of her work clothes and into a pair of comfy jeans and a sweater, but the notion was short-lived. It wasn't as if she really wanted to impress Nick, and it was pretty much going to be impossible to wow him with her sophisticated, glamorous life-style after he'd seen her buying toilet paper. With kittens on it.

Before Mr. Braun could knock again, she opened the door. "Hi Mr. Braun, Nick," she said.

Nick's startled double-take convinced her that he hadn't followed her, or even known that she lived in the building. "It's Carol, right?" he asked, a bright smile lighting up his face.

"You know each other?" Mr. Braun shook his head in disgust. "You're hopeless," he told Carol. "You have access to a handsome young man like this and you're still single?"

"We just met at the store tonight," Carol protested.

Mr. Braun's grunt conveyed his assessment of her argument.

Nick winked at her before saying, "I would have asked for her phone number, but I'm pretty sure she was fingering her pepper spray."

"Kids," Mr. Braun muttered. "You still carry that stuff? I thought you put it away after those self-defence classes."

Carol shrugged. "The teacher recommended we carry it."

"Well, I'm glad you're protected," he admitted grudgingly. "But what about all the nice young men out there? Like Nick?"

"She's right, Mr. Braun," Nick said. "You can't be too careful these days. I'm glad that Carol is cautious."

"Well, you don't need to be strangers anymore," the elderly man decided. "Carol, this is my nephew Rick's friend. He's making a few deliveries for friends before he heads to his parents for Christmas. Nick, this is the girl I keep telling that no-good nephew of mine that he needs to come up here to meet."

"Oh!" Nick exclaimed. "I've heard about you."

She glared at her neighbour before politely responding, "Oh?"

"Yes," Nick continued, "something about fire trucks?"

"That wasn't my fault! I swear! Mr. Braun, what have you been telling Rick?"

Mr. Braun grinned. "Rick likes his girls adventurous. I had to play up some of your, um, more dramatic moments."

She covered her face with her hands, then brushed back her chin-length red hair when it fell forward.

"I really should be going," Nick said. "I have a few other deliveries to make this evening."

"See what a nice young man he is?" Mr. Braun nudged Carol's side. "He's dropping off Christmas presents that his friends sent along with him."

"That's very sweet," she agreed, forgetting her own embarrassment and laughing as Nick took his turn at looking uncomfortable.

"Yes, well, it's the least I could do, seeing as I was passing through."

"Surely you have time to take a young lady out for coffee," Mr. Braun suggested. "You can't have that many presents left to deliver."

"No, not that many, but they appear to be spread out over the entire city," Nick responded. "And since I'm not that familiar with the roads here, I thought I'd better start early."

"Carol's lived here all her life! Haven't you, Carol?"

"Yes," she admitted. "Would you like me to take a look at the addresses? I can make sure you're planning the best route."

Nick shrugged. "Why not? Here's a map with the locations marked."

She glanced at the well-worn map marked with red dots in the four corners of the city and winced. "You weren't kidding. You'll need to leave now if you want to deliver these before people start turning in for the night."

"I thought I'd take Fermor and work my way downtown."

"Fermor's under construction. What you want to do is take Osborne."

Nick moved closer to look at the map over her shoulder. With a sigh, he asked, "You have a pen?"

"Don't be ridiculous," Mr. Braun interrupted. "Carol will be happy to go along with you."

"She will?"

"I will?"

"Of course you will," Mr. Braun told her. "I'd consider it a favour."

There was no way she could back out gracefully. After a longing look at the bag of microwave popcorn still sitting, unpopped, on her counter, she nodded. "Sure. No problem. I didn't really have plans for tonight, anyway."

Mr. Braun snorted. "You never have plans, honey."

Carol felt her eyes narrow. It was true, but still! Did he really need to say it out loud?

"You really don't have to—" Nick started, but she cut him off.

"You'll be driving around until midnight if I don't," she told him. "It's no trouble."

"And I'm sure Nick would be happy to take you out for something to eat afterward," Mr. Braun added.

"He would?"

"I would? I mean, of course, I would." Nick reached for the map, and his fingers brushed hers. For the second time that evening, she felt the tingle of warmth and caught a whiff of peppermint. "It would be my pleasure."

✳ ❄ ✳

"I thought you said to turn onto Osborne," Nick said, squinting at the street name on the sign.

"I did," Carol said, glad that Nick was driving. The roads were slick with a fresh snowfall, and many of the signs were hard to read.

"But this is Balmoral," he pointed out.

"Osborne turned into Balmoral."

"Oh."

"But only after it turned into Memorial," Carol added helpfully.

"Who planned this city?" Nick wondered out loud.

"I'm guessing no one," was her cheerful answer. "We consider it part of the charm."

He snorted. "Is that also why the street signs are about two inches big? So you can't read the names of the unplanned streets?"

"Yup. Keeps life interesting. We like our driving to be a challenge." She settled back in the passenger seat of Nick's late model SUV with the map spread across her lap. Outside, the wind swirled huge, sticky snowflakes around them, but she felt a sense of encapsulation in the cozy vehicle. She was trying to remind herself to be cautious of this man, but the heated leather seats were clouding her judgement.

When they pulled up in front of the first address on his list, he left the vehicle running and hurried to the back. She watched as he navigated the icy walk to the front door, carrying a gaily wrapped package. He handed the package to the occupant, exchanged a few words, and came back to the vehicle.

"No chit-chat this time?" she asked. "I thought you were going to have a sit-down visit with each of them, just like Mr. Braun."

"Not this time."

She raised her eyebrows at the cryptic response, but didn't comment.

"Where to next?" he asked.

She turned her attention back to the map. "We're going to head to the north end now." She frowned as she studied the address. "Are you sure this is right?"

"I double-checked all the addresses. Why?"

"It's just not a good part of town." She bit her bottom lip.

"How not good?" he asked.

"Probably ninety percent of the murders in this city take place within a few blocks of this address."

The information didn't seem to surprise him.

"Who are you delivering presents for?" Carol asked before she could stop herself.

Nick leaned further back in the driver's seat and shifted his hands to a more relaxed grip on the steering wheel. "Whoever needs it."

"You're starting to sound like the mafia," she told him.

His bark of laughter surprised them both. "I can assure you that I'm not a part of organized crime. Or disorganized crime, for that matter. I'm completely trustworthy and above-board. Left at the light?"

The closer they came to their destination, the more desolate and bleak the neighbourhoods became. The houses were poorly maintained and close together. She shivered when she saw a young woman without a jacket pushing a baby stroller despite the late hour and frigid temperature. A car filled with teenage boys pulled up alongside them, their music so loud that Nick's vehicle shook.

"Not the best part of town," he agreed. He didn't seem overly concerned, but she couldn't hide the helpless pity she'd felt watching the young girl. She was probably still a teenager, and already saddled with the care of an infant. Carol could only hope that the baby had been better dressed than his mother. And that they were on their way to warmth and safety.

"I wish I had presents for all of them," Nick said softly. "But not everyone is ready." He met her eyes as they pulled up in front of the worst street on the block. "Will you come with me?"

She almost snorted. As if she was going to stay by herself in a freezing car in a terrible part of town! Something in his eyes stopped her, though. He seemed to be asking more than just the words of the question, but she couldn't figure out what she was missing.

"Would you like me to?" she finally asked.

"It would probably be best," he said. After a pause he added, "And yes, I would like you to come."

Tucking her bag under her arm, she followed him to the back of the SUV, where he retrieved a package from a box of gifts. He held it for a moment, and a thoughtful smile crept over his face.

Carol shifted nervously in the cold. "So, you know these people, right?"

"Never met them."

"But you're delivering gifts from friends of theirs?" She glanced at the dilapidated house with trepidation.

"Something like that."

"Do you ever actually answer a question?" she demanded in exasperation.

"It's happened." He smiled broadly, and she felt some of her tension dissipate. After all, there was probably nothing to worry about. Still, she fingered her cell phone in her jacket pocket and made sure it was in easy reach.

Nick rapped on the door, a friendly and relaxed expression on his face. His expression didn't waver when the door was answered by the biggest man Carol had ever seen.

He had to be two hundred and fifty pounds, she guessed, and he was all muscle. His skin was dark, but in the poor lighting she couldn't determine his ethnicity. She involuntarily took a step backward, but no one seemed to notice.

"Elliot Smith?" Nick asked.

The man's eyes narrowed. "Who's asking?"

"I have a delivery for an Elliot Smith. Do you know where I can find him?" Nick's voice was polite without being overly friendly, and it was obvious that the big man didn't know what to make of him.

"I'm Elliot," the man said. "But most call me Big Guy."

Carol choked back a nervous giggle. Of course they called him Big Guy! Elliot's eyes flickered to hers, and she regretted her lapse and fidgeted under his scrutiny.

"Could we come in?" Nick asked. "It's pretty cold out here."

She shot him a panicked glance, but he kept his eyes trained on the Big Guy. She really hadn't counted on going inside. The car was looking better and better. At least she could lock the doors. Not that that would stop anyone from getting in if they wanted to, but…

Elliot's eyes swept over her from head to toe and lingered in strategic places. "Either of you carrying?" he asked.

Nick shook his head.

"Pepper spray," Carol admitted, not relishing the thought of explaining if it were found on her later.

Elliot let out a bark of laughter, and for the first time, his eyes showed a glimmer of warmth. "Bring it on, baby. If we can't dodge your pepper spray, we deserve to get hit."

She frowned. Was he making fun of her ability to use the pepper spray? Involuntarily, her hand slipped into her pocket and she fingered the cool canister.

"C'mon, Trigger Finger," Elliot called over his shoulder as he turned back into the house. "You, too, Delivery Boy."

Carol and Nick knocked the snow off their shoes and followed him into the cramped foyer. A powerful aroma nearly overwhelmed her, and she couldn't help a small cough. "What is that?" she whispered.

Nick grinned. "You didn't go to college, did you?"

"I did too!" she protested.

Nick merely shook his head. "We won't stay long," he assured her.

101

She studied her surroundings curiously as she followed Elliot. Three men almost as large as Big Guy were sprawled on threadbare furniture, watching a big screen television in the living room. Multiple tattoos were visible, some in full colour, others in varying stages of completeness. All eyes turned to Nick and Carol.

"They're here to make a delivery," Big Guy told them, not pausing as he walked through to the kitchen. The other men nodded and turned their attention back to the car chase on the television. Apparently deliveries were not out of the ordinary, she surmised.

She gulped nervously as they entered the kitchen. The counter tops were covered in dirty dishes and take-out containers. Despite the frigid temperature, the back door was open, and they were protected from the elements by only a screen door. Elliot cleared a space on the battered kitchen table and motioned for them to sit.

Reluctantly, she lowered herself onto a kitchen chair with a ripped cushion that allowed yellowed stuffing to spread freely. Nick sat beside her, his arm resting on the back of her chair but not touching her. No warmth, and no smell of peppermint, Carol noted. Although it was doubtful that her nose would be capable of smelling anything other than the terrible stench that pervaded the house.

"You got something for me?" Elliot asked.

Nick shrugged. "That depends. You ready for it?"

Elliot studied him, and for the first time, Carol noted the intelligence in his eyes. Elliot might be big and scary, she decided, but there was more to him than that.

"You wouldn't be here if I weren't," Elliot said, his eyes still fixed on Nick's.

Nick nodded imperceptibly and slid the brightly wrapped package across the table. The look on Elliot's face when he opened the box, however, had Carol fumbling for her pepper spray.

"What is this?" Elliot asked, his voice deathly quiet.

Nick shrugged. "Christmas present."

Elliot shoved the box back toward him. "There's been a mistake."

"No mistake."

Carol felt as if she were following the action at a tennis match. Curiosity finally got the better of her. "What is it?" she asked.

Neither man looked at her, though she thought she felt Nick's arm edge closer to her shoulders. Still without breaking eye contact, Elliot gestured for her to take a look in the box. Dividing her attention between the two statue-like men, she lifted the lid of the box.

"A stuffed animal?" she questioned, her voice incredulous. She turned her full attention to Nick. "You gave Big Guy a stuffed animal?"

Nick shook his head. "I'm just the delivery man. And it's not just a stuffed animal, is it, Elliot?"

Elliot's eyes dropped to the box. "Where did you get it?" he asked, his voice a gruff whisper.

"Does it matter?" Nick countered. "The point is, you have it."

Since Elliot didn't appear to be reaching for a gun, or calling in for reinforcements, Carol took a chance. "What's the big deal? It's not even new."

"It holds sentimental value," Nick said. "Doesn't it, Elliot?" It wasn't so much a question as a statement.

"Do I look like a man who does sentimental value?" Big Guy questioned.

"No, you don't," Nick agreed. "That's why it's here."

She added a third player to the tennis match, spreading her attention between the two men and the stuffed rabbit. The muted sounds of the television in the next room filtered into the kitchen. No one spoke.

"How did you get Bugsy?" Elliot finally asked. He reached toward the stuffed rabbit, but stopped short of touching it.

"Doesn't matter. He's yours, now."

She could tell that Elliot didn't like Nick's cryptic answers any more than she did, but he held his tongue.

"What am I supposed to do with it?"

Nick stood up, clapping the massive man on the shoulder. "That's up to you."

Carol stood up and prepared to join Nick in leaving, but Elliot wasn't ready to let them go.

"I haven't seen this in almost twenty years," he whispered.

"Not since she died." Nick's statement was simple, and no one doubted its veracity.

Carol sucked in a breath of air.

"She was only five," Big Guy mumbled. "Five years old! Who gets cancer and dies at the age of five?"

"Louisa did," Nick answered the rhetorical question. He reached into the box and gently withdrew the faded rabbit. "And she gave this to you before she died. She wanted you to have it, Elliot."

Elliot stared at the rabbit in Nick's hand.

"Are you ready to accept it now?"

Carol watched Elliot battle himself. The desire to touch the stuffed rabbit was there, but it was as if he couldn't force himself to extend his arm to take it.

"What am I supposed to do with it?" Elliot demanded. "Sleep with it under my pillow?"

"If that's what it takes." Nick continued to offer the stuffed animal.

"It won't bring her back." Elliot's voice was low, but clear.

"Certainly not her body," Nick agreed. "But there are other parts of her it can bring back."

"Like what?" Elliot asked suspiciously.

"Like her unconditional love and trust." Nick moved closer to Elliot and placed the rabbit in his hand.

Elliot sucked in a sharp breath. The urge to recoil was firmly printed on his face. "She shouldn't have felt those things to begin with," he hissed. "What good did it do her? I didn't live up to her trust. I didn't save her."

"You were eight years old," Nick reminded him. "All she wanted was for you to love her, and to be there for her. You did both."

A single tear slipped down the big man's face as he pondered the words. "Why bring this to me now?" he asked. He fingered one of the long ears as he waited for Nick's answer.

"Because you've had enough time to be angry at the world. It's time to remember what's important, Elliot. Before it's too late."

Elliot frowned. "What does that mean? And what's important?"

Nick smiled, probably amused at the picture of the massive man holding the rabbit to his chest. "You'll figure it out." He turned and walked out of the kitchen. Carol followed, her confusion growing with each step she took.

"Wait!" Elliot called. "Who are you?" He followed them through the living room, ignoring the men watching television.

"I'm Nick," he answered before they slipped out the door.

Once on the sidewalk, Carol planted her feet. "What was that?" she whispered, not wanting to be overheard by either the occupants of the house or anyone roaming the streets.

Nick placed an arm around her, and the cold night disappeared in a wave of warmth. The heightened awareness, nerves, and anxiety that she had felt in the house abated. "That was a Christmas delivery. Now come on. We need to keep moving if we're going to deliver all the presents tonight." He guided her back to the car, keeping her firmly tucked under his arm as they navigated the snowy sidewalk. "You were right. This isn't the best neighbourhood."

She stared at him in disbelief. "That's it?" she asked as he opened her car door. "That's all you're going to tell me?"

"What else do you need to know?" he questioned. He slid into the driver's seat and started the car. She held her hands to the vents and waited for the air to heat up.

"Who was that guy? Who sent the rabbit? And who are you? Are you really just delivering presents for friends? That was more than a little weird back there." The questions tumbled out one after the other.

"How about you ask me again later?" he suggested. "Right now I need directions for getting to the next address." He must have caught the uncertainty on her face because he hastened to add, "I can always take you home before I

106

continue. You don't have to come with me if it makes you uncomfortable."

She pursed her lips. As awkward as it had been dealing with Elliot, she was somehow loathe to call it quits for the night. For the first time in years, she was doing something unexpected, and it felt good.

"Turn right at this corner," she said. "The next address is about ten minutes away."

Their eyes met briefly, and he gave her a short nod.

✳ ❋ ✳

"Shouldn't 336 be across the street from 335?" Nick asked.

"Hypothetically, yes," Carol agreed.

"But you're telling me that I have to go another block to get to 336."

"Yes."

"And the numbers across from 336 will be in the two hundreds?"

"Yes."

There was a moment of silence.

"I'm guessing that there's a reason for this."

"Yes."

"Do you know what it is?"

"Yes."

"Do I want to know what the reason is?"

Carol grinned and fumbled in her purse for her lip balm. The cold weather dried them out almost instantly, and she could feel the tell-tale cracks forming when she smiled. "Different district of the city," she told him. "Oakland is the dividing street between East Kildonan and North Kildonan."

"And this explains the numbering system exactly how?" Nick squinted into the dark night and flipped the windshield wipers to a higher speed.

She shrugged. "I don't know for sure, but that's the explanation I've been told. If it makes you feel better, the street numbers start to match up in the 800 block."

"So one side of the street skips about a hundred numbers."

"Yes."

He shook his head. "Unbelievable."

"Yup," she agreed cheerfully. "I keep telling you—driving is like a sport in Winnipeg. Obstacles like this up the level of difficulty."

"And you live here by choice?" he questioned.

She laughed as she pulled out her hand lotion and slathered on a thick layer. "You should be here for construction season," she teased. "You'd never want to leave! Oh! I think that's it," she said, pointing to a small one-and-a-half-storey home.

He pulled to the side of the street and hesitated before turning off the engine. "This shouldn't take long," he said. "Would you like to come with me?"

She glanced at the well-maintained house on the quiet residential street. "It's okay?" she questioned.

"I wouldn't offer if it weren't okay," he told her. He turned off the ignition and pocketed the keys. "Come on. This one should be fun."

She raised an eyebrow, but willingly joined him when he opened her door for her. After he extracted a cumbersome package from the back, they walked up the snow-dusted walk. The door was opened by a tired-looking young woman with an infant cradled on her shoulder. She let them in, holding a finger to her lips.

"He just fell asleep," she whispered. "If you'll wait a minute, I'll put him in his crib. Please, have a seat."

Carol looked at Nick in surprise as the young woman disappeared up the staircase. "She just invited two strangers into her home! Or does she know you?"

Nick shook his head. After waiting awkwardly for a few minutes, they picked their way across the toy-strewn living room and sat down on the couch. From the collection of Barbies, trucks, Little People, and books, Carol determined that there was more than one child in the home. The house wasn't tiny, but the sheer volume of toys and clean clutter gave her a sense of the walls closing in on her. She took a deep breath to calm her claustrophobic tendencies and sneaked a look at the man beside her. Nick appeared perfectly calm and at ease, just as he had while navigating the slippery and snow-rutted streets. With a second deep breath, she felt her calm return.

Several moments later, the young mother returned. "They're all asleep," she sighed, dropping lightly onto the love seat. "I'm sorry. Where are my manners? You must be from Ryan's work; he said that someone might be dropping by. What can I do for you?"

Nick's easy grin was designed to put her at ease. "We're just here to make a delivery."

"A delivery?" she questioned, puzzled.

Nick produced the heavy box and placed it on the love seat beside her. "It's for Caitlin."

"Okay," she said, sounding even more puzzled. She moved to put it under the tree, but he stopped her.

"It's okay to peek, Jess," he whispered conspiratorially.

Jess hesitated a moment, and then lifted the wrapped lid of the box. Anticipation turned to confusion. "Skates?" she asked.

He leaned back on the couch and crossed an ankle over the other knee. "Skating is a great sport," he said.

Jess nodded, her confusion still evident.

"You might consider enrolling her in lessons," he continued.

"She's already in gymnastics," Jess said. "One sport per kid. That's the rule." She gestured to the mess that surrounded us. "Do you have kids?"

Carol and Nick shook their heads.

"Four kids. One sport each. There's no way we can keep up with more than that." There was a touch of panic in her voice. The strain of parenthood was evident in her drawn and pinched face.

He moved to the tree and placed the box underneath it. "Think about it," he told her. "You won't regret it." He paused to look at a framed picture on the wall.

Carol followed his gaze. Jess was posed with who she assumed to be her husband and four children. Three boys, one of them an infant, were dressed in identical blue shirts while one girl wore a dainty yellow blouse.

"You have a beautiful family," Carol told her.

Motherly pride erased the earlier fatigue. "I'm very lucky," she said softly. "Even when it takes until," she checked her watch, "ten o' clock to get them all asleep." She took a second look at the box under the tree, nestled among all the other presents. "Skating?" she questioned, her voice soft. "Really?"

Nick nodded.

"Maybe," she said thoughtfully. "I'll think about it."

"You won't regret it," he repeated.

Taking that as their cue to leave, Carol stood up, only to find that she'd been sitting on a toy. She handled the Little People figure to Jess with a laugh.

"I am so sorry!" Jess exclaimed, face flaming. "I'm always finding toys in the strangest places." She took a second look at her. "Do you work with Ryan, too?"

Carol exchanged a quick look with Nick. "No. I'm just along for the ride."

"And we really should be going," he put in. "We still have a stop or two to make tonight."

Jess walked them to the door. "Thank you very much for the skates. I'm sure that Caitlin will enjoy them."

"I'm sure she will," he replied. "Merry Christmas, Jess."

As they walked down the steps, Carol took several deep breaths of the freezing air and enjoyed the feeling of being outdoors, rather than confined. "I'm confused. Why did Jess think that you work with her husband? You don't, do you?"

He beeped the doors unlocked and opened the passenger door for her. "Don't you have another address to look up?"

She narrowed her eyes. "You're avoiding my questions again."

"This surprises you?"

She sighed. "Left. We're heading to one of the new developments."

As he followed her directions, the houses changed from modest bungalows and two-storeys to individual works of art. They stared up at one of the most opulent homes on the street, a sprawling two-storey house complete with wrap-around deck.

"It's huge," she gasped.

"You like it?" he asked.

Taking in the vaulted ceilings and open concept lay-out visible through the floor-to-ceiling windows, she finally shook her head. "I like the deck," she decided.

With a shake of his head, Nick opened her door for her without asking whether or not she wanted to come with him. He slipped a tiny box into his jacket pocket before leading her up the driveway, past several expensive vehicles. After ringing the doorbell, they waited uneasily for several min-utes. When the door finally opened, they were greeted by a beautiful woman in her late fifties, by Carol's estimation.

"Can I help you?" she asked, her gaze sweeping them from head to toe. The mingled sounds of music and conver-sation drifted out the ornate double doors, and Carol real-ized that she was hosting a party.

"You aren't here for the party," the woman continued, taking in their casual clothing, "and the catering staff arrived hours ago. Is there something I can do for you?"

Carol felt her hackles rise at the woman's condescend-ing tone, but Nick's smile remained firmly in place. "We have a delivery for a Constance Bjorn."

"All deliveries are to be made at the back entrance," she instructed, starting to close the door.

"This one needs to be delivered personally to Ms. Bjorn," Nick objected politely.

"Constance, dear, where are you?" a voice called. "There's someone here you really must say hello to."

"I'll be right there," Constance promised, glancing back over her shoulder as she replied to the summons. "As you can see," she told them, "I'm very busy. If you could please take your delivery to the back…"

Nick shook his head, but Constance had already closed the door in their faces. He stared at the ornamental knocker a few seconds before turning toward their car. "Let's go," he said.

She frowned. For the first time that evening, he sounded... defeated. "Aren't we going to take it to the back entrance?" she asked.

"No."

The reply was no more cryptic than many of the others he had made that night, but she couldn't help feeling that something was different. Another glance to his face confirmed that something was wrong. His lips were pressed tightly together, and he seemed suddenly older, and worn down. The questions she was itching to ask disappeared on the tip of her tongue. Instead, she slipped her hand into his as they walked down the driveway. As the faint aroma of peppermint again tickled her senses, she couldn't help wondering if he could smell it, too.

"She wasn't ready," Nick finally said when they were both in the vehicle.

She tried to read his expression, but they weren't under a streetlight, and he was lost in the shadows.

"Maybe next year?" she suggested. The fear she had felt earlier in the evening when she met Nick at the store was completely forgotten as she struggled to find something reassuring to say.

"Maybe," he said, but his tone was more resigned than optimistic. In an obvious effort to change the topic, he glanced at the map. "Only one more, right?"

She nodded. "South Lake Drive."

As if searching his memory banks, he stared into the distance. "This one may not be pretty," he warned.

"It's not a bad area of town," she said, studying the map.

"That's the least of my concerns," he said shortly.

"Are you okay?" she asked, frowning at the nose-dive his mood had taken.

He scrubbed his hands over his eyes. "Sorry. Sometimes…sometimes it's harder than it should be. And I'm not sure how this one will go."

"Okay," she replied slowly. She gave him the first directions, and then sat back. "You know, I would appreciate an explanation about some of this before the end of the night."

Nick glanced at her out of the corner of his eye before turning his attention back to the road. "Would you?" he asked softly. "Would you really?"

Her mouth gaped open. Her earlier fear may have been replaced with concern, but he still gave her the impression of being surrounded by mystery, and possibly danger. Since she wasn't entirely sure that she had an answer to his question, she stared out the passenger window as the houses drifted past.

✳ ❋ ❄

It was late by the time that Carol and Nick arrived at the spacious bungalow at the far west side of the city. The house was dark, and the outdoor light had already been extinguished.

"Are you sure this is a good idea?" she asked. "They're probably in bed already."

He patted the box under his arm. "I have a feeling that they'll think this is worth the late-night visit."

After waiting for several minutes, the door was opened by a middle-aged man shoving his arms into a gray tattered robe that had seen better days. "Hello?" he questioned, his eyes bleary with sleep.

"We have a delivery for a Mr. and Mrs. Colton," Nick told him, holding up the package. "May we come inside?"

"Who is it, Frank?" a voice called from within the house.

"Delivery people," the man replied, frowning. "Kind of late for a delivery, isn't it?" he questioned.

Nick shrugged. "It is the season," he reminded him.

"Frank?" A woman entered the foyer, also dressed in a robe. She secured the fuzzy pink belt before asking, "What's going on? Who are these people?"

"We have a delivery for you, ma'am," Nick repeated.

"May we have it then, please?" Frank asked. "It is late, and I'm sure you need to be on your way."

"Frank," his wife scolded. "Is that any way to talk to guests? Won't you come in for a cup of coffee?"

"Maxie!" her husband exclaimed.

"Oh, hush. They're obviously nice young people. Please, come in." Without waiting for a reply, Maxie headed to the kitchen to start the coffee.

Frank threw up his hands. "Fine. You might as well come in," he grumbled, motioning for them to follow him.

Carol struggled to keep her expression neutral as she watched the antics of the husband. It was evident that Maxie's welcome was genuine, and that Frank's gruff exterior was only for show.

"We won't take up too much of your time," Nick promised.

Minutes later they were seated around a round kitchen table, enjoying an assortment of desserts and tarts with their coffee. Maxie insisted that the guests try one of each variety, while making sure that her husband didn't. Carol's stomach rumbled in appreciation, reminding her that she had yet to eat supper. She tucked in gratefully, sighing over the decadent delicacies. Nick placed the package on the table, between the husband and wife.

"You can open it now, if you like," Nick told them, leaving his dessert untouched.

Frank nudged it closer to Maxie. "Go ahead."

Maxie removed the wrapping paper and opened the box to reveal a photo album. Her puzzled frown disappeared when she saw the first picture.

"Frank! It's Sara!"

Frank's already wary expression turned dangerous. "Put it away."

Maxie ignored him in favour of flipping through the pages. "Look at her, Frank!" she breathed. "Just look!"

Frank focused his eyes steadfastly on his coffee while Carol struggled to keep from sneaking a peek at the album.

"It was a boy! Frank, she had a boy!" Maxie's voice was full of wonder. She pushed the album toward her husband.

"I don't want to see it," he said, his dark eyes flashing furiously.

Carol was riveted by the expression of pure pain on his face. Again, she could see that his anger was covering a deeper emotion, and she couldn't look away from the scene playing out before her.

"Well, I do!" Maxie exclaimed. "Oh, Frank, he looks exactly like you." She wiped a tear from her eye and continued to flip pages. "They decorated his bedroom in trains," she told him.

Frank's eyes softened for a second, and he started to look at the picture. Stopping himself, he told her, "She's out of our lives now. Put the album away."

Carol held her breath as Frank turned away from the album. Biting her lip, she peered at Nick, and saw that beneath his calm exterior, he was just as interested in the conversation as she was.

Maxie's voice was edged with steel. "She's our daughter. And this is our grandson. I will not put the album away."

"It's been three years," Frank protested. "No word from her in three years! You know you're only going to get hurt by looking at those pictures."

"We should have supported her and accepted her choice to marry Don. You know that."

"He's no good!" Frank thundered. "Any man who would get a sixteen-year-old girl pregnant and convince her to drop out of school and marry him is no good!"

Carol started at the loud voice and winced at the harsh tone. Involuntarily, her hand sought Nick's. The faint aroma of peppermint reassured her just as much as the contact. He gave her fingers a comforting squeeze without turning away from the Coltons.

"He was good enough for Sara to choose him over us. And, from these pictures, it looks as if they're very happy together." Maxie, unaffected by Frank's display of temper, edged closer to her husband, bringing the photo album with her. Nick and Carol sat, forgotten, as she continued to pore over the pictures.

"They have a lovely home," Maxie told Frank when it became apparent that he was still refusing to look at the album. "And Peter is so big!"

"They named him after my father?" Frank asked.

"Sara was always close to her grandfather. You know that."

Carol watched as Frank's eyes drifted to the album, but he turned his head away. Maxie continued to flip through the pages, giving a commentary of the pictures they held. At the last page, however, her breath caught.

"Frank. She's pregnant again!" Tears rolled down her cheeks. "She's pregnant, and she's beautiful. Frank, she looks so happy." She placed her hand on his. "Please."

Swallowing hard, Frank lowered his eyes to the last picture in the album. From her seat across the table, Carol could just make out the form of a young woman, swollen with child, glowing with happiness. Beside her stood a young man holding a toddler in his arms.

A phone number was written on the bottom of the page.

"Thank you for the dessert, Mrs. Colton," Nick said, pushing his chair away from the table. "It's time for us to be on our way."

Both of the Coltons looked up in surprise, evidently having forgotten that they had guests. Carol felt like an intruder, infringing on an intensely private moment, but neither Frank nor Maxie showed any sign of irritation.

"Thank you," Maxie breathed, clutching the album to her chest. "You have no idea what this means to us."

"It was our pleasure," Nick assured her. He and Carol slipped out the front door while the couple stood watching them. Frank was gripping the album tightly, and gripping his wife even tighter.

Carol let out a slow breath as they buckled themselves in. "That went well," she said, sneaking a glance at the couple still standing in the doorway.

"Yes, that went well," Nick agreed, his eyes regaining some of the warmth that had been missing since they had left Constance Bjorn. "That went very well." He started the vehicle, but made no move to drive away. "I promised Mr. Braun that I would take you out to dinner," he said. "I know it's late, but I'd still like to do that."

"Oh, you don't have to," she assured him, her cheeks flaming. "Mr. Braun is always trying to set me up with—"

118

"I'd like to," he interrupted her, his eyes even warmer. "And I thought you still had some questions for me."

"Are you volunteering to answer them?" she asked.

"I wouldn't say that," Nick teased. "But that doesn't mean that you can't have fun asking."

"Well, you did cost me a dinner. I ruined my stir-fry trying to figure out if you were a mass-murderer who had followed me home."

He burst into laughter. "A mass-murderer?"

"I also considered stalker," Carol retorted. "Although, they're probably related."

"And do you feel safe going out to eat with a possible stalker slash mass-murderer?" he questioned, still laughing.

Carol folded the map. Strangely enough, after the events of the evening, she felt more than comfortable with him. "Safe enough," she told him. "But I'm picking the restaurant. There's a place on Osborne that has good food and cheesecake. Think you can live with that?"

Nick nodded. "Sounds good. Just tell me how to get there."

Twenty minutes later, they pulled up in front of a remodelled brick building in a trendy area of the city. Through the uncovered windows they could see that it was filled almost to capacity with happy, brightly dressed people.

"Sorry," she said, making a face. "I forgot that this is a really popular place to hold Christmas parties. It's probably packed."

He shrugged. "We'll check it out. If the wait's too long, we can go somewhere else."

They were soon seated in the last available table of the restaurant, tucked in a back corner booth.

"So, what's good here?" he asked, scanning the menu and shrugging out of his navy coat.

"Everything," was her immediate answer. "But I always go for the clubhouse." She unbuttoned her own coat and draped it beside her on the bench. Though she wasn't as dressed up as most of the other patrons, she was comfortable in her favourite little brown v-neck sweater. Nick, too, looked comfortable in a long-sleeved black T-shirt. Rubbing her hands on her legs to warm them, she asked, "So, do we get to play Twenty Questions now?"

"Sure," he agreed. "How come Mr. Braun is so determined to get you a date?"

Carol choked on the water the waitress had delivered while they perused the menus. "No fair! I thought I was going to get to ask the questions." She wiped her mouth with a cloth napkin.

"Well, that's not much fun," Nick told her, eyes twinkling. "Fair's fair, you know."

Carol dabbed at the wet spot on the table. "Okay, but I get two questions for each of yours. You're much more mysterious than I am."

Nick inclined his head.

"Mr. Braun is like a surrogate father. Or maybe grandfather. A really old-fashioned surrogate grandfather. He thinks it's time for me to settle down and get married."

He laughed at the quotation marks she indicated around "settle down". "You're not ready to settle down?" he asked, leaning back and placing one arm along the back of the bench.

With a snort she told him, "I'm the most boring person I know. If I were any more settled down, I'd be a sedentary rock formation. And that was question number two for you, so I get four now." She leaned forward in anticipation, moving her glass to the side.

120

"But the second question was related to the first!" he protested. "It doesn't count."

"Nice try." She smiled at the waitress hovering beside them and ordered her usual clubhouse sandwich. When Nick ordered the same, she raised an eyebrow. "Copying me?" she asked.

"I just figured if the clubhouse was so good that you had to get it every time, it must be worth trying," he told her. "And that was question number one."

She narrowed her eyes. "You're a hard man."

"Yep," he agreed. "Question number two?"

"Do you really know Mr. Braun's nephew?"

He nodded. "Yes. He's a good guy. Bit of an adrenaline junkie, but a good guy. I met him at the local gym."

She took a sip of the Coke the waitress had delivered. "Are you really delivering presents for friends, or is this something else?" She studied him carefully, waiting for his answer. The background noise of the crowded restaurant faded to a low murmur as she concentrated all her attention on the intriguing man across the table from her.

"Kind of."

"That's not an answer," she protested.

"You asked if we could play Twenty Questions. I never said that I would answer the questions."

"Spoilsport," she mumbled, narrowing her eyes. She settled back in the booth, trying to think of a different way to coax information out him. And trying to decide if she really wanted to. She somehow had the feeling that Nick was a very private person, and that nothing she could say or do would cause him to reveal anything he didn't want to. As curious as she was, it didn't feel right to continue pressing him. To her surprise, after a few minutes of silence he volunteered more information.

"I know the people I'm delivering the presents for," he told her. "They don't always know about the presents, though. So, yes, I'm delivering presents for friends. No, they didn't ask me to."

She digested the information thoughtfully and contemplated her next question. The entire evening had been so confusing, and so intense that it was difficult to hone in on what she most wanted to know. Studying the man across from her, she noticed for the first time the fine lines around his eyes, and was struck by the sudden impression of how very solitary he was. "Why do you do it?" she asked, convinced that the giving of these gifts cost him much more than he would ever let on.

Nick raised an eyebrow.

"Never mind. After watching Elliot and the Coltons, I think I know why you do it."

He swirled the straw in his Coke. "I do it just as much for the people like Constance and Jess, too."

She frowned. "I thought Jess was coming around about the skates."

"She won't be in time. The window will have passed before Caitlin gets those lessons."

She caught her breath at the undisguised remorse in his voice.

"Time for a break," he said, shifting his attention to the food the waitress was setting in front of them.

"I get one more question," she reminded him.

He looked up from the huge plate loaded with sandwich and fries. "I know. Maybe it could wait until after we eat, though."

If she had thought it was difficult to stay objective around heated leather seats, it was even trickier to keep focused when there was a clubhouse sandwich begging to be enjoyed. Her taste buds roared to life with the first bite of turkey, bacon, and mayonnaise goodness.

"So. Good." She flushed when she realized she was speaking with her mouth full. She swallowed and wiped her lips.

"It is good," he agreed, sinking his teeth into the tall sandwich for a second bite. When they finished, he pushed back his plate. "Okay. Hit me."

Carol took her time, trying to decide on the question she most wanted answered. Though the name of the game was Twenty Questions, she had a feeling that Nick wouldn't allow the game to go past the four he owed her. This last question had to count.

"How do you know what to give them?"

Nick didn't appear to be surprised by the question. "I can't really answer that. All I can tell you is that one year, I was given a very special present. And ever since then, it's been my responsibility to give gifts to others."

"You're right. You didn't answer at all," she complained.

"Is that a problem for you?" he asked.

"Not really," she admitted, thinking of the people they had visited that evening. "I think I'm just glad that there really is someone like you in the world, giving gifts that matter."

"Even if people don't accept them?"

Carol nodded. "There's only so much you can do, Nick. And I don't think it would work to force them. Do you?"

He shook his head. "No. It doesn't work."

"Not everyone is ready," she said, remembering Nick's comment when they had passed the young mother pushing a stroller. "Are people ever given more than one gift?" she asked suddenly, forgetting that she had already used her questions. "Or is it a one-time-only deal?"

He placed his hand over top of hers, and the scent of peppermint was even stronger than when he had touched her before. "People are given gifts every day. Some are open-ended, others have definite windows of opportunity. It's just a matter of recognizing them."

She flushed under the intensity of his gaze. "We should go," she whispered. "I think the restaurant is trying to close."

Without a word, he helped her into her coat and guided her back to his vehicle. He didn't ask for directions, and she didn't offer as he guided them straight back to her apartment.

"You don't have to walk me up," she said when he followed her up the walk.

"But what if I want to?" he asked, his hand at the small of her back.

When they reached her apartment, Carol slid her key into the lock, but didn't turn it. Instead, she turned. "Thank you," she said. "Thank you for taking me with you."

"I'm glad you came," he returned, taking her hand to tug her closer to him.

She swallowed hard, staring into his crystal-clear blue eyes. Though it had been, by far, the strangest evening of her life, she found that she wasn't ready for it to end.

"Don't move," he whispered. "I have something for you."

Her eyes widened as he knocked once on Mr. Braun's door. Without a word being exchanged, she saw her neighbour hand him a large box.

"For you."

Carol stared at him, not touching the box. "Is this a gift, or is it a *gift*?" she asked nervously.

"Relax. I thought this was your gift, but I'm pretty sure you accepted your real gift when you agreed to come with me."

"So you didn't knock on my door by accident." She shivered, despite the warm air being pumped through the hallway.

"I'm not in the habit of making mistakes," he told her. "Take the gift, Carol. Please. I'm pretty sure you'll like it."

She lifted the lid of the box slowly, and nearly dropped it in surprise when a ball of white fur flew towards her. She blinked in shock at the quivering, clawing ball that had attached itself to the front of her coat.

Nick burst into laughter and attempted to disentangle the kitten's claws. "I think he likes you."

"A kitten?" Her jaw dropped in astonishment. "You brought me a kitten?"

"Haven't you always wanted one?"

"Well, yes, but…"

"Then enjoy," Nick said simply. He succeeded in freeing the kitten from her coat and stroked it until it began to purr so loudly that it vibrated.

She stared at the mysterious man in front of her cradling a kitten. Before she could change her mind, she slipped her hand behind his neck and tugged him down towards her. He reacted instantly, holding the kitten to the side and lowering his mouth to hers. They tasted each other, rubbing gently, for only a moment before drawing apart.

"Thank you," she murmured, reaching for the squirming kitten.

Nick's eyes twinkled. "No, thank you," he insisted. He grazed her lips with his finger tips. "I get the feeling you don't make the first move with many men. Why…"

She cuddled the kitten to her cheek. "I had to see if you tasted like peppermint, too," she told him with an impish grin.

He threw back his head and laughed, startling the kitten. "I'll see you around, Carol."

"Will you?" she asked. "Will you be back?"

Nick nodded. "Yes."

She felt a surge of relief at his answer. "And you'll let me know if you need a navigator?"

"Of course. And if you're not available, I'll just have to make do with the GPS."

Her eyes widened. "You had GPS? The whole time?"

He grinned and brushed his lips across hers one last time. "Just so you know," he whispered, "I'm pretty sure that you were my gift this year."

Before she could react, he was gone, and Carol was left standing in the hall with a snow-white lump of impatient kitten. "Looks like it's just you and me," she told the cat as she pushed open the door to her apartment. "I hope you like popcorn."

She laughed as the kitten headed straight for her ruined supper. "You know, Peppermint, I think you and I are going to get along just fine."

The End

About Ryl Regehr

Ryl Regehr (pseudonym) is a piano teacher and mother of two who makes her home in Manitoba, Canada. Christmas has always been her favourite holiday.

"The Bringer of Gifts" was inspired by a desire to celebrate the magic and mystery of the season, and to pay tribute to the many gifts she has received over the years. The idea of a modern day St. Nicholas captured her imagination, along with the idea of gifts tailor-made to suit the recipient.

Where We Love

Where we love is home,
Home that our feet may leave, but not our hearts.
~Oliver Wendell Holmes, Sr., *Homesick in Heaven*

December 25th

Tracy Fraiser pulled a silver backed hairbrush through her tousled blond curls, trying to restore them to some semblance of order. She caught her husband John watching her, a bemused expression on his handsome face.

Moving behind her, he nuzzled her neck and whispered, "Resistance is futile. The hair always wins."

She scowled at him in the mirror, knowing the twinkle in her eyes would reveal her true feelings. "My hair was fine, just fine, right up until you decided to exercise your marital rights."

"I didn't hear you complaining during the exercise," he offered, his lips travelling the distance between her earlobe and collarbone.

"No. No, you didn't," she agreed with a giggle. Turning to face him, she set down the brush, her lips curving into a sultry smile. "Studies show that daily exercise is essential for good health."

"Then we should be very healthy." He bent down to kiss her. "In fact," he said, his sultry voice making her shiver, "we could probably use a little exercise. You know. For our health."

"Oh, no!" she protested, pushing him away from her. "No more exercise for you, Mr. Fraiser." At the dejected pout of his mouth and puppy dog look in his green eyes, she laughed and revised her statement. "No more exercise until after Christmas dinner."

His face brightened immediately, and he reached for her discarded hairbrush, pulling it quickly through his thick, dark hair. "In that case, woman, let's get a move on. The sooner we eat, the sooner we can come home and… exercise."

His order drew another laugh, but she took the brush from his hand and gave her hair another pass. Fastening the sides of her hair with two sapphire blue glass clips, she gave her face a quick swipe with the powder puff and ran a tube of pink lipstick over her lips. The whole family, John's and hers, was going to be at this dinner, and Tracy worried a little about how they would take the news she had to tell them.

Frowning at her reflection, she tugged at the silver sequined straps of her deep blue gown and asked her husband, "I know we agreed to tell them tonight, but is the timing really the best? I mean, it is Christmas."

"Dad already knows," John pointed out. "He's completely supportive, and everyone else will be, too. It's a wonderful opportunity for you, Trace, and you'd be a fool not to accept it." He wrapped his arms around her, and they both looked at their reflections in the mirror. "And one thing you've proven, over and over again, is that you are nobody's fool. Besides," he added with a grin, "if we don't tell them tonight, we won't have them all together in one place until next year. Talk about bad timing…"

"You're right." She covered his hands with her own. Taking a deep breath, she said, "Okay. Let's go do this." Hand in hand, they headed for the door.

✳ ❋ ✳

It didn't matter how many times they had traveled up the long, tree-lined drive leading to the elegant yet unpretentious home Michael and Genevieve Fraiser had built, the sheer grandeur of it always left Tracy a little awestruck. The large and stately Georgian style mansion sat on over twenty acres. The five acres surrounding the house had been cleared and landscaped to provide an elaborate garden. A boxwood maze, interspersed with heirloom roses, wended across two acres that bloomed spring and summer with every color of the rainbow, and ended at the center at a wrought iron gazebo hung with stained glass wind chimes. An expansive stable sat just beyond the house, its manicured pastures nurturing several healthy and happy horses, but the rest of the acreage remained preserved forest land, complete with a small lake, a creek, and a labyrinth of packed earth trails used for walking, jogging, and riding.

It was a beautiful location. She and John had said their vows there in early October two years earlier, at the edge of the lake, with the leaves changing into their autumn colors behind them.

As the butler took her coat, Tracy remembered how intimidated she had been by him, and even more, by all of the Fraisers when she had first visited them at their estate.

The Fraisers were old money. John's great grandfather, Tavis Fraiser, had opened an inn near the turn of the century. He had been successful at his endeavors, and had left each of his four sons an inn of their own. In turn, the Fraiser sons had expanded their interests, creating a chain of hotels. By the time the next generation of Fraiser men took the reins in the mid-sixties, their name was synonymous with good quality lodging at a fair rate.

The nine strapping Fraiser boys of that generation were more than enough to run a small empire. Michael and his brother Alec branched out, diversifying their interests. By the time the eighties rolled around, there were few pies into which a Fraiser finger had not been poked.

Tracy took a moment to look at her favorite picture in the hall, a portrait of Tavis Frasier, his sons, and grandsons. As always, she giggled.

John wagged his finger at her. "Don't say it! I do *not* look just like Uncle Mungo!"

She laughed again and looked back at the portrait, at the line-up of rich, powerful men.

It was into this life that John and his brother Daniel had been born; privileged lives and high expectations. Both sons had been raised to assume the mantle of business, beginning as bellhops and mail sorters, and working their way through the various jobs as they found the positions best suited to their strengths and skills. The Fraiser family firmly believed that with great privilege came great responsibility, and they lived their motto.

As Tracy stepped into her mother-in-law's welcoming embrace, she internally shook her head at the ease with which she had adapted to the Fraiser lifestyle. "Merry Christmas,

Genevieve," she said, returning the hug. "I'm sorry we're late, but it really was your son's fault."

"True," John admitted, stepping forward to shake his father's hand and kiss his mother on the cheek. "I am completely to blame: *Mea culpa* and all that. Have we ruined dinner?"

"Not at all, darling," Genevieve said with a laugh. "David and Hannah arrived with Kim exactly on time, but your brother and Jenna beat you here by only five minutes."

It didn't surprise her that her parents and sister had arrived on time, Tracy thought. David and Hannah Baxter, a high school history teacher and a part-time nurse, had raised their three children to be responsible and punctual. Tracy, along with her older brother Brendan and younger sister Kimberly, had always been expected to help with the cleaning and operation of their suburban three-bedroom ranch style house. They did chores and worked for their spending money.

Despite the work, it had been a happy life, marred only by the devastating loss of their brother Brendan when Tracy was fifteen. Brendan, whose lifetime ambition had been to join the FBI, was killed when a semi truck driver fell asleep at the wheel and crossed the dividing line. The truck slammed into a school bus carrying the Selah Falls basketball team as they returned from the state championship game, killing five of the passengers.

Brendan's death had had a profound effect on her. She developed an overwhelming drive to succeed, and to—as she explained to John on their fifth date—live every moment of her life for both herself and her brother.

That determination won her a full scholarship to Stanford University, where she studied criminal science and pre-law. It was at Stanford that she reconnected with business student, John Fraiser.

She stopped her reflections as Genevieve waved them towards the study. "Everyone's already in there. Why don't you go visit, and I'll tell Stella she can begin serving in about five minutes."

"Sounds perfect. We have some exciting news to share after dinner." John took Tracy's hand.

"It must be going around," Michael told them as he walked with them. "Dan and Jenna said they have news as well. Somehow I think their news is different than yours." He winked at his daughter-in-law, and Tracy had to laugh.

"Would you like a cocktail before dinner?" Michael offered as he ushered them into the cozy study. "Or coffee?"

Tracy shot a sideways glance at John. "Coffee would be nice, right, Mr. Klutz?"

"Hey!" John protested. "I apologized for that. Besides, that cup of coffee brought us together."

Coffee had brought them together, she remembered, thanks to a serendipitous encounter at Stanford University.

They had met before then, back in high school. Although, being a year behind John in school, Tracy had not traveled in the same circles. Other than one notable exception, their previous relationship had been more of a passing acquaintance than a friendship.

Once at Stanford, their paths did not cross for years, as John was enrolled at the school of business while she was caught up in the criminal sciences department. Quite by accident, they met in a Starbucks on an unusually chilly California autumn afternoon. She had just finished her daily five-mile run and was rewarding herself with a grande skinny mocha. John had finished both a brainstorming session with his Paths to Power project group and a venti Americano.

It wasn't exactly love at first sight. As Tracy stepped away from the counter with her drink, John had flipped back his backpack and bumped into her, knocking both her and her drink to the floor. She had snarled, he had apologized, and somewhere over the course of mopping up the spill and purchasing her a new mocha, recognition had dawned.

John ended up asking her to lunch. Lunch had led to dinner, and dinner led to the festivities of homecoming weekend. Before long, they were an official couple, sharing weekly dates despite their diverse scholastic interests. It was a short step from there to traveling home together to Selah Falls for holidays and breaks. After that, fate led them down the path to matrimony.

And now fate was leading them in a new direction, Tracy thought, worried about how everyone would react to their impending news.

Dinner began with a delicious Caesar salad. That was followed by French Onion soup, moving through perfectly prepared prime rib roast, grilled potatoes, green bean bake, glazed carrots, and John's favorite, corn pudding. The meal ended with a selection of pies and pastries to tempt the individual sweet tooth of each guest and family member. And each course was accompanied by the perfect wine pairing.

Although Tracy found the formal setting—with the plethora of silverware, golden apple place card holders and embroidered napkins—somewhat amusing, she knew that her mother-in-law took care and pride in her decorations and seating arrangements. She and John had been seated next to her parents, Hannah and David, and across the table from Jenna and Dan. Her sister Kim sat to Dan's right, with Michael and Genevieve stationed on either end of the table.

Unable to put aside her detective training, even at a family Christmas, Tracy couldn't help but notice that her sister-in-law seemed a trifle pale and didn't actually drink any of her wine. Jenna nearly turned green, in fact, when a slice of very rare roast beef was laid upon her plate, and Dan had quickly and quietly transferred the offending slab to his own plate. The look Jenna gave her husband of four years was full of love, relief, and gratitude as she helped herself to the vegetarian selections on the table.

Tracy watched them for a few more seconds before leaning over and whispering to John. "I'll bet you five dollars I can guess your brother's news."

"You're on," he whispered back. "What's your guess?"

"They're pregnant."

John looked at her, something between astonishment and skepticism in his eyes. "If you're right," he murmured, "you have to tell me how you figured it out."

"Deal," Tracy told him, her words hidden behind the toothy smile she gave him. With a small laugh, she turned to her mother and joined the overall table conversation.

When dinner was over, they all retired to the sitting room. The sixteen-foot Douglas fir stood in the corner opposite the river rock fireplace, golden orbs and green velvet ribbons dancing in the reflection of the strings of white lights. The heady scents of cinnamon and fir needles merged with the aromas of Kona coffee and Darjeeling tea as Genevieve poured tea and coffee from the matching silver serving sets, while Michael, John, and Dan sorted and passed around the gifts from under the tree.

When the majority of the gifts had been opened and admired, Dan Fraiser rose. "We have one more gift. Here, Mom. You open it." He handed Genevieve a package, about six inches square and two inches tall, wrapped in white paper with glittery silver snowflakes.

As Genevieve slipped one perfectly manicured fingernail under the fold of the paper, Tracy reached for John's hand, squeezing it and whispering, "Wait for it. Wait for it."

The paper fell to the floor, revealing a pale green photo album embossed with the words "Grandma's Brag Book". Genevieve looked at the book for a long moment, then at her husband, and then at Dan. As a wide grin of affirmation spread across his handsome face, she let out a squeal of excitement that was in complete contrast to her usual calm demeanor. She vaulted to her feet, enveloping Dan in a hug and then turning her attention to Jenna.

"When are you due? Have you seen the doctor yet? I thought you looked a little pale, darling. How are you feeling?" The questions flowed like the waterfall after which the town was named.

Jenna, looking a little overwhelmed and a whole lot happy, answered the barrage of questions calmly. "July seventh. Yes, I'm seeing Dr. Esser. I'm feeling a little tired, and this baby is apparently a vegetarian; he or she definitely doesn't want me eating meat." She shuddered dramatically, the smile on her face belying the action. "But otherwise, I feel great." She reached for Dan's hand. "We're very happy."

"And we're happy for you," David interjected, shaking Dan's hand and clapping Michael on the back. "For all of you. Babies are a blessing."

Hugs and congratulations finished, they all settled back in their seats. Michael looked expectantly at John, who nodded. "Our news is a little less exciting for the family," he said, "but I'm still excited, because it is really amazing news for my wife." He looked at Tracy. "Babe?"

Tracy leaned forward. "Well, you know that for the last eighteen months I've been working out of the San Diego field office," she began.

"Did you get the transfer to San Francisco?" her mother interrupted eagerly.

"That's wonderful, darling. You can be closer to home!" Genevieve enthused.

"No." Tracy raised her eyes to her husband, silently pleading for his assistance.

John held up his hand. "Let her tell you, please."

The room grew quiet, and Tracy continued. "There is this internship of sorts, with SO15. That's Special Operations, section fifteen. The agent selected trains for a year with Scotland Yard counterterrorism units. It's really an honor to be chosen; over eight hundred agents applied, only three were accepted." She grinned self-consciously. "I was one of them."

All eyes focused on Tracy, so John continued the tale. "We leave for London on January tenth. I'll be working for Fraiser's European interests for the next year, while Trace gets to play James Bond."

Stunned silence was the only reaction from everyone except Michael Frasier, who had already been aware of the award.

"You're moving to Scotland?" Tracy's sister Kim asked. "Seriously?"

"Not Scotland," Tracy corrected. "London. Scotland Yard is just the nickname of sorts. The actual physical location is in London."

Jenna burst into tears. Dan wrapped his arms around her and sent his sister-in-law a helpless shrug. "Pregnancy hormones," he mouthed.

Pushing her husband away, Jenna wiped her eyes and said, "That is wonderful news, Tracy. I'm so proud of you, but I'm going to miss you guys so much, and you won't be here when the baby is born."

Tracy moved then from her couch to the one holding her sister-in-law. Enveloping Jenna in a big hug, she assured her. "We'll manage, Jen. I promise. If we miss the big arrival, we'll find a way to get here for at least a few days. You don't think I'm going to miss spoiling my niece or nephew, do you? Seriously?"

"No?" Jenna asked, her eyes a little watery.

"No." Tracy stated emphatically. "Besides, with the internet, you can send me daily updates and pictures. It'll almost be like being here in California, you'll see."

"That's true," Kim added. "In fact, we might hear from her more while they're in England than we do now when they're in San Diego." She grinned at her sister. "It's not like she's a championship communicator or anything."

"Hey!" Tracy protested, but since the rest of the room was laughing, and the crisis seemed to have passed, she gave in. Laughing along, she accepted the hugs and congratulations that followed.

February 15th

"I still don't understand why I have to leave my weapon here," Tracy complained, unbuckling her shoulder holster and handing over her Glock. "I'm a fully trained and certified professional agent with the FBI."

"You are also an agent here on a temporary visa," Detective Sergeant Molly Brant told her as she took the weapon, locked it in the gun safe, and handed Tracy her receipt. In a flat monotone, she repeated the phrase she told Tracy each time the subject arose. "You may carry your firearm while on duty. Not when you are off duty." She affected a very bad American accent and added, "Them's the rules, Toots!"

Tracy shook her head, grumbling as she gathered her coat and ever-present umbrella. Over all, she was finding her assignment to the British counterterrorism unit to be exciting and informative. The two things she found difficult were the inability to carry her personal weapon when not working and the rain that never really seemed to stop. Thirty days in London, and the sun still hadn't made an appearance. Her coworkers assured her that the sun did shine in England, but Tracy, being a California girl, wasn't so sure.

At least they had found an apartment, or flat, as she was learning to call it. Staying in the owner's suite at the Fairview Hotel had been fine for the first week, but hotel living was never going to be something she enjoyed. She liked having her own space, with her own things. They had found a very nice two bedroom, located within walking distance of the tube system both she and John used to go to and from their respective workplaces.

It had come partially furnished, but she had actually enjoyed replacing the rickety double bed with a larger, more comfortable one, as well as finding a comfy couch and recliner combo. Her favorite room though, was the spare bedroom, which housed the computer with its camera and internet connection. It was the place she and John both checked first after arriving home; it was their lifeline to the family they had left behind.

John was in the kitchen when she let herself in. The smells of garlic and tomatoes wafted past her nose, and she let out a sigh of appreciation. "Mmmmm. Smells like pasgetti."

"Pasgetti baloney-ese," he teased. "It'll be ready in about ten minutes. You have six e-mails waiting for you, and your mom sent us a Valentine's Day card. It's on the desk."

"Did our moms get the flowers?" she asked, kissing his cheek as she slipped out of her coat.

"They did," he replied, turning quickly to claim her lips for a longer kiss. "And Jenna got the chocolates. She sent a note, something about making her look like the Goodyear blimp?"

"As if," she snickered, turning away. "I'll check the mail and come set the table."

A few minutes later, she returned, looking stunned.

"Kim's engaged. Engaged! Can you believe it?"

Her husband spun away from the stove, sending spaghetti sauce flying off the wooden spoon in his hand. "Really? Wesley finally got up the nerve?"

"Evidently." Tracy slumped in a chair, her head in her hands. "I can't believe it. My baby sister is getting married."

"She's not exactly a baby any more, Trace."

"Feels like it sometimes." She pushed herself up and wandered over to the mantle, picking up one of the many family photos they had placed there. Staring at Kim's college graduation photo, she realized that her baby sister was, indeed, all grown up. "Okay. Maybe she is an adult."

"Have they set a date?" John asked, looking over at her with an expression of concern.

"Next Valentine's Day, so you can wipe that worried look off your face. We won't miss it. Kim said she wanted to make sure I would be able to be there to help with all the pre-wedding stuff. When we go home to meet our new niece or nephew this summer, I'm going to help her pick out the dresses and flowers and everything. Still…" She sighed and put down the picture.

"Still?"

"It's okay. I'm just a little sad we can't be there now, to celebrate their engagement." She shook her head to clear away her melancholy thoughts, and started to set the table. "So, how was your day?"

"It was very exciting, all those numbers and engineering schematics. How was saving the world?"

"Same old, same old," she responded pertly. "If only they'd let me carry concealed, I'm sure I could save twice as many… uh…worlds."

"Tracy Fraiser. Savior of the Universe," he teased.

"I think that was Flash Gordon, dearest."

"You could flash me, Mrs. Fraiser."

"Tempting." She looked over. "What's for dessert?"

"Ice cream," he told her. "Left over from our Valentine's dinner last night."

"With hot fudge and whipped cream?" she asked, her eyes gleaming wickedly.

"Of course, oh…" He turned off the burner. "Want to have dessert first, Mrs. Fraiser?"

"Well, Mr. Fraiser," she told him, stripping off her blouse. "Life is unpredictable."

"Indeed." John set the pan in the center of the stove. "I'll get the whipped cream."

Dinner was late. Very late.

✳ ❉ ❆

April 10th

Tracy bounded up the stairs to the flat. It might be called Good Friday, but it hadn't been good for her. Jenna's last e-mail was weighing on her mind. Her sister-in-law, usually so calm and level-headed, seemed completely convinced that her husband was having an affair.

Tracy had brought up the subject with John, but he had just laughed. "Are you kidding me?" he had asked, shaking his head incredulously. "Dan? Having an affair?" He had laughed again. "Dan hasn't looked at another woman since the day he met Jen. It's ridiculous."

She knew that he was right. Fraiser men were like wolves. They mated for life. Still, the difference between Jenna's e-mails and Dan's was striking. Something was definitely wrong with her brother-in-law, and she wished she were back in the States. It wasn't just because the upcoming holiday had her missing her family, but because she would be able to track down the truth.

As she stepped into the flat, a chill ran down the length of her spine. Somehow, she knew she wasn't alone in the apartment; her senses were on full alert. She froze, reaching automatically for the weapon she wasn't carrying. Silently cursing the UK's policy on concealed weapons, she shifted her closed umbrella to her right hand and pulled out her cell phone.

Holding the umbrella in front of her, she silently pushed the door closed, her eyes scanning the area for danger. The kitchen and living area were clear. Moving slowly, Tracy approached the bathroom. Clear. The bedroom was next, and she stopped only to unlock the gun box and remove her Sig Sauer. She might not be able to carry her weapon with her, but she did have a certificate to keep one for home protection.

A thud from outside the room caught her attention, and feeling more secure now she was armed, she headed for the last room: the guest room.

Hand on the doorknob, Tracy took a deep breath, centering herself. The door opened smoothly, and she led with her gun. "Freeze!" she yelled.

"Holy crap!" Dan Fraiser exclaimed, his eyes wide, his hands outstretched. "It's me, Tracy. Don't shoot!"

She lowered her gun. "What are you doing here, Dan? How did you get in?"

"Johnny gave me the key. If I'm not in danger of being shot, may I sit down?" He stared down at her hand, which still gripped the pistol.

She nodded, flicked on the safety, and moved all the way into the room as he began to explain.

"I flew in a couple of hours ago. I was at the construction site in Lyon, but I thought I'd drop in on you for a couple of days before I headed home. The hotel's full for the Easter weekend, and I didn't want to rattle around the suite by myself, so John said I could crash with you."

"Wait a minute," Tracy said. "I need to put this away." She stepped out of the room, and returned the Sig to its locked box.

As she left the bedroom, she saw that Dan had moved to the living room and was pacing in front of the couch. "Sit down, Danny. I'll make us some tea."

"Tea?" he asked, a grin breaking the tension on his face. "Are you going British on me, Trace?"

"I can make coffee, if you'd rather," she retorted, "but you look like you've already had way too much caffeine."

"That's truer than I'd like to admit," he said with a sigh. "I'm all messed up, Trace. Totally."

The hot water pot beeped, and she quickly poured the water into the waiting teapot. Setting the tea set on a tray, and adding a few peanut butter cookies, she carried it to the coffee table. "Sit," she instructed.

He sat. Pouring tea through the strainer and into the waiting cups took time. It was time spent in silence.

He sipped his tea and picked up a cookie, turning it in his hand.

She waited. She waited some more.

Finally, unable to tolerate the silence any longer, she burst out. "So, first you take a completely unnecessary trip to inspect a construction site where they haven't even broken ground yet, and then you just decided to pop in here before going home to your pregnant wife? What's going on, Dan? What are you hiding?"

"Nothing! " To her surprise, his eyes filled with tears, and his voice dropped significantly. "I don't know," he whispered. "I really don't know."

"Are you having an affair?" she asked bluntly.

"What? An affair? No!" Dan was stunned, that much was obvious. "Why would you say that? I love Jenna. She's my wife. Why would you think that?"

144

"Because that's what your wife thinks," John said from the doorway before coming in the rest of the way.

He dropped a kiss on the top of Tracy's head and went to the kitchen. Coming back with another cup, he joined her on the couch, and poured some tea. Then he gave his brother a long look. "Any idea why Jenna thinks you're having an affair?"

Dan flushed guiltily and looked away, and Tracy knew. "You are an idiot, aren't you?" she asked. "When was the last time you touched your wife?"

"I don't want to hurt the baby," he mumbled. "And Jen was so sick at the beginning, and when that passed, she was so sensitive and tired, and…"

"And now she's getting stretch marks, and feels like she's the size of a house," she scolded. "You're working late, leaving the house early, flying halfway around the world for no good reason, and then delaying your trip home? All that makes her think you aren't interested in her anymore."

"That's not true." Dan raised his glance from the floor to meet hers. "She's more beautiful than ever. All round and, well, I know it's a cliché, but glowing. I love her more than ever."

"Then tell *her*, you dolt. Not me." Tracy stood up. "I've had a long day. I'm going to take a shower. You, brother dearest, are going to call your wife and tell her that you are a selfish jerk. Next, you are going to tell her exactly how beautiful and desirable you find her, and then, first thing in the morning, you will get on a plane and go home to spend Easter with her. Understand?"

"Yes, ma'am." Dan looked a little stunned, but relieved at the same time.

"Good. Any other time, Dan, you'd be welcome in my house. But right now, I'm afraid your stupid juice might contaminate my guest room. Fix this." Tracy turned and left the brothers alone.

"You'd better go and call Jenna," John said, taking a sip of tea. "I'm pretty sure you don't want to suffer the wrath of Tracy."

"That's for sure," Dan agreed. "She's pretty good at calling me a selfish bastard when she thinks it's warranted."

"Actually, she called you a selfish jerk. The day she called you a selfish bastard was the first time I fell in love with her," John said with a grin. "Man, did she wale on you!"

"The first time?" Dan asked. "At the Falls? Bro, she was only fifteen!"

"I know." A wistful look came over John's face. "Fifteen, and hurting, and so determined to wake you up from your self-destructive funk. How could I not fall for her? She saved my brother."

"Does she know?"

"I don't think so." John smiled sheepishly. "We've never really talked about that day. We've made so many, better memories, that one sort of fades to the background for us."

"You're a lucky man, little brother."

"So are you, big brother." John picked up the tea tray. "We both have a lot to be thankful for."

"Wrong holiday, Little John. This is Easter, not Thanksgiving."

"Whatever. Go tell your wife how lucky you are, before my wife comes out and rips you a new one. Again."

"I will." Dan rose. "And when I'm finished groveling, I'll take you and my amazing sister-in-law out to dinner." He grinned. "Tracy's choice. You tell her."

"I will." John rinsed the tea things and set them on the drain board. As his brother disappeared into the guest room, he walked to his own room, hoping he could convince his wife to choose a very expensive restaurant.

✳ ❄ ✳

"What did you mean when you told Dan that day at the Falls was the first time you fell in love with me?" Tracy asked, snuggling into her husband's arms.

"You heard that?" John asked, raising his head from the pillow long enough to look into her eyes. "I thought you were in the shower."

"I was conducting covert surveillance." She rolled over to face him. "That's my job. So, what did you mean?"

John sighed. "I fall in love with you a little bit each day," he said. "Little things, like the way you scrunch your nose when you're concentrating, or the spark you get in your eyes when you solve a puzzle. The first time, the very first time was the day you took down my very drunk and suicidal brother. You rounded on him with such passion; such fury. You didn't have to hit him over the head with a boulder; you just told him how it was.

"I was in the trees, frozen, but you got it. When you told him you understood, he listened. He talked. I didn't know until that moment that he had switched seats with Brendan. I had no idea how deep his guilt went, but you did. You understood, and you told him that no matter how horrible he felt, it didn't give him the right to harm himself and bring that sorrow to his family."

147

"I'm glad it worked," she whispered. "If he'd actually... I'm glad you were spared that."

She sighed as the grief that never fully disappeared rose again in her chest, so she sought refuge in the comfort of John's arms. It had been years since the accident had taken Brendan, yet still the grief would sneak up on her when she least expected it.

Holidays were the worst. Even his birthday and the anniversary of his death had faded so that they were just slightly sadder days. But holidays were hard, even more so this year, separated by an ocean from the majority of her family.

John held her close, and whispered in her ear, "Still, I fell in love with you that day. Five years later, I fell in love with you again, over a spilled latte."

"It was a mocha," she corrected, rolling over so that they were spooned together. "And you are a keeper, Mr. Fraiser. Definitely a keeper."

"As are you, wife of mine. Always." John stifled a yawn. "Goodnight."

"Goodnight, love," she whispered, listening as his breathing deepened, becoming more regular as he slipped into sleep. She remembered the day in question.

It had been during the dark period in her life, those months after Brendan had died. It had been a dark time for her family, for the whole town. Tracy's parents were struggling to maintain a façade of normal for their daughters, but they couldn't hide their grief. Kim, at thirteen, was in turns sullen and withdrawn, followed by sudden violent outbursts of emotion. Tracy was just...lost. She had made the hike to the Falls in order to connect with her brother; it was one of his favorite places.

Drunk and cursing, Dan had come crashing through her reverie. Tracy watched him stumble to the edge of the waterfall, a bottle clutched in his hand. He smashed the bottle against the rocks, holding the jagged edge against his arm, tracing lines from his wrist to his elbow, and leaving thin lines of blood in his wake. Tracy had moved quickly, distracting him, and then had raged at him for his selfish and self-destructive behavior.

Lying in bed, she could still feel her anger that he would even think of killing himself and causing his family the grief she and her family had been suffering.

He had broken down, and she had gone to him, wrapping her arms around him and letting him cry on her shoulder.

And then, silently, John was there, pulling his brother away from Tracy and into his own embrace, quietly thanking her. Dan hadn't protested, just allowed his brother to lead him away. Tracy had trailed behind them, watching as the younger brother comforted the elder, leading him away from the darkness, and toward the light of home.

Lying next to her husband, Tracy whispered, "I think I fell a little bit in love with you that day, too." Lacing her fingers through his, she closed her eyes and fell asleep counting her blessings.

July 4th

"Come out, now!" Tracy threatened the mound that was her sister-in-law's belly. "Seriously, dude. I only have two weeks, and four of those days are gone. I want to hold you, not just poke you through your mama." She looked at Jenna. "Can't you do something? You're the mom."

"I might be the mom," Jenna said solemnly, "but this one is every bit as stubborn as his or her daddy."

"We're doomed," Tracy exclaimed, rolling her eyes. "If this kid is half as stubborn as Dan and John, we might as well give up now."

"Hey," John interjected, placing his hand on Jenna's stomach. "Stubborn is not just a Fraiser trait. I know a couple of wives who possess that same little trait."

"No," Tracy argued. "You and Dan are stubborn. Jenna and I are determined and tenacious. There is a difference."

John snorted, but otherwise kept his mouth shut, contenting himself with rolling his eyes.

"Maybe baby here likes fireworks," Tracy said, leaning close again. "Baby, tonight is fireworks night. If you decide to be born, you get to see the fireworks. Big bangs for your birthday."

As if in answer, Jenna's stomach wobbled, and she laughed, pushing down on the bulge with one hand. "Foot," she gasped. "I can't decide if I've got a field goal kicker or a gymnast in here."

"I'm betting on gymnast," Tracy told her. "Right, Nadia?"

"I am not naming my baby Nadia," Jenna protested. "If she's a girl, we like Arabella."

"Arabella Fraiser." Tracy rolled the name around on her tongue. "I like it. It's very Scottish. What do you think for a boy? Angus?"

Jenna wrinkled her nose. "No! For a boy, we're thinking Declan or Duncan. Dan liked Tavis, after his great-grandfather, but I think that's a little too Scottish for me."

Dan spoke up for the first time. "Tavis is a great name. Any boy would be proud to wear it."

"I like Declan." John put in his two cents. "Duncan is good, but it's awfully close to Dan. Dun. Dan. Yuck. Go with Declan."

"No need," Tracy told him. "I'm pretty sure this is Arabella."

"Considering there hasn't been a Fraiser daughter born in three generations, I think I'll stick with Declan. Or Tavis." Dan grinned at his sister-in-law and kissed his wife.

Tracy leaned down again. "Nope," she said with complete confidence. "This is definitely Arabella. Come on, Bella. Auntie Tracy wants to take you shopping for shoes. Hurry it up, Miss Arabella." The baby kicked again, and sent them all into peals of laughter.

✳ ❄ ✳

"I can't believe it worked!" John said, looking at her with amazement. "How did you do it?"

"I bribed her," Tracy said calmly. "I bribed her with shoes and fireworks. She had no choice but to be born." She looked down at the pink wrapped bundle in her arms. "Isn't that right, Arabella?"

The baby, less than two hours old, looked up at her with curious blue eyes. Tracy moved to the window, and pointed out into the dark night. As the sky lit up with flares and sparks, she whispered into the infant's ear, "Happy birthday little one. We'll get to those shoes in a couple of days."

✳ ✳ ✳

October 31st

"Don't turn on the television, okay?"

The fist squeezing John's heart loosed its grip at the sound of Tracy's voice on the other end of the telephone connection. "Too late," he said tersely.

"Oh." She sighed. "I was hoping you'd be too busy to catch the news."

"No such luck." Shifting the phone to his other hand, he asked, "Are you okay?"

"I'm fine," she assured him. "Perfectly fine. No holes, no blood, not even that much dirt. Really."

"What happened?" He knew she wouldn't be able to answer, but he couldn't help asking.

"Bad guys. Good guys."

John could almost see his wife struggle to keep her comments vague.

"This time, the good guys won, but it was a little messy."

"Messy as in you won't be home for dinner?" he asked. "Or messy as in we have to leave the country?"

"I won't be home for dinner," she responded. "Or breakfast, most likely. As for leaving the country, since we didn't really do anything for our anniversary, what do you say to a belated celebration in Paris?"

"Trace…"

She sighed again, this time louder. "I love you, husband of mine. You know that, right?"

"I know." He ran a hand through his hair. "Are you sure you're okay?"

"I'm fine. Seriously. But this whole thing is going to break in the international media very soon. I'm going to be

152

tied up in debriefings, so could you call home and warn the family? You know how Jenna worries."

"I'll take care of it. So, Paris? Or California? We could spend another week or two. You could help with the wedding plans and take Bella shopping for new shoes."

"That sounds like heaven, but more than four days away could be problematic. Besides, we've already missed Bella's first Halloween. Did you see the picture Jenna sent? The pumpkin costume was adorable." She was silent a moment. "We're going to miss her first Christmas too."

John winced at the catch in Tracy's voice.

"Tracy," he started, but she cut him off, her voice stronger.

"I know. We knew this was going to happen when I took the job. I need to suck it up; I can have a pity party later. Back to the subject at hand. I think Paris is a better option. We get away, and I'm within shouting distance. Besides, I think Miss Bella needs some sparkly shoes from gay Paree." She giggled, but it sounded a bit forced.

"I'll make the arrangements," he said. "When can I expect to see you?"

"Uh… hopefully before lunch time tomorrow. I've got to go. I love you."

"I love you, too." And she was gone.

John looked at the receiver in his hand. Most days, he could deal with having a special agent as his wife, but when the job involved poison on the subway, and exploding apartment buildings, it made him wish Tracy had chosen a somewhat less dangerous line of work. Sometimes.

Then again, would she still be his Tracy if she had chosen to be an accountant? It was hard to say.

153

Right now, Paris sounded perfect. Four days in a luxury suite with his wife, checking to make sure she was as undamaged as she claimed. He grinned to himself as he turned on the phone and checked his watch. Automatically subtracting eight hours, he realized it was just after eleven in the morning in Selah Falls: A good time to call home and offer preemptive reassurances. And, thanks to one of Tracy's comments, an idea was beginning to percolate.

After calling the family, he would make the arrangements for a romantic weekend in Paris and pop in a movie. It would be a long and lonely night without Tracy.

✳ ✳ ✳

December 23rd

The sigh was quiet. So quiet, that John would have missed it, had he not been highly tuned in to his wife's mood. For all Tracy's outward appearance, it had been a long year, and he knew that spending Christmas away from Selah Falls was tearing at her heart.

"We can still fly home," he offered. "If we leave from Edinburgh, we can be in Selah Falls before Christmas morning."

"What?" She turned confused blue eyes on her husband. "Why would we do that?" she asked. "We're headed back in three weeks. Why would we waste the money on something as silly as flying home for what amounts to a weekend?"

It was his turn to sigh. With an ironic grin, he shook his head. "First, wife of mine, much as we might pretend otherwise, money isn't really a problem. We have more than enough. Second, if it makes you happy, if it's what you want for Christmas, then it wouldn't be a waste. I know you miss being home for the holidays."

Tracy smiled at him, and his heart skipped a little. "First, husband of mine," she teased, repeating his words, "just because we have access to more money than either of us needs, doesn't mean we need to spend it unwisely.

"Second, I do miss being in Selah Falls for the holidays, but, as I discovered at Thanksgiving, home is not a place. Home is wherever there's family—even if we're only together on the computer."

She reached over to squeeze his hand. "This year, home is going to be at a hunting lodge in Kirkcaldy, Scotland. Your Uncle Alec promised we'd have internet access by Christmas, so we can connect with the family—just like we have all year. Then, when we get back home, we'll redo Christmas in person, just a few weeks late."

John squeezed back, one hand firmly on the wheel. This year abroad had been a struggle, but they had really made an effort to stay connected with their families. In a few weeks their self-imposed exile would be over, and they would be headed home.

Thanksgiving had been the hardest so far, he thought. Tracy had been sad all week, and had taken Thursday off as a sick day. But when he had arrived home at their London flat on the twenty-fifth of November, carrying a ten pound roasted turkey with all the fixings, her sadness had turned to surprise and pleasure.

Inside their tiny flat, it had been a homemade American Thanksgiving. They had laughed and stuffed themselves while the rest of England simply observed another rainy Thursday.

A sly smile slid across his face as he remembered putting away the leftovers...

"What are you grinning about?" Tracy asked.

He sent his wife a wicked smile. "Cranberry sauce," he intoned solemnly.

A furious blush swept up her neck, and across her face. "You...oh..." she sputtered.

"It's okay, Trace," he told her. "We are married."

He started to laugh at the embarrassed glare she sent his way, and she dropped the glare and joined in the laughter.

"Keep it up, buddy boy, and you won't be getting any cranberry sauce for your Christmas dinner!"

"Oh no! I *looooove* my cranberry sauce!" His free hand moved to her waist, his fingers tickling at her sweater clad ribs.

Squirming closer to the door, she slapped at his hand. "Uhn-uh. No touching! Keep your hands on the wheel, and your eyes on the road, husband dear. I think our turn is coming up."

"Aye, aye, wife." John good-naturedly turned his attention back to driving. The road to Kirkcaldy was, indeed, approaching. There would be time for touching... later.

✳ ✳ ✳

The lodge was stunning. Tracy gazed at it, astounded by its size. "Whoa," she breathed, "when your Uncle Alec said he'd bought a lodge, I was thinking more along the lines of, you know, a *lodge*. Wood and logs. This is a... a..."

"Castle?" John suggested.

It was impressive. Three stories of sandstone and rough timbered wood, the lodge sat proudly on a wide expanse of lawn, green still, despite the winter chill. Leaded glass windows sparkled in the dying sun. Tracy wondered how long it would take to walk to the river. She couldn't see it from here, but from what she'd heard, it was just beyond the house.

"It's going to make a lovely inn, isn't it?" Tracy asked, shivering slightly as the wind picked up.

"It's gorgeous," John agreed, taking her hand. "And I bet it's even better on the inside—and warmer." Hand in hand, they approached the front door.

An elaborate brass knocker in the shape of two doves hung from the door. John rapped it twice, and the door was opened by a thin woman with rosy cheeks and bright blue eyes.

"Welcome," she said cheerfully. "Welcome to Sìochaint." She ushered them inside. "I am Mrs. Hay. Meredith Hay. My husband and I will be running the inn for Mr. Fraiser."

"It's a pleasure to meet you," Tracy said, looking around the foyer. "My goodness, this is lovely, Mrs. Hay."

"Thank you, but please, call me Meredith."

"Only if you call me Tracy," Tracy told her, "and this is my husband, John."

"It's lovely to meet you," Meredith said, beckoning to a tall man standing in the hall. "This is my husband, Colin. He will take your bags."

Colin Hay stepped into the room, a smile lighting his dark eyes. "Welcome to Sìochaint, Mr. and Mrs. Fraiser. It is a pleasure to have you as our first guests."

"Please, we're just John and Tracy," Tracy said. "We're quite glad to be your practice guests. I understand there is going to be a soft opening celebration?"

"Yes," Meredith explained. "Tomorrow night. Just a few people coming for Oidche Choinnle, to light the Yule log and raise a glass in celebration. The real opening is next week, in time for Hogmany, or rather, the New Year."

"That sounds like fun," John said, as he and Tracy followed Meredith up the polished mahogany staircase. "But, what exactly is Oidche Choinnle?"

"That would be the Night of Candles," Colin explained, as he followed behind with the bags. "On Christmas Eve, we put out candles to light the way for the Holy Family. A fire to warm you and a light to guide you." Meredith stopped in front of a door, and Colin stepped past them to put down the bags.

"And, in case you were wondering," he continued, "the word *sìochaint* means peaceful, or restful, which is exactly what we're hoping your stay is."

"Now," Meredith said as she shooed her husband into the hall, "why don't you two get settled? We've already had tea, but dinner will be at seven, in the small dining room. I have a nice leg of lamb, and some decent greens. I thought we could give you the history of Sìochaint and a tour, after we eat. Mr. Fraiser suggested that we share meals, as you are our only guests until tomorrow. I hope that is suitable?"

"It sounds perfectly perfect," Tracy said sincerely. "Which room is the dining room?"

Meredith laughed. "That would be down the stairs and to the left. If you see a big silver stove, you've gone too far." With that, she gave Colin a gentle shove in the back, and left them alone.

"Wow." John stated, as the door closed behind the Hays. "This is spectacular." He took in the stone fireplace with its gentle flames dancing behind the metal screen, then moved on to the plush burgundy curtains drawn back from the cathedral window. When his gazed landed on the large, four-poster bed with its lush satin spread, his mind went into sexual overdrive. Especially when his wife kicked off her shoes and sank her bare feet into the deep pile of the area rug.

"I know," she said. "Jenna said that Uncle Alec put a lot of time into getting the restoration just perfect. He even brought in local artisans to work with the sandstone facade. I guess sandstone grows around here."

John snickered, and Tracy glared at him.

"Yes, I know that sandstone doesn't grow, Mr. Know-it-all. Don't laugh at me."

John moved quickly, scooping Tracy into his arms. "I wasn't laughing at you, babe," he said, depositing her on the high bed.

"That so? What were you laughing at, then?

John nuzzled her neck, his lips nibbling at her earlobe as he whispered, "I was just wondering if Meredith has any cranberry sauce."

✳ ❄ ✳

Tracy and John nearly danced down the stairs, hand in hand, and found the dining room without any trouble. Dinner was delicious, despite the lack of cranberry sauce. Roast lamb, studded with rosemary and garlic, was served with tiny potatoes and roasted vegetables, and was followed by a delicious concoction Meredith called apple butterscotch pie. Meredith and Colin made enjoyable dinner companions.

Pleasantly full and enjoying the company, Tracy agreed enthusiastically when Colin suggested a tour of the lodge. They followed Colin, listening intently as he supplied fascinating details about the history of the lodge and some of the previous occupants.

The main floor consisted of eight rooms: a formal dining room, the smaller dining room, a parlor, the grand room, a small but well-appointed library, a state-of–the-art kitchen and two luxurious powder rooms.

Upstairs housed ten suites, each with a fireplace, four-poster bed, and full bath. The color and decor of each suite was unique, yet equally as elegant as the suite designated for John and Tracy. A second set of stairs led to the third floor.

"Meredith and I have an apartment on the third level," Colin explained. "There are two other apartments on that level that will be kept for overflow and family, but Mr. Fraiser wanted the two of you to be the first guests in the new suites."

"The inn is beautiful," John said. "I didn't know that a hunting lodge could be so elaborate. I have to admit, I was expecting something a little more rustic."

Colin laughed. "Aye, I'm sure. A Victorian era hunting lodge was much more like a country estate." He shook his head. "I canna believe the changes. You should have seen this place when Mr. Fraiser purchased it. It was a disaster, literally falling down in huge pieces." He took a look around. "Your uncle has worked wonders."

"Uncle Alec has the touch," Tracy agreed with a smile. "It's a Fraiser trait. It goes along with the stubbornness."

"Indeed, he does have the touch," Meredith said, joining them at the top of the stairs. "But stubbornness is, I think, a male trait, not just belonging to the Fraisers." She moved to join her husband, leaning into him as he slipped his arm about her waist. "Tomorrow, Colin and I are going to get the tree and holly for our decorating party. Would you care to join us?"

"That sounds like fun!" Tracy exclaimed, turning to her husband with a hopeful look. "What do you think, John?"

"I think we'd be honored to join you," John replied, "But I did want to take Tracy into Kirkcaldy to see the town. When did you want to go?"

"We'll go in the morning," Colin said. "After breakfast. It shouldn't take more than a couple of hours, so you can have the whole afternoon to sightsee."

"I have a couple of suggestions for lunch and tea," Meredith offered, "unless you'd prefer to pack a lunch."

"No, I think I'd prefer a pub or a restaurant," John told her. "What time should we be back?"

"I'll have a light tea out at half past four, and I expect people will begin arriving near the six o'clock hour. We'll have a buffet supper, after the lighting and decorating." Meredith stifled a yawn. "Oh. Sorry."

"No, it's late," John said. "Thank you, Colin, for the tour, and thank you Meredith, for the delicious dinner. We'll see you in the morning."

"Breakfast will be out a wee bit before nine, if that is acceptable." Meredith took her husband's hand, allowing him to pull her toward the staircase.

"It sounds perfect," Tracy said, as John opened the door to their room. "Good night."

She closed the door and turned to her husband. "They seem nice. Your Uncle Alec does a good job hiring his caretakers, doesn't he?"

"He does," he agreed, moving to the window and pulling the curtains closed. "He also has good taste in beds.

What say you, wife? Should we retire to our slightly disheveled, luxury mattress?"

"Yes, husband," she answered pertly. "Just as soon as I check out the soaking tub and double shower." She pulled her sweater over her head and glanced over her shoulder. "Care to join me?"

John's throaty growl was all the answer she needed.

December 24th

Bringing in the greens turned out to be a whole lot of fun.

Tracy knew that for her husband, it would be the first time ever he wasn't cutting his own tree for the holiday. She and John had been a little surprised to find out that in this area of Scotland, most trees were precut and imported from the Highland forests.

Colin and Meredith drove them all up to Cupar, to the Bethany Delivery Center, where they picked up and netted an eight foot tall Nordic Spruce. The trip was filled with joking and laughter. Tracy felt as if she and John had found kindred spirits in the young Scottish couple.

After the men secured the tree firmly to the Peugeot wagon, they all headed off together to cut holly.

Armed with clippers, they traipsed around the holly bushes, looking for prime boughs.

"Make sure you clip us some smooth ones," Meredith whispered to Tracy. "Avoid the prickled ones."

"Okay," Tracy said, moving toward a bush that held smooth branches. "Why?"

"Because the smooth ones represent the lasses, and the prickly ones the lads. If we take more smooth ones into the house, it means that the women will rule the household for the year."

"Sounds good to me," Tracy said with a giggle. "Girl power!"

"Not happening." John slipped his arms around her, stopping her from clipping the holly. "Colin says he needs to wear the pants at Sìochaint for a change." He lowered his head, nibbling on her neck.

"All right, you two," Colin interrupted, snaking his arm around his own wife's waist. "If you ever intend to get your sightseeing done, we need to gather the holly. How about we compromise, and cut equal amounts of prickle and smooth?"

"That sounds like the name of a solicitor's office," Meredith giggled. Pulling away from her husband, she brandished her shears. "But, the nature of marriage is compromise, so I must agree. Balance in all things, you know."

"To balance!" John released Tracy, and raised his shears in salute.

✳ ❊ ✳

"Deck the Halls with boughs of holly,
Fa la la la la, la la la la
'Tis the season to be jolly,
Fa la la la la, la la la la
Don we now our gay apparel,
Fa la la la la la, la la la
Troll the ancient yuletide carol,
Fa la la la la..."

Tracy finished her third chorus of the carol with a dramatic pause, and a resounding,

"*La la la laaaaaaaaaaaaaaaaa!*"

Turning his eyes briefly from the road, John asked, "Is it out of your system yet?"

She wrinkled her nose slightly, as if pondering the question. Shaking his head, he turned his gaze to the road again.

After hauling the tree and bunches of holly into the house, they had headed off to explore Kirkcaldy. They had had a marvelous time, picking up a few knickknacks and last minute gifts, checking out the historical sites, and having a wonderful lunch at a small, and obviously local favorite pub. Pleasantly tired, they were headed back to Sìochaint, planning on catching a nap before the party.

Although Tracy must still have energy, John thought when she grinned impishly at him, and belted out,

"*Fa la la la la, la la la la!* Now I'm finished."

"Good." He let out an exaggerated sigh. "Much as I love to hear you singing, I admit to being tired of that song. Do you have any others in your repertoire?"

"I might," she mused, tapping her chin with her finger. "But I think I'll save it for later. We're here, and I'd hate to frighten the Hays."

"Let's sneak upstairs before they notice that we're here," he suggested. She nodded her agreement, and they slipped quietly into the inn, carrying their shopping bags.

Safely in their room, John kicked off his shoes and flopped down on the bed. "Care to join me?" he asked.

"In a moment," Tracy answered, grabbing a bag and heading into the bathroom. "I want to freshen up first. My hands are still a little sticky from the lemon curd at lunch."

"It was good, wasn't it?" he called through the closed door. "Especially with those currant scones. Mmmmmm."

"Delicious." Her voice was muffled by the closed door and running water. John leaned back against the pillows and closed his eyes.

"John?" Her voice was a little hesitant. "John, do you remember asking me what I wanted for Christmas?"

"Yes." He kept his eyes closed. "If I remember correctly, you said you wanted peace on earth and a concealed carry permit."

"Well, I've thought of something else."

The voice was closer now. He opened his eyes, and nearly swallowed his tongue. There stood his normally non-girly wife, clad in a red satin teddy, trimmed with white marabou. Her feet were bare, and a perky Santa hat sat precariously atop her tumbled blond curls. As he attempted to sit up, hoping he wouldn't choke on his drool, she moved toward him. "What?" he managed to sputter. "Dressed like that, I'll give you the moon if that's what you want."

She giggled, and shook her head. "Nothing that grand," she told him. "Just you. All I want, all I've ever wanted, is you."

He found his voice, hoarse and raw, as he reached for her. "And you are my wish come true."

✳ ❄ ✳

"John! It's almost six thirty. What's taking you so long? I'm hungry. We missed tea, you know!"

Tracy checked her dress in the oval floor mirror once again. The deep blue stretch velvet was simple in design, with capped sleeves and a scooped neckline, and was extremely comfortable, as well as festive. The skirt ended mid calf, and swirled slightly as she paced.

"I thought I was the one who was supposed to preen in front of the bathroom mirror," she called through the door.

The door flew open, and John snorted. "I've never known you to preen. Would you like to start now?"

She looked him over from head to polished shoes. His dark hair was neatly combed, and his cream-colored dress shirt and sapphire tie were the perfect compliment to her dress.

"No, thank you," she said a little breathlessly, "I'd rather stare at you."

"Likewise, I'm sure." He spun her around. "You look delicious. Hmmm. Something is missing, though."

"What?" She glanced in the mirror. Dress on straight. Two shoes, matched. Slip not showing. Pantyhose. Wedding ring. "What did I forget?"

"This." He held out a small box. "Merry Christmas Eve, my love."

She took the box and opened it, unable to stifle her gasp. "Oh, John. It's beautiful!" She pulled the gold chain out of the box, her eyes drinking in the circle of sapphires and diamonds.

He took it from her, and she turned to allow him to fasten it around her neck. The circle nestled just below her throat, glittering in the light.

"It's an eternity circle," he said, his voice husky and deep. "Because that's how long I will love you. For an eternity."

She blinked back tears, speechless with emotion. She stood on tiptoe, and pressed her lips against his. "Thank you," she managed to whisper.

"No. Thank you. Thank you for loving me." Her handsome husband offered his arm, and she took it. "Now let's go downstairs and have a Christmas party. I want to show off my beautiful wife."

Arm in arm, they descended the stairs. She felt as if she were a fairy tale princess on the arm of her own Prince Charming. Outside the double doors leading into the grand room, John stopped. "I have one more gift for you, Trace."

"What?" She gazed up him, bemused.

John pushed open the doors, and she stared in shock and amazement.

There, gathered around the tree and the fireplace was the whole family. John's parents, Michael and Genevieve, sat on the large sofa, along with Tracy's folks. Her sister Kim cuddled on the loveseat with her fiancé Wesley, while John's brother Dan stood with Jenna, their little Arabella snuggled against her father's shoulder, her tiny feet clad in pink sequined slippers.

"Home."

The End

This story is dedicated to my family, especially John, Elizabeth & Olivia, and in memory of Grandma Catherine and M-i-L Sandra.

About Ronda Russell

Ronda Russell has been a writer almost as long as she has been a reader. Her physical coordination just took a little longer to develop than her word decoding skills. She writes because it fulfills her. She writes because she needs to, just like she needs to eat and breathe.

She's been fortunate enough to have a husband and daughters who encourage and support her, and she loves them dearly for that and so much more. But family doesn't end with blood. She also has a wide range of friends who are always willing to offer both encouragement and critiquing.

In fact, this story sprouted from a connection with one of these friends, who loved reading about Scotland, spies, and strong family connections. "Where We Love" is Ronda's tribute to this friend's favorite things.

LELANI DIXON

In Hiding

A NOVELLA

Chapter 1

Brian Marsters tried to tune out the Christmas music—it was still two days before Thanksgiving, for crying out loud. It helped to focus his attention on the mystery lady working so tirelessly loading bag after bag with groceries.

For the past two weeks, since she had volunteered for the holiday season at the downtown Memphis food bank, she was one of the first to arrive each day and one of the last to leave. She unloaded boxes, counted inventory, bagged groceries, and even swept up at the end of the day. The only task she'd balked at was handing out bags to those in need who came each day for essential food items. She chose instead to remain behind the scenes. He couldn't fault her for that, but it did make him wonder.

She'd introduced herself as Cassie Weiss. Despite all of the probing he made in his capacity as the Director of the Food Bank, there wasn't much more he'd learned about her. She was polite and funny, but she used that sense of humor to deflect all of his questions about her.

She had a great body and a pretty face, but she didn't do anything to highlight either. Her hair was a dull light brown and she wore it pulled back in a ponytail every day. She wasn't much over five feet tall, but her body was that of a woman with curves in all the right places.

He didn't know what it was exactly that attracted him, but he was determined to solve the mystery of Cassie Weiss. Unfortunately, fate had another idea.

He watched as she finished the last batch of bags, sent them to the distribution line, and then began to clean up her work area, putting bags away and restocking the few left over items. The volunteers were welcome to take home groceries for personal use, and Cassie occasionally took advantage of that. Brian noticed she only took home enough for one person. He watched as she grabbed a can of soup, stuffing it into the backpack she carried over her shoulder each day.

Brian had to assume that she planned on heating the soup up for dinner. He had other thoughts. He shut off the sound system, relieved to cut off "Grandma Got Run Over by a Reindeer" before he had to hear it for the fifth time that day.

He watched her body tense and whip around as he approached her. She seemed to always be on the defensive, but she visibly relaxed when she recognized him.

"Hey, Brian, are you heading out?" she asked as she placed the last few canned items on the cart to be returned to the shelves.

"I am. You about ready to go?" He was working at developing a friendship with her and figured that she'd eventually tell him why she was so nervous.

At least, he hoped that one day she would feel close enough to him to do so. For now, his plan was to take things slow and to let her get used to him, maybe come to rely on him.

She looked around and must have realized that she was the last one in the bagging area and that everything had been put away. "Looks like it," she told him with a bright smile.

"Can I twist your arm and get you to join me for dinner at a gourmet restaurant?"

"I know your idea of gourmet. It consists of, 'Would you like fries with your order?'" she mocked.

They'd already gone out twice before. Her initial awkwardness had faded away when he played it cool and showed her that he was a nice guy. As is, it had taken her several days to accept his first invitation, so he had been careful not to press for more than company and conversation over a meal.

"Hey, I was going to splurge and treat you to a deluxe hamburger," he answered.

"Would that be a Big Mac or a Whopper?" she joked as she reached towards a nearby chair and pulled off the oversized navy blue pea coat she wore against the late November chill.

He stepped forward to help her into the coat and resisted the urge to tug the band out of her hair to allow the loose curls to spill over her shoulders. They reached to just below her shoulder blades and he imagined felt like silk. He placed his hands briefly on her shoulders and gave a light squeeze. Then he stepped back and presented his arm in an overly formal gesture, causing her to laugh. "Milady," he said as he gave a mock bow.

Brian worked on keeping up a light banter between them as they headed out. They ended up at a diner that he was always recommending to people. He considered the food and service to be top quality, even though customers still had to order at the counter and carry their own tray to a booth or table.

There had been some attempt to brighten the place with holiday décor. There were papier-mâché turkeys on the tables, cardboard reindeer and elves on the walls, and a large Santa spray-painted across the front windows. Brian groaned when he realized the song playing on the sound system was again about poor old grandma.

After carrying their respective trays over to a small two-person Formica tabletop next to the front window, they sat down to eat. He noticed that she gave a quick glance at the nearby windows. Was she feeling too exposed? What had happened to her to make her so cautious?

He wanted to ask, but knew better. Instead, he glanced down at their food. He had ordered his usual hamburger, while Cassie had ordered the grilled chicken breast salad with low-fat dressing on the side. Brian rolled his eyes as he looked at her plate.

"You really think you can live on that rabbit food?" he asked with a smile in his voice.

"There's meat in here. You know, if you manage to get your protein without all of the fat, you'll live longer."

"Uh huh," he agreed as he swallowed. "Want some of my fries? They're especially good if you dip them in Ranch dressing."

She shook her head at him. "You're heading to an early grave, Brian."

He looked up and grinned at her. "You think people who eat salad live longer?"

"I do," she agreed.

"All right, give me a bite." He stood up slightly to lean toward her with an open mouth, ready to receive a forkful of green salad. He was taking a risk, waiting to see how she would react. Feeding another person was an intimate act and he wasn't certain how she'd respond, but he needed to push her just that little bit.

It happened fast. Brian stood and leaned over the small tabletop with a smiling challenge in his eyes and an open mouth. Then he dropped face first into her salad plate. The blood dripped from his temple down the side of his face. She leaned back in horror and opened her mouth to scream when a spit of glass hit the side of her face and cut her left cheek.

Survival instinct took over and she dropped down onto the narrow bench seat and then onto the floor. The first bullet had hit Brian; the second had sunk into the back of the booth, flying right in front her face. Three more bullets came through the window before it shattered. Patrons screamed and ducked down. Someone shouted to call 911.

It all happened so fast.

Brian had known her as Cassie Weiss, though it wasn't her actual name. She didn't have time to regret that he hadn't known her real name and never would. She was already scrambling. She couldn't afford to be at the scene when the police arrived. She needed to get out of town, to run, as far and as fast as she could. Sitting on the floor of the booth, she looked at Brian's legs. She reached into his front pocket and found his keys.

She functioned like an automaton, with all of her emotions turned off. This was survival and there was no place

173

for the feelings that battered at her hastily erected façade of calm. If she made it out of this, she could fall apart later.

Grabbing her coat and the small backpack she carried everywhere, she scooted out from under the booth and, staying on hands and knees, headed for the counter. She crawled behind it and beneath the swinging kitchen half-doors. Small shards of glass penetrated her hands and knees, but she didn't even feel the sting. She focused only on her destination. The cook was crouched down behind the industrial dishwasher with his arms over his head. She passed the large grill, the freezer unit, the stockroom, and made it to the rear door without being noticed. The commotion of the panicked people screaming and yelling covered her escape.

She surveyed the lot. Brian's car was parked two rows back. Using the trash bins as cover, she darted from the bin to the car in the first row and then across the open space to the second row.

She ended up on the passenger side of the small Toyota Corolla. She unlocked the door and crawled across to the driver's seat, staying below windshield level as she inserted the key and started the engine. She reversed out of the space, jumped the curb, and ended up on a side road that wound through a residential area.

The sirens and lights informed her that the local police were nearing the diner from the main street. She headed away from the diner and blended into traffic without being spotted by them.

But that still left the person with the gun.

She wasn't so naïve as to think that this was a random act. If Brian hadn't shifted towards her at just that moment, she would have been the one face down in the salad plate.

The second bullet had only missed her because of her instinctive jerk away from the horror of Brian's murder. She began to shake as reaction set in. She had to get out of town, someplace safe. She was beginning to believe that such a place didn't exist for her.

She headed south and drove through the night, stopping only once for gas and a restroom break. When she reached Atlanta, she followed signs to the International Airport and headed for long-term parking. She fished around in the glove compartment and tucked the sunglasses she found there in her coat pocket.

She locked up Brian's car and headed to the shuttle stop, carrying only her backpack. She caught the parking shuttle to the terminal and headed for the gift shop. Her purchases included an Atlanta Braves ball cap, a travel first aid kit, and a small roll-on suitcase. She was digging deep into her remaining cash, but there weren't any thrift stores in the airport. Taking her purchases to the women's room, she headed for the larger stall reserved for people with disabilities. Inside, she opened up her backpack and pulled out the emergency change of clothes she kept with her at all times.

There were still a few shards of glass embedded in her palms, and she used the plastic tweezers that came with the kit to dig them out. Gritting her teeth, she treated the small cuts in the palms of her hands, her knees, and her left cheek. She grimaced at the sting of antiseptic and dabbed ointment on the larger cuts, adding a Band-aid to two deeper wounds; one in the left palm and the other in her right knee.

Tugging on form-fitting black jeans and an oversized gray hoodie, she stuck her feet back into the same black sneakers. They were the only shoes she had.

175

Finally, she placed the baseball cap on top of her head with her hair tucked up inside. She stuffed her backpack and her pea coat into the roll-on luggage and headed out of the stall. Looking in the mirror, she pulled the hood of her sweatshirt up so that only the bill of the ball cap showed. She tossed the dark-framed glasses she'd used when she was Cassie Weiss into the trash and replaced them with Brian's silver-tinted sunglasses. Satisfied that she had altered her appearance despite her limited resources, she headed out.

She stopped to buy a small carton of milk and a granola bar, her breakfast, and then went out to the ground transportation area and looked for a way to get to the Greyhound bus terminal. She took a shuttle out to the main street and walked to a local bus stop. Two transfers later, she was at the terminal. She looked at the board and found that a bus heading to Charlotte was scheduled to leave in a half hour.

North Carolina would have to do for now. She was determined to stay as close to Washington, D.C. as she could throughout the holidays.

Samuel Kragen's trial was scheduled to begin just after the New Year and would be held in Federal Court. She was low on funds and the more she spent on traveling, the less she'd have to return in time for the trial to begin.

She was, after all, the key witness for the prosecution.

Chapter 2

U.S. Deputy Marshal Jonah Carter rubbed the back of his neck as he waited at Dulles Airport for the shuttle to the parking lot where he'd left his car early that morning.

Three weeks ago, the report of a drive-by shooting in downtown Memphis, which had resulted in one death, had caught his attention. Mention of a potential female witness who had left the scene compelled him to follow up. He'd researched the reports and then headed down, following a hunch.

His hunch had paid off. There were several witnesses who identified Carina Woods as a volunteer at the local food bank, though they'd known her as Cassie Weiss. She was also identified as the woman who had been eating at the diner with the shooting victim, a Brian Marsters.

The crime scene team had pulled four bullets out of a booth of the two-person table where the pair had been eating dinner. Another bullet had lodged in Brian Marster's skull. It was lucky the shooter had used a small caliber handgun. A larger bullet would have taken the top of the victim's head off.

Reviewing the scene and witness statements, Jonah decided that Brian must have made a sudden move toward Carina and been hit by the bullet intended for her. Marsters had most likely leaned over the table to kiss her.

He couldn't blame the guy; Carina was a hell of a good-looking woman, even with the disguise she had adopted. But getting close to her was dangerous. Jonah rotated his healed shoulder, which had taken a bullet meant for Carina months earlier.

He had spent a day tracking Carina's moves in Tennessee. She'd lived in a weekly rate apartment that managed to depress the hell out of him. The few articles of clothing she'd left behind were clearly thrift store buys designed to camouflage her. Her work at the food bank was exemplary, or so the many volunteers who worked there had told him. He'd also checked out Brian Marster's apartment. It was in a slightly better neighborhood, but not by much.

An APB had been put out on Cassie Weiss, the name Carina had used in Memphis. Marster's Toyota Corolla had been missing from the diner parking lot and his keys were not listed as being found in his personal effects.

Jonah had pieced it all together, but had no idea where she had headed next. Until earlier that morning, when the car had been spotted and reported in the long-term parking lot at the Atlanta International Airport.

His flight to Atlanta had resulted in him finding that the steering wheel of the car had blood smears on it. He'd had the Atlanta P.D. run DNA tests that proved the blood belonged to Carina Woods. He imagined that she had been cut by some of the glass from the shattered window in the Memphis diner. Based on the amount of blood, he had reason to believe that the injuries had been minor.

He'd spent the remainder of his Sunday reviewing security tapes of the airport until he had spotted Carina heading into a gift shop. She had her hair dyed from its original sunny blond to a light brown, wore large dark-framed glasses, and a wool pea coat that disguised her very feminine figure. He followed her on camera into the women's restroom and then waited over thirty minutes for her to come out. She'd done a great job altering her looks. He watched her walk out of the airport, board a shuttle, and disappear once again.

Christmas was less than a full week away and he had to get her safely to the trial that was set to begin on the Wednesday after the New Year. He wondered if she thought she would be able to remain on the run indefinitely. She had to be out of money by this time. She'd taken a large sum with her, cleaning out her savings account, prior to taking off from the cover identity the Witness Protection Program had established for her in Arizona, but she'd been on the run for more than five months now.

He'd met Carina after she had presented documents from Samuel Kragen's private files to the FBI. Carina had been involved with Samuel Kragen, a very powerful and wealthy man. What she hadn't known was that the man made most of his money through illegal means and had ties with some very nasty people in the Russian mafia.

She had unwittingly mentioned to Kragen a conversation she had overheard while catering an exclusive dinner at a well-connected senator's home. The senator was backing a bill that would cost Kragen and his associates a great deal of money. Later that week, she had been at Kragen's house and had overheard him order a hit on the senator. The next morning, she had gone into his home office and used her cell phone camera to take pictures of enough documentation to put the man away for a very long time. She had also copied e-mails and other files from his hard drive onto a thumb drive. She provided evidence on crimes including loan sharking, extortion, and weapons running.

Knowing how powerful Kragen was, the federal prosecutor had arranged for Carina to be protected by the U.S. Marshals. It was at that point that she had been assigned to Jonah's caseload.

179

Jonah coordinated Carina's protection while she gave her testimony to the grand jury. He coordinated her transportation to and from court, chose the personnel who guarded her twenty-four hours a day, and oversaw all security measures related to her safety.

While returning from giving testimony on the third and final day, Jonah had been escorting Carina down the hall of the hotel where she was being housed. Carina had taken off her high-heeled shoes while they were in the elevator, complaining that her feet were killing her. After they exited the elevator and headed down the corridor, a shot rang out.

Jonah had instinctively shoved her to the floor and had taken the bullet in his left shoulder. He had spent a few nights lying awake wondering what would have happened if she hadn't taken her shoes off and the bullet had been aimed higher. Would it have missed him altogether? Or would he have been shot in the head? There were too many variables to decide one way or the other, but it didn't stop him wondering.

The gunman had planned his escape well, and the marshals on the detail hadn't caught him. While Jonah was having the bullet surgically removed from his shoulder, the Justice Department had moved Carina to Arizona and placed her in the Witness Protection Program to await Kragen's trial.

Then Carina had escaped that protection, apparently of her own volition. And Jonah had been looking for her ever since.

The woman had gotten under his skin. Despite the vulnerable position she was in, she had an inner strength that had impressed him. Hell, he was even babysitting her cat! He was glad that his brothers hadn't caught wind of that one. Christmas with the Carter clan would be miserable if his brothers knew that their ex-Marine, U.S. Marshal brother had taken on cat-sitting for one of his witnesses.

He was dog-tired as he let himself into his apartment just before midnight, reminding himself that he had taken his position knowing that it wasn't going to be a nine to five Monday through Friday kind of job. He heard a slight sound and looked for the cat, Mr. Darcy, who usually greeted him.

His gun was in his hand before his brain had time to tell him to draw it. He stared down the barrel at the woman standing in front of his couch, holding the cat and stroking his medium length gray fur.

"Hello, Marshal Carter," Carina said calmly.

"What the hell?" Jonah said as he lowered his weapon. He pulled the door closed behind him and locked it, shooting the bolt home. "How did you get in here? How did you get my address?" He returned his gun to his shoulder harness.

Carina shrugged. "I palmed your keys the day you took that bullet for me."

"I wondered where they'd gone. I thought they'd been lost in the ambulance or at the ER. I had to use my spare set. Damn, I'm a U.S. Marshal. I can't believe I didn't change my locks. I know better." He shook his head at his oversight. He wouldn't even excuse it to the fact that after he had healed from his shoulder wound, his time and attention had been focused on tracking her down. She'd fled Arizona just prior to him being cleared to return to duty.

"I figured that's what you would think when you realized you'd lost the keys. I took them on impulse. They were sticking out of your hip pocket when you went down. It was all so chaotic: I was trying to put pressure to the wound and then someone dragged me away and I just kept the keys in my hand. Then I was being hustled out the back of the hotel under guard and relocated to Arizona while you were still hospitalized. I kept them for you."

That explained how she'd gotten into his apartment, but didn't explain how she knew where he lived. "I still don't get how you knew my address."

She shrugged. "In court, I was locked up in that room until it was time for me to testify to the grand jury. You went to go get coffee and left your jacket on the back of the chair. Your wallet was in the pocket. I recognized your address on your driver's license since I have a client just a block over." She shrugged again. "Sorry."

He looked at her holding the cat against her chest, as one hand continued to stroke. There was a slight tremor in the hand and he knew that she wasn't nearly as calm as her voice portrayed. "You don't seem the nosy type," he observed.

"I'm not under normal circumstances. Maybe if I had been, I'd have known what Samuel Kragen was up to sooner. I always gave him his space, respected his privacy. I should have taken up snooping long ago." She looked up at him with a plea for understanding in her eyes. "I was bored, nervous. I was just trying to distract myself. Your wallet was all I had available. Anyway, I've kept your keys with me ever since you shoved me back and took the bullet that was meant for my head. I trust you. I know you'll risk your life for me, you've proven that. I know that there are procedures and rules you're supposed to follow. But this time, I only want you to know where I am until the trial begins. No one else you work with. Just you."

"Me?" he asked, a sinking suspicion of what she meant.

"Yes, just you. Someone tipped Kragen and his goons off that day so that they knew which hotel I was staying at during the grand jury testimony. And then there was Arizona."

"Yeah, what happened there? As far as I knew, your cover was secure and then you were just gone."

"It's a long story. Why don't you come on in and get comfortable? Are you hungry? I helped myself to your kitchen and made some pasta primavera. You want garlic bread to go with it? Coffee?"

He shook his head. This woman was in his apartment offering him his own food and drink. "I'll be back out in a few minutes. The pasta and garlic bread sound good, but let's open a bottle of wine to go with it. I need to get some sleep. The last thing I want is coffee."

She nodded and headed towards the kitchen while he went down the short hall and into his bedroom. After washing up and changing into a pair of comfortable jeans and a pullover, he followed the tantalizing scents coming from his kitchen.

He stood in the doorway of the small kitchen and watched her. She was wearing a pair of sweatpants and the same oversized hoodie he'd seen her wear on the security tape in Atlanta. Her hair was back to its natural color, so he assumed she'd been using some kind of rinse on it so that she could change her color frequently. The mass of blond hair was pulled away from her forehead by a headband so it tumbled over her shoulders in loose soft waves to frame her face. Her face was bereft of make up and she could have passed for fifteen, except for the worry line just above the bridge of her nose.

"Smells good," he commented as he walked into the kitchen.

183

"Yes, I love the smell of garlic cooking. The bread will be a few more minutes, but the pasta is ready if you want to go ahead and get the wine poured." She nodded her head to the bottle standing open on the counter.

He got two glasses from the cupboard and poured the wine before carrying it to the dining room next to the kitchen.

Carina followed him, carrying a plate of pasta and silverware for one. She set them in front of him as he took a seat, and then sat adjacent to him and picked up the wine he'd poured for her. She took a long, slow swallow. "Don't let me forget to get the bread for you," she said as he dug into the pasta.

"Mmm," was his only response as he chewed.

He watched as a slight smile crinkled the corners of her mouth. Then, on a long sigh, she launched into her story. "I was working in Arizona at that boring government job you guys set up for me. Processing Medicaid claims." She sighed again and rolled her eyes. "Thanks for that, by the way."

He grunted, then paused in his chewing to take a sip of wine. The pasta was better than any he'd ever ordered in a restaurant. He'd been hungrier than he'd realized. Now that meals weren't served on domestic flights, it was hard to get something decent to eat when traveling for business, especially on unplanned trips.

"I kept feeling as if I was being watched. At first, I thought it was the Marshal's Office just doing its job, but then I got a glimpse of this guy in a suit. A couple days later, I saw him again. One evening, I went home and knew that my apartment had been searched. Nothing was missing, but things had been shifted enough for me to notice. Then, the next day, I went down to a sandwich shop to get lunch. The man in the suit was talking to another guy—slick looking.

Small in stature, but he had that look, you know, like he could kill without remorse."

Jonah nodded, he knew that look.

She continued. "I don't know how to describe it, but he looked up and looked directly at me. It was like he was looking through me. I knew I had to get the heck out of Arizona. I walked back to the building where I worked, took the elevator up to my floor, and then took the stairs straight back down. I went to my apartment and packed a bag.

"Before I left, I looked out the back window and saw Mr. Slick sitting in a black sedan. I altered my appearance and snuck out through the laundry room door, around the pool, and over the fence. I hailed a cab, made sure I wasn't being followed. After a quick trip to the bank to clean out my savings, I hopped on a bus and wound up in Oregon."

"And didn't let me know where you were," he said.

"No, I…oh no!"

Jonah braced when she cried out, then relaxed again when she just hopped up and rushed into the kitchen.

"It's not ruined," she announced as she brought in a cookie sheet she'd put the bread on and slid the toast onto his plate. "It's a little crispy." She shrugged. "But it's not burnt."

She headed back into the kitchen to dispose of the hot sheet and the oven mitt. When she returned, she brought the wine bottle and topped off both of their glasses. She looked questioningly at Jonah as he sampled the garlic bread.

"It's good," he said, and followed the bite with another sip of wine and a questioning look. "You were going to tell me why you decided to keep me out of the loop."

She sighed. "I wasn't sure who to trust. I trust you. You took that bullet for me. You saved my life," she clarified when he looked expectantly at her. "And maybe that's part two. I thought that if I could just fall off the radar screen for a bit, I could maybe get back to you before the trial started and maybe stay safe. I've always planned to show up at your door near the start date of the trial. I didn't want you, or anyone, risking their lives for me until the trial began. Not that that worked out." She got a sorrowful look on her face and Jonah knew that she was remembering Brian Marsters.

Before he could say anything comforting, she spoke again. "I know—I mean, I can't prove it—but I know that there's a leak somewhere, maybe in your office. It wasn't an accident that they found me in Arizona. I believe that."

"Because you saw some guy in a suit talking to a slick guy who followed you to your apartment?"

"But he didn't follow me there. He got there on his own. He knew where to go to find me. He knew where I worked and where I lived. If I had come home at my regular time, he would have ambushed me. I only escaped because I caught onto what was going on and was able to sneak in and out of my apartment building when they weren't expecting me. Look, you don't have to believe me, but you won't convince me that I'm wrong."

"The Marshal's Office hasn't known where you were since Arizona, and Kragen still managed to track you." He set down his fork before he stuffed himself any more.

"I know. I don't know how he's doing it. I really don't. Your keys are about the only thing I still have with me from when I left Arizona. I've been as far north as Minnesota and as far west as Oregon. I haven't stayed in one place for more than a month at a time. I've been volunteering at thrift stores and food banks. I haven't attempted to get paid employment. I changed my look each time I moved on. I haven't told anyone my story and I've used false names. How are they tracking me?"

Jonah looked at her. With her scrubbed face and sweats, she couldn't have looked more innocent. He wanted to reach out and pull her into his arms and just hold her. He shook himself. He had a job to do and this woman's life depended on him doing it well. Fantasizing about tracing her lips with his fingertip and then his tongue was not going to get him anywhere.

He couldn't believe where his mind was wandering. He was a professional, for God's sake, and he'd protected some great looking women during his career. He'd never had trouble before staying focused on the job, on his duty. But he'd known from the moment he'd met her that Carina Woods was trouble. He'd been right.

"I don't know how they're tracking you. Were there any other attempts on your life besides the one in Memphis?"

"You know about that?"

"Yeah, I put it together. I just came from the Atlanta airport. I've had a trace out on Marsters' car. When it was reported in Atlanta, I flew out and checked the airport security tapes. Where have you been since then?"

"North Carolina. I was in Charlotte until this morning when I took a Greyhound bus to D.C. and then the Metro here."

He nodded. "We'll talk about it more in the morning. You look like you need some rest and I know I do."

"I do. I really appreciate you taking care of Mr. Darcy for me. That was really beyond the call of duty."

He shrugged. "I couldn't just abandon the cat now, could I?" he asked.

187

They carried the dirty dishes into the kitchen. Jonah checked to make certain that Carina had everything she needed before he retired to his bedroom, leaving her to use the guest bedroom. Mr. Darcy abandoned him for his mistress. Jonah lay in bed thinking about what Carina had told him.

If there was a leak, if someone was leaking inside information, he needed to find out who it was. But, he realized, that was going to have to take a backseat to keeping Carina safe. The trial was set to start in just over two weeks. Keeping her in his apartment might work for a few days, but he needed to get her out of town and to a safe place for the holiday week.

There was no way he could take her to his family Christmas, as that would be too obvious and put people he loved at risk. He'd have to contact his parents and let them know that he had a work assignment that was going to keep him busy through the holidays. His mother wasn't going to be pleased, but there was no way he could delegate the task of keeping Carina safe to anyone else. Even if he handpicked the people who guarded her, he knew that she would never trust anyone else at this point. She'd been through a great deal, so maybe she was being paranoid. Then again, he doubted that Brian Marsters would agree with that assessment.

Chapter 3

Carina was in the kitchen making pancakes from scratch when Jonah walked in. She didn't hear him enter the kitchen, she was just suddenly aware of his presence. When she turned around, he was leaning against the doorjamb, watching her intently.

His feet were bare and he was wearing a pair of gray sweatpants and a navy blue T-shirt. His square-cut face and strong jaw had the stubble of beard from the previous night's growth, and his hair was tousled from sleep.

He needed a haircut, she thought. His dark brown hair was beginning to curl over his ears and brushed a bit past his neckline. His warm aqua blue eyes twinkled with an echo of the smile still on his lips.

Why did he have to be so good-looking? Damn it. She was certain her body betrayed her attraction to him. Her life depended on this man doing his job and doing it well. Fantasizing about him wasn't going to help the situation any.

"Good morning," she said, forcing a cheerful note into her voice. "Coffee's made." She continued frying bacon and flipping pancakes while he wandered over to the coffee-maker and poured himself a cup.

"I wondered if you'd still be here this morning," he confessed.

She shrugged. "I've got nowhere else to go."

He nodded, seeming to accept the simple truth of that statement. "I have to go into work this morning."

"You won't…"

"No, I won't tell anyone that you've turned up. I risk my job keeping this a secret, but I thought about your theories and I can't guarantee that there isn't a leak. At this point, we've got just over two weeks to get through before the trial begins. I had planned to take some time off to spend the holidays with family, so I'll just alter my plans." He took a sip of coffee. "If I work the rest of this week, we can take off on Friday and head out to a beach house a friend of mine has down in North Carolina's Outer Banks. We can stay there through New Year's Day and then head back for the trial."

"North Carolina?" she asked, surprised.

"Yeah, he has a place on Nags Head. He's stationed in Afghanistan at the moment, so he won't mind. Plus, he's got his car stored at a garage near his home base at Quantico. We'll stop there and trade cars. It's on our way anyway. I have an open invitation to use the house and I have keys to his car and his beach house."

"And no one is likely to look for you there?"

"Why would they? They don't know you've turned up. Mac and I became friends back when we were new recruits in the Marines. I got out after my tour of duty to get my Masters Degree in Criminal Justice and become a Marshal. Mac stayed in, got the Marines to pay for his education, and now he's a full Colonel. He's been out of the country for the last year and a half. My connection to him should be off the radar. It's the best I have to offer in the way of a safe house."

"It sounds like you spent some time thinking about this," she observed. She appreciated his concern for her safety, even if it was only due to his dedication to his job.

"I have. I think it's best if you stay here in my apartment and I carry on as normal. I'll go in and file my report regarding Atlanta and act as if I'm still trying to locate you."

"How close have you come to locating me over the past months?"

"Not close. With all of my resources, I never would have found you in Tennessee. I don't know how they've been tracking you. You haven't used ID that could be traced to you or any type of bank account. Speaking of money, how low are you?"

She paused, reluctant to answer. "I lived frugally, but I'm down to my last twelve bucks in cash."

"I'll get us some cash, but we'll have to keep a low profile. I don't want to withdraw too much cash or use any credit cards that will tip anyone off if they're looking at me."

"I don't need much. I'm used to getting by," she told him. Gone were the days of manicures, pedicures, facials, salon days, shopping sprees; all the things she'd thought were integral parts of her adult life. She had two pairs of pants, two shirts, a sweatshirt and a pea coat, along with a couple pairs of underwear, socks, and a pair of shoes. Her toiletries included shampoo, a toothbrush, toothpaste, a hairbrush, some feminine hygiene products, and some basic makeup. What more could a girl need?

"I can tap a small savings account I keep for emergencies later today to get you a few things. I know you didn't bring much with you."

Did the man read minds? "If you've got a washer and dryer, I can wait until we're on the road to pick up a few things."

He nodded. "That would probably be best. I'll go ahead and get the money now though. It won't seem odd for me to spend extra money, not at this time of year. If you think of anything you need, let me know and I can stop and get it for you. Speaking of which, I better pick up a couple of throwaway phones so that you can reach me if you need to without anyone tracing the calls."

Carina slid a small stack of pancakes onto two plates, added a couple slices of bacon to each, and carried them to the small kitchen table. "You want some orange juice or milk?" she asked.

"No, the coffee's fine. It looks good, thanks," he said as he sat down and poured maple syrup onto his pancakes and started to eat. "I'm not used to having a beautiful woman in my kitchen fixing me a hot breakfast before I go to work. I usually just grab a bowl of cereal."

She warmed to the "beautiful" comment before struggling to shut down her hormones. "You're welcome," she managed.

She needed to be careful not to confuse a man doing a job with a man she could easily become attracted to. Very easily. She lectured herself while he made appreciative noises and polished off the remainder of the breakfast she'd fixed him.

Jonah left a half hour later and she was alone in the apartment. She went into his bedroom and pulled open a couple of drawers until she found a T-shirt that she could wear while she did laundry. She stripped off the clothes she was wearing and pulled the T-shirt over her head. It was clean, but she could still smell traces of his scent. It was a good scent: subtle, masculine, and sexy. She grabbed up her small pile of clothes and then looked around for his dirty laundry.

She liked his apartment. The predominant colors were warm browns and tans. The furniture was oversized wood and leather, made for comfort. There were pieces on the walls or on shelves that showed he enjoyed traveling or examples of what she thought of as masculine artwork. There were some carved wood pieces and a few small metal sculptures. There were also photos scattered throughout the apartment.

There was no sign of a woman's things, so he apparently lived alone.

He seemed to pick up after himself though. She found his laundry hamper in the bathroom and began sorting the clothing. After adding her things and the few towels she found hanging, she managed to get three medium loads worth and began the process of washing them all in the small laundry closet just off the kitchen.

Having begun the laundry, she wondered how she would spend the rest of her day. She checked out his CD collection and put on some music as she began to give his apartment a thorough cleaning. She needed to keep busy. Her volunteer work while she was on the run had kept her sane.

She was used to a very busy life. She and her partner, Phoebe, had a thriving catering company that was patronized by the movers and shakers in Washington, D.C. They had a niche business that fulfilled a very specific need. Both she and Phoebe were accomplished chefs and went into private homes to prepare meals for groups of up to twenty people, avoiding the large affairs that required trays of already prepared foods to be brought in.

They cooked primarily in their clients' kitchens and kept their staff small and well-trained. Owning her own company had been a lifelong dream, but it had taken sixteen-hour days to realize that dream. Now that they were successful, she and Phoebe hadn't rested on their laurels, but continued to work hard. That is, until that fateful night when she'd overheard Sam on the phone.

Carina shook her head. She didn't want to think about that now. Cleaning the oven would be the perfect task to help take her mind off of her troubles.

That evening, when Jonah entered his apartment, he found that it sparkled. Everything had been dusted, vacuumed, scrubbed, polished, and put away. Carina had even unearthed his few Christmas decorations, and the ceramic Christmas tree and swags of plastic greenery never looked better.

The mouthwatering scents emanating from the kitchen told him that dinner was about ready as well.

"Hello, Carina?" he called. The last thing he wanted to do was startle her.

"In here," she responded.

Walking into the kitchen, he found her bent over the oven. He felt a tightening low in his belly as he watched black denim stretch over her well-formed backside.

"It's done," she announced, withdrawing a steaming tray and setting it atop the stove.

"Smells good," he said with a smile. "It pays to have a live-in chef."

She pulled off her oven mitts and brushed a stand of hair from her flushed face. Transferring the contents into a serving dish, she said, "I found the chicken breasts in your freezer and added some vegetables and rice with a light gravy. I hope that's okay."

"It's more than okay, but you didn't have to cook," he said.

"I wanted to. I like to cook."

"Well, I like to eat, so I really appreciate it. Do you think we have enough food for the next few days? We'll stop and shop on the way down to the beach house, but if we can make it through the rest of the week without buying up too many groceries, it'll help us save on our cash supply." He decided that he'd defer to the professional caterer when it came to meals. She seemed happy enough to be in charge of the cooking.

194

"Yeah, I set out some other frozen meats and vegetables I found to defrost. We just need a few fresh things. I'll make a list," she said.

"I usually buy in bulk. I'm not much of a shopper, so I go to a warehouse store and buy enough to fill the freezer every few months," he confessed as he helped her carry the steaming dishes to the dining room table.

"You must enjoy cooking as well. There isn't a frozen dinner in sight."

He smiled. "I enjoy eating more than cooking, but yeah, I have a mother who believes that every man should be self-sufficient in the kitchen."

"Do you have a big family?" she asked as they served themselves and began eating.

"Damn, this is good," he stated after his first bite. He wasn't sure what she'd done to it, but it wasn't any typical casserole he'd ever eaten.

She smiled in response. "I love to cook. I think of it as a form of art."

"This is certainly art," he said as he took another bite.

"Your family?" she prodded.

"Mmm, yeah, my parents and two brothers. Mom and Dad live out in New Mexico. They have a motor home they travel around in for about seven months out of the year. When they're not on the road, they live about a mile from my brother Jason's home. Mom said that since Jason was the only one sensible enough to give her grandkids, she was going to base herself near him."

"What about your other brother?"

He paused to savor another bite of food. "Justin? He's a computer genius. He works for a software company out in

Seattle. My parents spend a couple of months visiting him each year."

"And you? How often do you see them?" She brushed a few strands of hair away from her face.

He caught himself following the action and shook his head to clear it. "Oh, I join them at various points along their journey a few times a year. They park themselves at Mac's beach house for about a month each year. Mac is sort of a surrogate brother. I brought him home on leave once and the family adopted him. He grew up the only boy with four sisters, so he was certain that he had landed in heaven with all the testosterone dripping down the walls at my house. He said that his main reason for joining the Marines was to get away from all the nagging."

She laughed. He realized he hadn't heard her laugh often. Then again, the circumstances behind their meeting hadn't really been a reason to laugh.

"And did you ever visit his family?"

"As often as possible. I had an on again off again thing going with his sister, Shannon, but it finally ended for good just before I moved to D.C."

He politely asked Carina about her family, although he already knew most of it. She'd lost her parents in a car accident when she'd been fourteen. Her family had been on a trip to Italy. On the way from Pisa to Venice, the car had been hit head on by a drunk driver. Both of her parents had been killed instantly, as had her younger sister. Carina had suffered serious injuries.

After prolonged rehab, she'd been placed in foster care until she was eighteen. There had been no other relatives willing to take on the responsibility of giving the injured and traumatized girl a home. She'd made her own way in life without any family support, and he sensed the loneliness in her.

He regaled her with stories of his childhood and living with two brothers, and enjoyed watching her unwind inch by inch. He suspected she hadn't allowed herself to relax since she'd overheard Samuel Kragen making that phone call all those months ago. He built a fire and then sat next to her on the couch, not too close. Since she seemed to be fascinated, he continued to tell her stories about his life, something he'd never done with a witness. Then again, he'd never had a witness in his home, either.

She smiled at him as Mr. Darcy curled next to her thigh and purred loudly under her stroking hand. "This is nice. I forgot how nice it could be to just relax," she confessed.

He wanted to keep her that way, safe and relaxed. "It is nice. I've enjoyed talking with you tonight. With my apartment so clean though, I'm wondering what you'll do with yourself tomorrow."

"I was thinking about organizing your sock drawer."

He smiled at her. "I may have something else to occupy you, if you're interested."

"Yeah? Like what?"

"I'm being promoted after the New Year. The current supervisor is retiring and I'll be taking his position. I have several years of case notes I need sorted and organized. They're my personal notes and aren't considered confidential. The confidential documents are already filed with the Justice Department, but I always keep my personal notes here in case something comes up and I need to refresh my memory. I had planned to get to it after returning from my trip out to my parents' home for Christmas. It's tedious work, but if you're interested…"

197

"I'll do it," she agreed readily. "I'm rather desperate for something to occupy my mind. The more I dwell on my situation, the less healthy it is for me."

He'd figured as much, that's why he came up with this project. "Yeah, you've had a lot of alone time to think, haven't you?"

"A lifetime's worth," she agreed.

"Okay. In the morning, I'll show you what I need and let you get started. In the meantime, I need to get some sleep. I've got quite a bit of wrapping up to do so that I can take off until after the New Year."

"Did you have any trouble getting the time off?" She stood up and took their empty glasses into the kitchen.

"No. I had already arranged for some leave over the holidays, I just extended it."

"I hope you don't mind, but I borrowed one of your T-shirts and I thought I'd use it as sleepwear."

Jonah had a mental flash of her wearing one of his T-shirts, nothing but her well-shaped legs below the hem. He closed his eyes. "No, I don't mind, not at all."

Later, Jonah lay in bed imagining Carina slipping between the sheets of the guest bed. The thought wasn't conducive to sleep, and it took a great deal of self-discipline to finally train his thoughts to a less erotic image and drift off to sleep.

The screams woke him. They were bloodcurdling, and he was instantly awake, but disoriented. For a short time, he thought he was once again in a war zone. It wasn't often that he had nightmares from his days in the Marines, but every once in a while they paid him an unwelcome visit.

Then he heard quiet sobbing and realized he was in his own home, in his own bed. He reached into the bedside table and eased his gun out. He released the safety and slipped out from his bed, moving silently into the guestroom.

She was sitting huddled in the bed, her arms wrapped around her legs. Her face was pressed into her knees. Her body shook with the sobs. He scanned the room quickly for signs of an intruder or a forced entry, but saw nothing. Only the cat, pacing on top of the dresser, his ruffled fur and slitted pupils evidence the woman's screams had startled him.

Mr. Darcy stared at him, then back at his mistress as if he wasn't sure if he should stay away or approach. He could sympathize with the cat's dilemma.

"Carina." He said her name softly.

The sobbing stopped and her head came up. She grew perfectly still and stared at him through her drenched eyes.

"I'm sorry. I heard you scream and I thought…" He didn't want to tell her he thought that someone had broken in and gone after her. She was smart enough to figure it out for herself.

She wiped her face with the backs of her hands. "I'm sorry. I had a nightmare. I…" Her body shook with the sob that wracked it. "I saw Brian leaning towards me and then he was lying there, his face in my salad plate, the blood trickling down from the hole in his temple. I didn't scream when it happened in real life. I opened my mouth to scream, but then I was sprayed with glass from the next bullet and I just reacted. In my dream, I just sat there staring at him and screaming."

He went with instinct and sat on the side of the bed, pulling her against his chest. He slipped the safety on and placed his gun on the nightstand. He brought his free hand up and just sat stroking her hair with it as she cried into his shoulder. It was several minutes before her sobs quieted into occasional hiccups. He continued stroking her hair.

"Were you very close to him?" he asked.

She shook her head against his chest and then pulled back slightly. He let her go reluctantly.

"I worked with him at the food bank. He was a nice guy. He sort of hit on me, but not aggressively. Just, you know, testing the waters. When I didn't give him the green light, he backed off right away and stuck to friendship."

"But he was leaning over to kiss you at the diner," Jonah said.

"No, he wasn't. I had been teasing him about his childish diet. I made some remark about him heading to an early grave. He said that since I believed he'd live longer if he ate salad, he'd have a bite of mine. He was leaning over for a bite of my salad."

Her voice cracked and her eyes filled again. In a tortured whisper, she said, "He didn't live longer."

His hand left her hair to wipe the fresh tears from her cheeks with a gentle brush of his thumb. "It wasn't your fault."

"How can it not be my fault? The gunman was aiming for me and Brian got in the way."

"That's right. The gunman was trying to shoot you and Brian happened to get in the way of the bullet. You didn't aim the gun at his head. You didn't pull the trigger. You're a victim in this." He made certain to keep his voice low and firm.

"People who try to help me, people who are nice to me. They get shot. You might be killed protecting me."

"It's my job to protect you. I'm good at my job. Trust me." He reached over to the nightstand and pulled out some tissues.

"I do trust you." She wiped away tears. "But they've already shot you once. Then they killed Brian. It's me they want dead, but other people are being hurt and killed in my place. I can't go on living like this."

He pulled her back against his chest. "That's why you're going to testify and end it. Samuel Kragen is responsible for all of those things you just listed and more. You saved the senator's life by coming forward. Who knows how many other people he's ordered hits on?"

"Besides me, you mean," she said bitterly.

"Besides you. He's gotten away with murder and you're going to put an end to that. Of course he wants you dead." He felt her shiver. "But that's not going to happen, because I won't let it. We're together in this and we're going to finish it."

She sighed and drew back. "I'm sorry. I don't usually fall apart like this. I guess I've just been dealing with the shock and fear of what happened in the diner by suppressing it and tonight it all came bubbling up."

"Don't apologize. I saw some things back when I was in the Marines that haunt me to this day. I get the whole PTSD thing. And if anyone has been under an inordinate amount of stress, it's you. You've been on the run and hiding ever since you overheard that phone call. You made a tough decision, coming forward and providing evidence to the federal prosecutor. I'm going to see to it that you get your day in court. And when Samuel Kragen is stripped of all of his power and money, you'll be able to get your life back. Now, do you think you'll be able to get back to sleep?"

"Yeah, sure," Carina mumbled as she pulled back, embarrassed. She noted that Jonah was wearing another pair of sweatpants and a T-shirt similar to what he'd worn to breakfast. Did he usually sleep with so many clothes on, or was that for her benefit? She almost told him that it didn't seem to be working to keep her hormones in check, but she thought better of it.

"All right, I'll go back to my own room, but if you need me, just call." He reached past her to pick up his gun.

She looked at it, puzzled. "You brought a gun?"

"I did. I wasn't certain if what chased you was real or not."

"Oh," was all she said. Her body trembled once with the thought. "You don't think…"

"No, I don't think anyone tracked you here. I woke up and reacted without thinking about the logic of the situation. I'm certain you're safe here and in another three days, we'll leave and go to an even safer location. Do you think you can handle that?"

"Yeah, I'll be okay." Mr. Darcy decided to rejoin her now that the storm had passed. He bumped his head against her arm and she automatically reached out to comfort him. Or to be comforted, she wasn't certain which.

Jonah started to reach out to her, but must have changed his mind. He pulled his hand back and stood up. "Get some sleep. I'll see you in the morning."

She lay in bed thinking about what he'd said for a long while. The feel of his arms around her had felt warm and safe and secure. She wanted to just abdicate all of her worry to him and let him take care of it. Real modern woman thinking, she admonished herself with an eye roll. She gave herself a stern lecture about not becoming a damsel in distress and then began to fantasize about Jonah climbing into bed with her. Her sleep was restless, but not because of nightmares.

Chapter 4

The next three days fell into a comfortable rhythm. Carina woke up early enough to prepare breakfast for herself and Jonah. He left for work and she set about sorting and filing his old case notes.

She learned a lot about the man by reading his observations. His notes were meticulous: detailed descriptions of people's actions, appearances, and possible motivations. If anything, she began to trust his ability to protect her even more.

Beyond that, she often found herself daydreaming about him. There were pictures of him with family and friends playing basketball or at the beach. She'd caught herself staring fixedly at pictures in which he was shirtless. She liked his chest. She'd certainly enjoyed leaning against it the night he'd come to her room after her nightmare.

She'd even found a shot of him in a racing swimsuit. He'd been in his late teen years and little had been left to the imagination. She wondered if she should feel guilty drooling over a picture of a man when he was little more than a boy.

Maybe finding that photo had been a mistake. Because ever since, her brain seemed determined to superimpose the image of the nearly-nude younger Jonah onto the adult living model. It had been embarrassing as hell when he'd walked in that evening and all she could picture was his hard strong body in a little black Speedo.

Not that the view, front or rear, of him in his jeans wasn't fine, too. Very fine, indeed.

What was wrong with her? She enjoyed sex, but had never been overly sexual. She'd never had the type of response to a man that she had to Jonah. And all he had to do was walk into the room.

Maybe it was the stress. The running and hiding. It heightened her responses. She'd read about that happening after battles and near-death experiences. Yeah. That was it, had to be.

All she had to do was make it through the next two weeks.

✳ ❄ ✳

Jonah had woken up the past two nights from dreams of her legs wrapped around him, his face buried into her long silky hair. Cold showers weren't working. And it didn't help that the more time he spent with her, the more he liked her. She was a witness he was sworn to protect. He really needed to remember that.

Not to mention he had to remember the fact that he was at work and he had cases to wrap up and pass off.

"Rodriguez, you got room for one more follow-up?"

"Shit, Carter, you planning on dumping your whole caseload on me?" she asked, her small, fine-boned face screwing up into grimace.

"Hey, you're the one who told me that you were the best," he reminded her.

"I am the best, but I got a personal life, you know. You want I should give up all my free time?"

"That's my diabolical plan. Look, this guy is settled in a long-term cover, I just want him to have a contact while I'm out of the office. It'll just take one phone call."

"Yeah, yeah, one phone call, my ass. Every time you go out of the office, your whole caseload starts whining. And who gets to pick up the slack? Me. I'm not your mama, Carter, you clean up your own messes."

Jonah grinned and tossed the file at her. She'd do it. "Stewart won't give you any trouble. He's cake. I'm giving the whiners to Davis."

"Good. Davis loves to babysit a bunch of pussies."

He shook his head and didn't respond. Rodriguez could swear better than any sailor he'd ever met. In fact, she'd been a sailor. And she could swear in English, Spanish, and Arabic. She was a damn good marshal who played down her abilities. He'd been keeping his eye on her; she was going places.

He called Davis over and handed him a stack of files. "The two on top are the hottest. I'd like you to read the files and then I'll meet with you in an hour to brief you on them."

"If something comes up, can I reach you on your cell?" Davis asked.

He was a seasoned marshal and Jonah had worked with him on several cases. They were friendly, if not friends. Jonah liked him, but felt Davis had reached a plateau in his career. When Jonah became his supervisor, he was going to give him some challenges and see if he could step up. For now, all he wanted was for the other marshal to competently cover his ongoing cases.

"I'm going to be out of contact, but you can ask Rodriguez for back up. She's hot for you."

"Shit," Rodriguez responded from where she stood making copies.

"See? She's practically speechless." Jonah grinned.

He continued making calls, making notes, and filing away everything still on his desk. He met with Davis to answer questions and give him some tips. Davis once again asked about contacting him, but Jonah assured him that nothing was hot and that he could handle anything that might come up. What was up with him? He was a veteran marshal and shouldn't need such hand-holding.

Despite a few snags, Jonah arrived home from work early on Thursday afternoon. It was the day before Christmas Eve, and it was best to get on the road as early as possible. Traffic was going to be bad, but that would play to their advantage. Getting lost in D.C. traffic was one way to avoid being followed.

Carina was packed and ready to go when he arrived. He suspected this wasn't just due to her efficiency and preparedness. After all, she hadn't been out of his apartment since she'd arrived and let herself in. She was probably more than ready to breathe fresh air again.

"Hi. I just want a quick shower and to change. I'm packed and ready to go. Shouldn't be more than twenty minutes," he told her.

"That's fine. I'm ready. I just have to pop Mr. Darcy into his carrier."

He tossed a bag to her. "I thought maybe you should do the disguise thing, until we get there anyway."

He grinned in anticipation of her reaction and watched as she opened the bag. Inside was a wig, long, straight, and black, that would fall just past her shoulders. There was also a bright red sweater and a white jacket with faux fur around the collar and cuffs.

When she got to the bottom, Carina held up a pair of large-framed mirrored sunglasses. She raised her eyebrows at him. "Brilliant disguise."

"I know it's not your usual style, but I thought that was a plus." His smile grew into a grin at her expression.

She held the jacket out away from her body, as if it was alive and ready to attack. She grimaced at it, took a deep resigned breath, and headed back into the guest bedroom.

Just over fifteen minutes later, Jonah found a transformed woman standing in his living room. The long black hair changed her appearance completely. She'd pushed the sunglasses up on top of her head, pulling the hair back from her face. She was wearing her black jeans and black tennis shoes. She'd topped this off with the red sweater that showed off her figure.

"Nice. No one will see you and think Carina Woods," he said with approval.

"I don't even recognize myself," she said with a nervous smile as she pulled the white jacket on over the sweater.

"Let's get on the road." If he didn't get out of the apartment, he was very much afraid he would give in to the urge to run his hands over that tight sweater.

Once they were outside in the hall, Jonah moved so that he was slightly in front of her. They walked to the elevator and headed down to the parking lot. "I parked the car near the door," he told her as he opened the apartment building's back door.

He heard her take a deep breath and watched as she squared her shoulders and stepped through.

Jonah headed to his four-door sedan and used his remote to open the trunk. He put his suitcase and battered satchel in and reached for Carina's carry-on bag. She looked terrified to be outside, her face pale and her eyes huge.

"Go ahead and put the cat on the back seat and get in," he suggested, knowing she wouldn't want him to mention her fear, or to offer reassurance.

Once the luggage was stowed, he got into the driver's seat and started the engine. It wasn't cold, but when he noticed the shivering from the woman in the passenger seat, he flicked the heater on. He hoped the warm air would steady the nervous chill that shuddered her body.

He knew her taste in music, and he tuned in a station that played a mix of pop and soft rock. Not exactly his preference, but he didn't pay much attention to music while driving, anyway. Especially when he had to drive and make sure they weren't followed.

Once on the interstate heading south, he felt sure no one had followed them. Which was good, since already the traffic was bumper-to-bumper. Someone following them would just have to get out of their car and jog up to them.

"This should clear up more as soon as we're out of the general area," he said aloud, more for her benefit than his.

"Uhm," was all she responded.

"We'll take 95 South down to Quantico where we'll swap cars. Then we'll head down to Richmond and stop at a mall to let you pick up a few things. We'll take Interstate 64 over to the beach cities. I think we'll stop somewhere in Chesapeake to do our grocery shopping. I'd like to stay anonymous in crowds, as much as possible. At the mall, you can change your look again and I'll change my clothes as well."

Slowly, with his talking, the familiar music, and the warmth from the heater, Carina began to relax slightly. She reached forward to flick the heater off when it began to get too warm. "I'm sorry, I don't know why I freaked."

"I didn't see you freak, far from it."

She huffed out a breath, blowing up the bangs of the wig. "Well, I definitely sympathize with people who suffer from agoraphobia. Leaving your apartment was hard enough; let alone leaving the building. I'm sorry I was so tense."

"Don't apologize for reacting to everything you've been through. If you need something, speak up. Let me know how you're feeling, if you need some time, whatever."

"Thanks. You're a really nice guy, you know?" She slid a glance over at his handsome profile.

"I know a lot of people who would disagree."

"I doubt it." Then she corrected, "Maybe the bad guys. I'm thinking that people on the other side of the law aren't real fond of you, but I bet most law-abiding citizens like you."

"I've worked very hard to cultivate my rep as a hardass. Please don't undermine it."

She smiled, which surprised her. "See, you're being nice again. You said please."

He reached over and pinched her arm. "I'm not nice."

Her smile grew. "Whatever you say."

The drive to Quantico took them over an hour, the traffic heavy, but moving.

"The car is parked at a garage where it's kept tuned and ready to go," Jonah said. "I'm going to drop you at a market that's nearby. I don't want the guys who work at the garage to see you."

"You're going to leave me alone?" She felt panic blooming and ruthlessly smothered it.

"Yes, for about ten minutes. It's probably an unnecessary precaution, but if anyone does follow me down, I don't want the guys at the garage to tell them that I had a woman with me."

"Okay, I'll wait for you at the market. Should I pick anything up in there?"

"Can you pick up some pistachios? The shelled kind, since I'm driving. And a soda, dealer's choice."

She suspected he didn't really want a snack, but was giving her something constructive to do while she waited. She appreciated his kindness and consideration. Still, she was embarrassed that she was now going to have to ask for something outright. "I might need some cash."

"Yeah, sorry. I stopped and got us some more cash today. I'll give it to you before I drop you off." He guided the car to the curb in front of a corner minimart.

She stared as he pulled out his wallet and withdrew what had to be several hundred dollars in tens and twenties.

"This will buy more than some nuts and a soda."

"You need to pick up some clothes when we get to the mall. I might as well give you the money now."

"Okay, thanks. I'll pay you back someday," she said humbly. He was leaving her alone with enough money to disappear again if she was so inclined. She knew that he was telling her that he trusted her. She appreciated it.

"When the case is over, I'll turn in a reimbursement form. Keep your receipts."

She returned his grin and nodded.

"Mac's car is a silver Maserati Gran Turismo. It's hard to miss."

"I'll say," Carina agreed. She slid from Jonah's car and hurried into the minimart. She perched her sunglasses carefully on top of the wig, then started scanning the aisles.

She settled on a package of peanut butter crackers and bottled water for her snack. She found what Jonah asked for and went to the checkout. As she stood at the counter, gathering her purchases, she saw the car pull up outside and nearly dropped the bottle of water she was about to tuck under her arm.

"Thank you, Merry Christmas," she said hastily to the clerk and ran outside.

It was absolutely beautiful. She wasted no time sliding into the passenger seat. "Wow, this really is some car," she said, running the palm of her hand over the butter-soft red leather seats. Italian leather. The feel of it was luxurious and she felt a sensual purr start up in her throat, as if the leather stroked her instead of the other way around.

"Yeah, Mac started his mid-life crisis early," said Jonah. "Buckle up."

"Did he rob a bank while he was at it?"

Jonah chuckled, a deep rich sound that made Carina's skin tingle. Being in a sexy car just magnified a budding sexual desire she wasn't sure she could quell.

"My buddy Mac owns two things, his beach house and this car. He's been deployed—racking in hazardous duty pay—or living in a bare bones bachelor pad for so many years now that he is able to put nearly all of his money in the bank. He rents the beach house out, so it's actually another income source for him. If he ever gets serious about marrying and starting a family, he'll have a lot of adjusting to do. For now, he lives the ultimate bachelor life."

"What about you? You're a bachelor. Ever been married?"

"No. The closest I came to it was when I lived with Mac's sister, Shannon, after I left the Marine Corps."

"What kept you from marrying her?" she asked, trying not to visualize Jonah living with another woman.

"It just wasn't right. I think I knew it almost before we moved in together. My mother would have been a great deal happier if I'd married Shannon first, both of our mothers, for that matter. I needed a test run, which, looking back, may have been the first clue. My parents are the kind of people who have a marriage that just works. Don't get me wrong, they work at it, but they're so in love with each other that they're two parts of a whole."

"That's beautiful," she said. "My parents had that too. I didn't know it at the time, or I didn't realize it at the time. But, looking back, I can see that they were deeply in love with each other. When we went to Italy, even though my sister and I were there, it was like a second honeymoon for them. Even though they were killed, I take comfort knowing that they were truly happy on that trip."

She had a memory flash. She and her sister were standing at the top of the Leaning Tower of Pisa, looking down over the edge. Her parents were on the grassy lawn below, sharing a kiss. At the time, she had resented the fact that they weren't sitting there waiting for their daughters to appear at the top of the landmark after the long climb. Now, her heart warmed at the knowledge that they had shared a dream come true—a romantic holiday in Italy.

"I think it's worth waiting for the right person. I want what my parents have. I loved Shannon, but we weren't... meant to be, I guess. Our families weren't happy about the split, but my mom came to me once and said that she was glad that we realized we weren't right for each other before we made a lifetime commitment."

"It must be hard at family gatherings."

When he cursed, she worried that the question had upset him and then realized he was upset at the SUV driver that had cut in front of them.

"It was, but one or the other of us usually finds an excuse not to be there. Last I heard, she's serious about some advertising guy she met up in New York. I wish her the best."

"Unlike what I wish for my last significant other."

"How in the world did you hook up with Kragen? If you don't mind my asking."

Carina shook her head.

They were back on the interstate heading toward Richmond, Virginia, the car purring like a sleek panther.

"He sparkled," she said finally. "I don't know how else to put it. I met him at a dinner I catered. He came back to the kitchen to ask for my number. I thought he wanted to book a dinner, but he wanted to ask me out to dinner. He's a really good-looking man with a very smooth manner."

"He wouldn't be as successful as he is if he wasn't," Jonah commented.

There was no censure in his voice. She was relieved that he wasn't judging her for her mistake with Sam.

"As far as I knew, he was a respected businessman. For whatever reason, he decided that he wanted me. The relationship happened fast, too fast in retrospect. He pressured me to move in with him and I did, but I kept my own place. I never felt, I don't know, maybe I should borrow your phrase and just say that it never felt right."

"Why didn't you end it?"

Carina released a big sigh as she stared at the window at the passing scenery. It wasn't terribly interesting. The fall leaves were gone and the trees were bare.

"You may not believe me, but I was in the process of trying to extricate myself from our relationship. I'd found an excuse to stay at my townhouse several nights leading up to the night I overheard that phone conversation. In fact, I wonder if Sam forgot that I was around when he made that call. We'd been drifting apart, but he didn't seem to want to let go. We didn't have any major arguments, but he's the type of man who gets what he wants through persistence. I think if he'd tired of me, it would have ended quickly, but because I was the first one to start to pull back, he insisted on holding on."

"His mistake," Jonah remarked.

"Yeah, if he'd only accepted that it was over, I wouldn't have been there to hear his phone conversation. I had stopped by to pick up Mr. Darcy. I'm not sure that Sam knew I was on the grounds."

"And his security people?"

"Well, obviously, they knew I was there, but I was still technically living there, as far as they knew. Sam saw me soon after he finished the call, but I managed to walk in casually, carrying the cat, and he didn't think it unusual that I was there.

"He seemed preoccupied. He said that he had some business to finish up, and we'd have a late dinner. I stayed the night and then went into his office the next morning after he left. His chief of security, Sergei Dvorkin, found me in there. I had Mr. Darcy with me and used him as cover, claiming that he'd wandered into the office and I'd come to retrieve him." She scratched an itch just below the front hairline of her wig.

"It was close. I had just tucked the thumb drive in my pocket and shut down the computer when Sergei walked in. I took Mr. Darcy and headed out with the evidence I handed over to the federal prosecutor."

He didn't say anything for a while. She figured he was wondering if she'd had sex with Kragen that night. She hoped he didn't ask. She held her breath when he finally glanced over and responded.

"That took guts, going back in for the evidence."

She exhaled in relief. "Without it, I knew that it would just be my word. I couldn't imagine anyone believing me, let alone acting on the information. As far as I knew, Sam was a respected businessman. Who would believe he was ordering the murder of a United States Senator? It was like something out of a Tom Clancy novel."

"You're an admirable woman," Jonah said.

She shook her head, even while her stomach clenched at his compliment. "No, I'm just a woman who was faced with a choice. I decided that I had to make the right choice if I was going to live with myself. Of course, at the time, I didn't know that there would be attempts on my life."

"You had to know that it was a definite risk."

She shrugged. "The reality is rather different from some obscure possibility."

They fell quiet until Jonah exited the interstate and headed to a mall. He parked near Macy's and they split up once they entered.

After her months of frugality and disguises, Carina enjoyed buying clothes in her size and in colors she liked. She bought two pairs of pants and three sweaters, and then headed to the lingerie department. Underwear, socks, a couple of bras, nightwear, and a thick robe joined her other purchases. She even managed to find a one-piece bathing suit hidden on a clearance rack in the back of the department. Jonah had told her to pick something up for the Jacuzzi at the beach house.

She stopped at the makeup counter and added moisturizer, some eye-shadow, and a new shade of lipstick. She hit the shoe department next for a second pair of shoes, in case her one pair got wet.

After picking out a hat and scarf set, she headed to the luggage department. Her purchases wouldn't fit into the carry-on bag she had. She bought a duffle-style suitcase with wheels and then looked over at the satchels near the check out counter.

She remembered the battered satchel Jonah carried for his job. The stitching had started to break. A new satchel would make a good Christmas gift. Refusing to question why she was buying a gift for a man who was only doing his job, she added it to her purchases and hid it in the suitcase. She'd shopped wisely, hitting the sales and clearance racks when she could, but she had pretty much wiped out the cash Jonah had given her.

Carina headed out of Macy's and towards the mall restroom. Inside, she was relieved to finally remove her disguise and change into a pair of navy blue jeans and a looseknit, oversize, cowl-neck sweater in deep maroon.

She stuffed everything else into her new suitcase and headed out to the mirrors. She pulled her brush out of her bag and took her hair down from the braids that had fitted smooth under the wig. She brushed her hair out to wave around her face and down her back.

Studying her reflection, she decided that her hair really could use a trim. Other than that, it was great to see herself looking like herself again. She could only hope Jonah was right, and they were safe.

As she headed back to the main thoroughfare of the mall, her suitcase in tow, she spotted a pay phone. Giving in to impulse and a deep-seated need, she put in coins and dialed a well-known phone number.

"Sally? Hi, it's me. Is she there?" She waited until the phone was passed. "Hi, Allyson, Merry Christmas. How are you?"

A few minutes later, she grabbed her suitcase and rushed down the hall, trying to swallow the lump in her throat. It was so good to hear Allyson sounding full of hope about her new family.

It was good to provide comfort to the girl as well. Carina understood well that hope often came with guilt and confusion. She could remember having similar worries herself, wondering if it was okay to be happy again.

She headed to the food court to meet Jonah. Spotting him in a crowd of last-minute Christmas shoppers was going to be a challenge.

It was his height and build that gave him away. He'd covered his hair with a black ball cap and was wearing a pair of black-framed glasses. He'd also changed into a pair of black jeans worn with an off-white cable knit sweater.

"Looking good, Carter," she said as she reached him. "You look like you should be teaching a history class at a university. Got any office hours?" She fluttered her eyelashes in an exaggerated flirtation to ensure he knew that she wasn't making a serious play for him. Unfortunately.

When he perused her up and down, Carina wondered if he was checking the suitability of her new look or noticing that she'd put on clothes that fit her better than anything she'd worn since arriving at his apartment.

"You'll have to stay after class," he told her with a teasing grin. "I think I'll splurge and take you out to dinner at a real restaurant instead of here in the food court."

"Big spender, huh?"

"Nothing but the best. Come on, let's blow this popsicle stand. There's a TGI Friday's across the parking lot."

"Nothing but the best, huh?"

"Okay, so it's not a five-star restaurant, but it's better than what's offered here."

"I can't argue with that," she said.

They went to the car where they stowed Carina's suitcase with all of her other purchases inside. She pulled her pea coat from her carry-on and slid into its familiar hug. Then she carefully set out her new scarf, knit hat, and a pair of gloves to wear later when they reached the beach, where it would be colder.

After making certain that Mr. Darcy was comfortable, she walked with Jonah to the restaurant. So what if it was a chain restaurant, it was better than the food court, and surprisingly deserted. Probably because everyone was shopping, she thought.

She enjoyed the leisurely meal. Even Jonah seemed relaxed, letting down his guard enough for casual conversation. It almost felt like a date. It should have been an awkward transition, but it felt... right.

All too soon they were back on the road again, the powerful Maserati growling softly as it sped toward Nags Head. It wasn't far to the I-64 interchange, where they picked up their new course towards Norfolk and Virginia Beach.

In the town of Chesapeake, they stopped at a grocery store. Carina made Jonah push the cart around as she filled it with carefully selected produce, choice cuts of meat, and the spices and herbs she would need to prepare the meals she was itching to create. Including a Christmas dinner for two.

"Do you want ham, turkey, or standing rib roast?" she asked.

"Can't we have all three?" he asked with a smile.

"Not on our budget. Choose, Carter, or you'll get nothing but Brussels sprouts."

"In that case, let's have ham."

She enjoyed trading quips and carefree banter as they cruised the aisles of the nearly empty store. Carina had been so intent on selecting ingredients for the meals she planned that at first, she didn't notice that the pile in the cart contained some items she hadn't picked out.

"You won't keep that girlish figure with these, Carter," she said, picking up a bag of bite-sized candy bars from atop the ham.

"Don't you worry about my figure." He reached for a package of cookies and tossed that into the cart, too.

She rolled her eyes as two more packages followed the first. She didn't mind. But after he tasted *her* cookies and muffins, he'd forget all about those plastic and cardboard ones.

They were the last people to check out, just before the store closed at ten.

They loaded up the groceries and began the last leg of the journey, nearly another two hours. Carina offered to drive, but obviously Jonah was enjoying driving Mac's playboy car and wasn't willing to relinquish the wheel.

She was nodding off when she felt the car slow to make the turn into the driveway of the beach house. That was enough to shake her alert, and she peered into the darkness, anxious for a glimpse of the house.

Jonah hit a remote control that lifted the garage door and he pulled the car into the garage, letting the door close behind him. The overhead light came on automatically. It was a roomy two-car garage. A Waverunner occupied the other parking space.

Stretching and yawning, Carina stumbled on stiff legs from the car. Then she reached back to pick up the cat carrier. Fortunately, Mr. Darcy was a good traveler.

She headed back to the trunk to help carry in their luggage. They were going to have to make multiple trips between their luggage, their purchases, and the cat supplies.

"Just take the cat and your carry-on bag. The bedrooms are on the third floor, kitchen and common rooms are on the second floor. The only thing down here is the garage and storage. I'll get the cat's things first and we'll set up his litter box in one of the second floor bathrooms. His food and water dish can stay in the kitchen. If you'll stay up there, I'll bring things up and you can put the groceries away while I make trips up and down the stairs."

"Don't wait for me to argue with you," Carina warned. She was so tired that she wasn't certain she'd make it up the stairs once.

Jonah dropped the cat's things off and headed back down while Carina explored. The place was huge. The second floor had an open floor plan with comfortable couches and chairs arranged into conversation groupings. There was a large flat-screen TV over a brick fireplace. The kitchen had counter-space to spare, and Carina ran her hand lovingly over the double oven.

She let Mr. Darcy out of his carrier and walked down a short hall. The hall opened onto a game room that contained a pool table, a pinball machine, a jukebox, and an arcade game. There was a bathroom off of the game room.

Across the hall was an indoor gym with an elaborate resistance machine, a treadmill, and a weight bench. There was another bathroom off of that. At the end of the hall, a door led out onto a deck with a privacy screen where the Jacuzzi sat. Though she was tempted, she left the door closed. As much as she wanted to feel the ocean breeze, she knew it would be too cold.

After setting up Mr. Darcy's litter box in the first bathroom, Carina showed him where it was and then headed back to the kitchen. Jonah had already set grocery bags on the counters and she busied herself emptying them and organizing the refrigerator, freezer, and cupboards.

She had hot chocolate ready by the time Jonah was done bringing everything in from the car.

"Do you want whipped cream or marshmallows?" she asked.

"Marshmallows, lots of them," he answered.

She smiled at him and poured the chocolate into two oversized mugs. She pulled out the bag of marshmallows they'd bought and added some to both mugs. She handed his mug to him and they wandered over to the couch in front of the fireplace.

Jonah picked up a basket of remote controls and, after fishing around, found the one that lit the gas log fire.

"All the modern conveniences," Carina noted.

"Yeah, like I said, Mac rents this place out. Storing wood was a hassle. The renters burned it all up, so he installed this. He shuts off the gas in the summer and it saves a lot on expenses. He has a realty company that looks after the place and I try to get down at least three or four times a year to check on things."

"Does Mac ever get to enjoy the place?" she asked.

"When he's not deployed, he spends several weeks a year and nearly every weekend here."

"When is he expected back?" she asked.

"His current tour of duty just ended. I expect him back any day now, but he hasn't given me a date. He may have extended if he was in the middle of something. The guy is nothing if not dedicated."

"He sounds like a good friend to have," Carina commented, hearing the affection in Jonah's voice.

"He got me through that first tour of duty we served together. He's always had my back and I'll always have his. He's just one of those lifetime friends, you know?"

"Not really," she confessed. "I met my best friend, Phoebe, after I was an adult. I learned at a young age to hold myself separate from others. When my parents and sister were killed in Italy, I didn't have any close family and I was put into the system. I was considered difficult. I still had medical issues from the accident, you know, and even more emotional baggage. I was shuffled around until I wound up in my third home. It was a good place and I thought I'd be there until I graduated from high school, but my foster mother had a mild stroke and wasn't able to foster after that."

"I'm sorry."

She inclined her head at the true sympathy in his voice. "So, I went back to playing musical homes again. Each time I started to get comfortable, I had to move again. It wasn't until I turned eighteen that I was able to find any stability. My parents had owned a restaurant in Baltimore. After their deaths, the restaurant was sold. The money was placed in a trust fund that I was able to access to pay for college when I turned eighteen."

She paused as she wondered if Jonah already knew all of this. Shrugging, she continued. "After I graduated, I went to culinary school and then went back to school and got my MBA. I wanted to run all aspects of my business. I met Phoebe in culinary school. She and I hit it off and decided that we wanted to go into business together. When I turned twenty-five, I received the remainder of my inheritance and that's when we started our business. My whole life has been consumed with that ever since. Phoebe is the closest friend I've ever had. She wanted to be my friend for some reason and just wouldn't take no for an answer. After all she's done for me—I really dumped on her when I suddenly disappeared like that."

"She knows why you disappeared, she's very aware of the case. I spoke to her last month."

"You did?" She turned to face him. "You talked to Phoebe?"

"Yes. I wanted to know if you had contacted her. She said that she hadn't heard from you and I had to believe her. She said that if I saw you before she did, to tell you that things are going very well and that she can't wait for you to come back. She loves you."

"I guess she does. I don't know what I would have done without her these last few years. She's been my only family."

"You'll have a family one day. You'll make a family of your own," he said in a quiet voice.

She gave him a wistful smile. "I hope so. That would be the ultimate dream come true. I had great parents and they gave me a wonderful base. I didn't handle it well when it was pulled out from under me so suddenly, but I hope that I can create what I had when they were alive for my own children someday."

They stared at each other for a while. Carina wondered if Jonah was going to make a move, but he just reached out to take her empty mug. She sighed inwardly.

He stood up. "We're both tired. I had the realty company send in a housekeeper today and make up a couple of beds and put out fresh towels. I took the master bedroom and put you in the large guestroom I use when Mac and I are both here. Both rooms have their own adjoining bathrooms, so they're prime real estate when there's a crowd."

Carina scooped up her cat and headed up the flight of stairs following him. The room he showed her into was painted a bright blue with a nautical theme.

"Sleep as late as you like," he told her. "There's no schedule here. I'll see you when you get up."

"Thanks, sleep well," she said. She closed the door, stripped, and pulled on the silky pajamas she'd bought. She was asleep as soon as she'd slipped into the crisp sheets.

Chapter 5

The wind was howling when Mr. Darcy woke Carina up the next morning. She lay in bed, luxuriating under the warm covers for a few extra minutes before getting up. She changed into a pair of comfortable pants and a sweater and headed down to the second floor to see what Jonah was up to. She found that Jonah had made coffee, but there was no sign of him.

Carina gathered the ingredients and made a batch of blueberry muffins. After putting them into the preheated oven, she squeezed oranges for fresh orange juice. She took a cup of coffee and headed down towards the gym where she'd been hearing the sound of weights clicking together.

Carina entered to find Jonah doing leg presses. He'd worked up a good healthy sweat and was only wearing a pair of shorts. She stood, leaning against the doorframe and watched his leg muscles ripple with each rep.

No wonder he could burn off those candy bars and cookies, she thought, almost salivating at the sight.

He finished his set and reached for a towel, the play of muscles under his sweat-streaked skin almost more than Carina could bear. She must have made a sound, because he turned.

"Good morning," he greeted. "What smells so incredibly good?"

She cleared her throat, hoping that he would think that was the kind of sound she'd made before. "Muffins. They'll be ready in about fifteen more minutes."

"I'll go take a quick shower and be down in fourteen," he told her with a grin.

She returned to the kitchen to clean up the clutter from her baking. Soon Jonah appeared, almost to the minute— she had checked the time—his hair damp, dressed in worn jeans and a black pullover. He headed straight for the tray of muffins on the counter, hand outstretched.

She turned around and slapped his hand away. "Let me get them out of the tray first," she admonished him.

He snatched up the first one before it hit the cooling rack, ripped off a steaming chunk, and stuffed it into his mouth. "Oh, wow! Oh my God. These are incredible!" He pulled off another piece and continued to eat.

Carina laughed. "If you put a bit of butter on them, they're even better."

"No, I have to eat them before they start to cool."

"They're good cold too," she promised. She took a muffin for herself, putting it on a plate, cutting it in half. Just a little bit of butter. By the time she looked back up, three more muffins were gone from the cooling rack.

He had the grace to look guilty, but never paused in his eating.

She figured it was the best compliment a cook could have: silence broken only by the sounds of chewing and swallowing. She smiled and poured him a glass of orange juice.

"You really are an amazing cook," he told her between a sip of orange juice and his next bite of muffin.

"Thanks. I was starting to burn out before all of this happened. I had put so much of myself into building up the business that I wasn't enjoying it any more. I guess having everything taken away is the best way to help you realize how much you love something."

"Do you plan to go back to it?" he asked. "It can't be easy for you—a small business owner in a Witness Protection Program. Even with Phoebe to run things while you're gone."

"I will. I hope. The first thing I'll do is to give Phoebe a much-deserved vacation and take over. We're lucky that we didn't go in for catering large affairs. If we had, I don't know that she would have been able to keep things going. It's just too much for one person to manage, all the additional wait staff and transporting large food trays.

"We really set ourselves up by sticking to our niche of smaller private dinners where we can really focus on the meal. I wanted to cook so that I could create and I wanted to go into catering instead of opening a restaurant, because I thought I'd have less management to do."

She grinned and shook her head. "Maybe I'll worry about getting back to it after they lock the cage doors on Samuel Kragen. Looking back, I realize that I had been backing out quite a bit while I was with Sam. He was very demanding of my time. It was one of my biggest issues with the relationship."

Jonah didn't say anything. He knew that she was intelligent enough to know that Kragen may not be convicted and that she may never be able to return to her life. If Kragen continued to be a threat, she might need to be relocated with a new identity indefinitely. It was something he didn't want to think about.

Kragen had been indicted for multiple crimes based on the files Carina had copied and turned over to the feds. Due to the lack of evidence regarding his attempt to contract a hit against a U.S. Senator, other than Carina's testimony, he was not facing "conspiracy to murder" charges. Even if he went to prison, that might not be enough to take away his power base. There was also the connection to the Russian mafia to consider.

There was always the possibility that Kragen would make a deal with the federal prosecutor, providing evidence against other bigger fish for a reduced sentence.

There were just too many possibilities, he thought. Ones neither he nor Carina had any control over. He just needed to concentrate on his job: making sure that Carina got to the trial, alive.

To change the subject, he decided to suggest a walk. "The wind is really blowing out there, but if we bundle up, we can go for a walk along the beach."

"I'd love to get out and walk on the beach."

Wrapped up in jackets, scarves, hats, and gloves, they headed out into the gale force winds. Jonah was glad for the sunglasses—they also helped deflect blowing sand.

The tide was out. The hard-packed sand was strewn with spume and jetsam from the raging surf. He reached for her hand, mumbling some excuse about not letting her get blown away.

For nearly a mile they walked, leaning into the strong wind. The wind, the stormy sea, the cries of gulls and the smell of the sharp, salty air was invigorating. She liked it too, he could tell.

The walk back was faster with the wind at their backs, pushing them along. Just as they passed the neighboring beach house, a man wearing fishing gear stepped out from behind the back fence. Jonah braced for action, but stopped to speak to the man.

"Morning," he called.

"Nice day!" the man called back with a grin. "My wife kicked me out of the house. She said that I was driving her crazy and I should come on out regardless of the weather to cast my fly into that surf," he declared.

"Good luck to you," Jonah said with a wave and guided Carina around to the side entrance of the house.

Once the door shut behind them, the quiet, after the roar of the wind, was nearly shocking.

"That was amazing!" Carina said.

They stripped off their sandy outerwear and left it in the small downstairs mudroom before heading up to the second floor.

After Carina settled down to read a book, Jonah headed upstairs to the deck outside the master bedroom. The deck was on the front of the house, overlooking the ocean. He watched his neighbor cast into the surf. Despite being slightly insane, fishing in the strong wind, Jonah didn't see anything suspicious about the man.

He had told Carina that he felt safe at the beach house. Safe didn't mean he was throwing caution to the wind, either. His guard was up and he was going to check out anything that seemed unusual.

* ❋ ✳

They passed the day companionably. He insisted on helping her prepare dinner, so she dubbed him her sous-chef and set him to chopping and stirring while she worked her magic.

He could get used to this. Cooking, eating, cleaning up; they made a good team.

Then he reminded himself, for probably the tenth time, that he was just there to protect her. Now was not a time to think about a relationship.

"How about I see if I can hunt down some Christmas decorations?" he asked as he hung a dishtowel neatly on a drying bar.

"Sure."

She didn't sound too certain, but the flash of wistful longing in her eyes was enough for him. He decided to start in the garage and wasn't disappointed.

In triumph, he transported his trophies to the living room, where he displayed them for her approval. An artificial Christmas tree, some lights and ornaments, a few swags of artificial holly. Not much, but enough to make her smile and get into the spirit. As he started unraveling a string of lights, she went to the sound system and tuned in a station playing holiday music.

She left him to finish hanging ornaments, disappearing into the kitchen. More heavenly smells wafted out. Jonah resisted the temptation to go in there this time, though. Feeling virtuous, he gave a few adjustments to the lights, hung the last satin ball, and bundled the containers back out to the garage.

The timing was impeccable. He returned in time to meet her carrying a tray of hot chocolate and fresh-baked cookies. And in the end to a perfect evening, they sat side by side on the couch to admire their handiwork and listen to the music.

The music was low and romantic, some tinkling piano piece that reminded her of happier times. She stared into the fireplace, watching the flames, the flickering and warmth lulling her into a doze. The next thing she knew, she was waking up with her head cradled against Jonah's chest.

She looked up and smiled into his eyes. "Sorry, I guess the walk on the beach did me in."

"No problem," he said in a hoarse whisper.

"What's wrong?" Her pulse quickened as she saw the look of hunger in his eyes.

"What's wrong is that you're a woman under my protection and I want you," he answered.

She shifted so that she was able to reach his chin with her lips. "The feeling is mutual," she said, feathering kisses along his jaw.

"This isn't right," he moaned, but clamped his mouth on hers, kissing her deeply.

Carina thrilled to the feel of him, the heat of his mouth, and the firmness of his body. She pulled back breathless.

230

"We'll blame it on the mistletoe," she decided and sank back into his kiss.

Jonah pulled his mouth from hers and trailed kisses over her face, her neck, and down to her sensitive ear. "We don't have any mistletoe," he told her with a sensual nip of her earlobe.

"I won't tell if you won't," she promised, pulling his face to hers and recapturing his mouth.

She let her hands and mouth roam as freely as his. She wasn't sure if it was several minutes or several hours before he pulled away, holding her back. She moaned in protest and stared at him, breathing hard.

She could actually see him clenching his jaw several times before he turned intense eyes her way.

"What's wrong?"

"I want you, Carina Woods, but I don't want to take advantage of this situation. I don't know if I could live with myself if I did. I'm going to take a quick walk outside, you go on up."

"Jonah…" she protested, reaching up to touch him.

"Please, just go on up," he begged.

Carina nodded and pulled away from him. After he went out, she stood and gathered up the mugs. After leaving them in the kitchen sink and making sure any food was covered or put away, she headed up to her room.

She couldn't help smiling. Even with all the intrigue and worry, this was turning out to be the best Christmas of her adult life. She was determined that Marshal Carter would get over his scruples and that they would enjoy the holiday week very, *very* much.

✳ ✳ ✳

Christmas morning, Carina woke up and pulled on a pair of sweatpants and a T-shirt. She decided to start her day in the gym. Jonah was running on the treadmill when she entered, so she started with some stretches and went on to some free weights.

When he moved on to weights, she hopped on the treadmill and did a five-mile run. Her muscles felt warmed and lax when she finished. She felt a bit out of shape, as she hadn't been able to keep up with her workout regime since being on the run.

She smirked at the irony. Shouldn't being "on the run" have kept her fit?

After a cool down, she pulled out an exercise mat and sat with her legs crossed doing some breathing exercises and meditating to center herself. This, she thought, was a crucial part of her daily life that she had been missing for months now.

When she stood, Jonah spoke up.

"After a workout like that, a Christmas morning soak in the Jacuzzi should be just the thing."

She considered. "Yeah, I could go along with that."

"Go get changed and I'll turn it on," he offered.

He was sitting in the heated bubbling water when she stepped out onto the sheltered deck.

"Man, it is *cold* out here!" she said. Her teeth began to chatter.

"Get in quick," he suggested.

Carina dropped the towel she'd wrapped around herself and climbed into the hot tub.

"Oh yeah," she said almost as a moan as she sunk into the water up to her neck.

Jonah's mouth went dry when she dropped her towel. The one-piece bathing suit skimmed her body and left nothing to the imagination. That didn't prevent his imagination from working overtime. It had gone from what she looked like to what she'd feel like under him. He didn't know how he was going to survive more than another week alone with Carina without touching her. More than touching her. His need for her grew stronger with each passing day. How was he supposed to survive eleven more?

He was in trouble and he knew it.

Last night, he'd very nearly succumbed. How much more was a guy supposed to take? And what kind of idiot in his position suggested a soak in a Jacuzzi? He must be masochistic, he decided as he watched her and struggled for self-control.

She had her eyes closed in pleasure as the jet-propelled water pummeled her. She remained low in the water and only shifted once to reposition herself in front of the jets.

He couldn't stop staring. He averted his gaze quickly when she opened her eyes and tried to erase any signs of desire from his face.

When she smiled, smug and cat-like, he figured he hadn't managed to hide it all. He was relieved when she didn't make a move; he wasn't certain he'd be able to resist if she had. Hell, he was certain he wouldn't have resisted if she had made any sort of move on him.

He managed to survive the hot-tub. She got out the same time he did, so he ran up to his room and took a shower. A cold shower. He dressed quickly and headed downstairs. He was going to cook her breakfast; he had a good hand with omelets.

The coffee was finished and his cooking nearly so by the time she appeared in the kitchen. She was wearing the bright red sweater he had given her the other day. He appreciated it, both because it was festive...and form-fitting.

He enjoyed the view even more when she walked to the tree and bent down to place a wrapped gift under it. He saw her do a double take at the package he had already left there for her.

They enjoyed the breakfast in a companionable silence. He wondered what her thoughts were. His thoughts focused on her.

After putting the plates in the dishwasher, he straightened. "Do you want to open gifts now?" He had to smile at the gleeful, childlike enthusiasm on her face as she nodded and rushed to the tree.

She smiled and handed him his gift. "I don't know that it counts considering the fact that I used your money to pay for it," she confessed.

"It counts," he said with a smile. "Open yours first," he suggested.

Carina unwrapped the gift and looked up at him in surprise at the complete line of her favorite brand of skin care products. "How did you know?" she questioned.

"That you use that brand?" he asked. At her nod, he answered. "I saw you take out a tube of something that was this brand back when I was first protecting you."

"And you remembered?" she asked.

"Let's just say that you made an impression on me," he stated. He didn't add that there was nothing about her that he'd forgotten.

She smiled. "I guess when you take a bullet for someone, it heightens your memories of that time."

He didn't correct her that getting shot had nothing to do with why she was so unforgettable.

After a few moments of staring at her, he glanced back down at his present. He opened the large flat box and found a leather satchel inside.

It was his turn to be surprised and he glanced over at her, raising one eyebrow in question.

"I noticed that the one you use is starting to fall apart. I figured that you should start your new supervisor role with a brand new satchel to carry files home in," Carina explained.

"Thank you, I really did need a new one." He smiled as he thought of the worn leather and busted out seams of his current satchel. "I thought I was going to have to break down and shop for one myself."

They took a long walk on the beach to work up an appetite for the traditional Christmas dinner they made together. They lit candles and turned out all but the Christmas tree lights, as the evening drew to a close and they sat to share their meal.

"You've outdone yourself," Jonah said as he tasted the apple pie she'd made. The crust flaked off and melted as he placed it into his mouth.

"You're the one who peeled all of those apples," she reminded him with a smile.

They finished their meal and cleared away the dishes before he took her hand and led her over to the couch to sit in front of the fire. He pulled her back against him and they sat snuggled together sharing stories of Christmases when they were children.

Carina told him of the first Christmas she'd had as a big sister and how she had wanted the baby to play with all of the toys, but her eight-month old sister had been more fascinated by the boxes the toys came in. But that was the year her Santa gift had been her very own CD alarm clock and she had felt very grown up.

He told about how he'd tried to convince his parents that he was ready for a gun at age twelve. "I was determined that I was going to grow up and be a cop. I wanted them to get me a gun so that I could be the best shot when I got to the academy. I was really bummed when I opened my present and it was a slingshot. My dad said that I could practice my aim with that.

"Then he handed me another package and it was a Nintendo game called Cops and Robbers. They'd gotten us a Nintendo as a family gift and each of us boys got our own game. I got over the disappointment about the gun."

After they were talked out, they sat listening to the music and watching the fire. "How determined are you that we not sleep together?" Carina asked suddenly.

"Oh, I have every intention of sleeping with you, of making love to you," he told her. "I just want to be sure that what you feel for me isn't mixed up with my role as your bodyguard. I don't want to have an affair with you. I want a relationship, a long one."

"But kissing is okay until then?" she asked, sliding those eyes towards him. She was irresistible.

"It's more than okay, it's required," he told her, as his mouth found hers.

He pulled her off the couch and led her up the stairs. He kissed her one last time at the door of her bedroom and gave her a gentle shove inside.

He turned away and headed to his own room. Maybe he was going to bed physically frustrated, but he'd never felt so emotionally fulfilled. Whatever happened next, he was fairly certain that he was well on his way to being in love with Ms. Carina Woods.

Chapter 6

Energized from her workout, freshly showered, and feeling happier than she had in weeks, Carina flew down the stairs towards the enticing aroma of sausage and coffee. She found Jonah at the kitchen stove, his hair still damp, loading a plate with scrambled eggs and sausage links.

"Sit," he ordered, nodding at a chair already pulled out and waiting for her.

"Mmm, looks good. Thank you." She sat and wasted no time digging in.

The morning workout had not only relaxed her, it had increased her appetite. For everything, she thought as she snuck a look at Jonah's denim-covered butt when he turned to get her coffee.

"Have you ever gone to the Wright Brother's Museum?" he asked.

Carina looked up. "No," she answered. She was surprised that he would suggest they leave the house. She thought that they were in hiding. "You want to go there?"

"Yeah, I think we can risk it. You can wear your black wig to alter your appearance, but there shouldn't be any problem going to a tourist spot."

The idea appealed and she started to brighten at the prospect of getting out into a public setting. "Are you sure they'll be open?" she asked.

"Yeah, they're open year round. They were closed yesterday for Christmas of course, but they're open for business today. There's a museum and then the walk up to Big Kill Devil Hill, where Orville and Wilbur experimented with their glider. The wind isn't as strong today, but it's still cold out there. December on the Outer Banks is cold." He looked at the sweater and jeans she was wearing. "You might want to put a thicker sweater on and wear the white jacket I got you the other day."

She grimaced at the thought of wearing the faux fur-lined jacket. "Okay, I guess if it means going out, I can manage to put the thing back on."

After finishing breakfast and donning her disguise, she followed him down to the garage. "Hey, do you think I can drive?" she asked.

He stared at her, keys in hand for a few moments. She figured he was weighing his friendship with Mac and wondering if it could withstand damage to the car.

"I won't wreck it, I promise. I'm an excellent driver," she deadpanned in a passable imitation of Dustin Hoffman in *Rain Man.*

He laughed and tossed her the keys.

He gave her instructions and they headed over to Kill Devil Hill with Carina at the wheel. She loved the feel of the powerful engine. The car responded to her slightest command, seeming to anticipate her. She almost hated pulling into the parking lot and turning the engine off.

"That was great! Can I drive back too?" she asked.

"I think I've created a monster," he mourned.

They spent a pleasant morning watching an informative video and looking at models and other displays that documented the Wright brothers' early flights. They hiked up the hill to where the sixty-foot pylon marked the place where the glider flights were conducted.

When they returned to the car, Carina's cheeks were warm from a combination of the fresh air and the excitement of being out and about. With Jonah, she felt safe and secure, a feeling that had been missing from her life for far too long.

He insisted that they stop at a quaint seaside restaurant to try the local fare. There, she enjoyed a bowl of clam chowder and told Jonah about a diner in Minnesota where on Fridays, she'd ordered the special, which was Thursday's leftover potato soup with canned clams dumped in for Friday's clam chowder. It was fun to laugh at moments and memories that she'd had no one to share with while she was on the run.

✳ �֍ ✽

When they went back to the beach house, everything seemed fine, but Jonah got a feeling of unease. He couldn't explain it, but something seemed off.

He went back out on the upper deck to see what their neighbor was up to, but there was no sign of the determined fisherman. He walked back into the bedroom and removed the shoulder holster he wore his gun in when not at home. He tucked the gun into the waistband at the back of his jeans before pulling a loose hoodie sweatshirt on to cover it.

He soon discovered Carina had pulled out all of the stops for a traditional Sunday dinner. She made a pot roast, with all of the fixings. They ate dinner, drank wine, watched some television and called it an early night.

They limited their touching to a few kisses and one long embrace before he gently pushed her away and sent her upstairs with a playful smack on her bottom. He checked everything one more time before going to bed. Out on the deck outside of his bedroom, he was able to see a light on in the house next to them, but didn't see any sign of the residents. He set his wristwatch to wake him in two hours and again got up to check on everything. Again, he saw no sign of trouble.

It was just after three in the morning when he heard a sound that brought him out of a light sleep into an instantly alert wakefulness. He picked up his gun and eased himself out of the bed. He first went out on the deck to see if there was any sign of anyone outdoors, but again, it looked all clear. He went to the hall door, opened it slowly and listened intently. There was someone downstairs. If Carina had gotten up in the middle of the night, surely she would have turned on a light.

Creeping down the stairs, careful not to make a sound, he pressed himself against the wall at the landing and listened. Whoever it was seemed to be in the kitchen. With his gun drawn and aimed, he crept the rest of the way down to the second floor. The figure standing in the light cast by the open refrigerator door was clearly male. The refrigerator door closed and the figure turned, quickly ducking down below counter level.

"You planning to shoot me?" asked a very familiar voice.

"Shit, Mac! What are you doing here?" Jonah asked. He flipped the wall switch to turn on the overhead light as Mac straightened into a standing position.

"Last I checked, this was my house," Mac said.

"You could have told me you were coming," Jonah complained.

"I was planning to drive down here and get settled and then call and tell you I was back. I figured you'd be with your family celebrating the holidays. If you happened to be in

240

D.C., I was going to invite you down to join me. How was I to know that you and my car were already here or that after eighteen months in a war zone I'd walk in to my own beach house and have my best friend aim a gun at me?" he asked.

Jonah walked over and grabbed Mac in a manly bear hug, patting him on the back twice. "Damn! It's good to see you," he said. He pulled back and looked at his friend. There was fatigue in Mac's face, he'd lost weight, but the cocky grin was firmly in place.

"Are you taking a vacation from work?" Mac asked.

"Yes and no," Jonah began as he heard a sound on the stairwell behind him.

Mac's jaw dropped when he saw the woman walk down the stairs. She was wearing a pair of silky pajamas with a thick fleece robe loosely belted over them. Her hair was a tumbled mass of blond curls that framed a face flushed from sleep. Her green eyes were slumberous and her mouth…

It hit Mac suddenly that if his friend was here with a woman, said woman was not available. He'd never poach another man's woman, especially not a man who was as close as a brother to him, but he was tempted.

Boy, was he tempted.

"Carina, this is Mac," Jonah said.

She nodded. "Yes, I recognize him from the pictures at your apartment." She walked up to Mac and held out a hand. "Jonah talks fondly of you. It's nice to meet you," she said.

"Yeah, I'm sorry, but he's been keeping you a secret, so you have the advantage."

She smiled. "You look hungry, can I fix you a late night snack?"

241

"You don't have to do that. I'm pretty self sufficient," Mac answered.

"Let her," Jonah advised. "The woman is a professional chef and her homemade muffins could even make a tough Marine like you weep."

"Marines only weep manly tears," he assured Carina.

She smiled at Mac. His face had too many angles to be called handsome, but she doubted he had any issues getting dates, with or without that sexy sports car as a lure. He was tall and fit, thicker-built than Jonah, with warm brown eyes and dark blond hair.

"Muffins?" she asked.

"Please," Mac said with a smile that melted her heart.

She pulled out the ingredients, including the remaining fresh blueberries, and began mixing them together. While she cooked, Mac and Jonah pulled up bar stools that sat on the other side of the kitchen counter and began catching up.

She listened to Mac talk about his flight through Germany and how he'd just kept on going until he got to the garage where he stored his car, only to find it missing. Since he also had a set of Jonah's keys, he'd driven Jonah's car down to Nags Head. He'd had to park out on the street, because the Waverunner was taking up the second parking spot in the garage. Carina could see that Jonah was reluctant to leave his car on the street where it could be spotted, but he didn't explain that to Mac.

In fact, he wasn't mentioning much to Mac, including that she was a witness that needed protection. She figured he would fill Mac in later, in private.

When the muffins came out of the oven, she had to threaten violence to get the men to give her the chance to get them out of the tray before they consumed them. Between the two of them, they polished off the entire batch.

Mac washed down the last muffin he'd arm-wrestled Jonah for with some of Carina's fresh squeezed orange juice, and then turned to her. "Will you marry me?" He enjoyed the pretty blush that came to her cheeks, but her glance at Jonah told its own story.

Looking at his friend, it appeared that his sister Shannon had been well and truly replaced. It was about damn time, he decided. Jonah and Shannon had never been right together. Why had he been the only one to see that right from the start? He was glad his best friend and sister had come to their senses before getting married. He'd been afraid that they would give in to family pressure and make both of their lives miserable.

"It's too late, or too early, to make such a life altering decision." Carina said, answering his marriage proposal. "I think I'll head up and sleep on it." She took her leave and headed back up to her bedroom.

"So, where did you meet her and does she have a twin?" Mac demanded.

"She's a witness," Jonah began.

"She's not just a witness," Mac disagreed. "I could see the sparks flying."

"We haven't taken it much beyond that. I'm tempted. Hell, I'd have to be a corpse not to be."

"So, how did my beach house become a safe house?" Mac wanted to know.

"Carina is testifying against a snake she used to be involved with named Samuel Kragen. Kragen has been a front man of the Russian mafia in D.C. for some time now.

Only, he's kept that connection hidden. Carina lived with Kragen in his Arlington mansion."

Mac raised his eyebrows, but didn't say anything as his friend continued. He knew his friend normally got very involved in the cases he worked on, but this was the first time he had seen Jonah so involved on a personal level.

"She co-owns an exclusive catering service." Jonah picked up some muffin crumbs from the table. "She has an elite clientele that includes many of the movers and shakers of this country. While she was serving a sit-down dinner at a certain senator's home, she overheard a conversation about a bill he was sponsoring.

"She'd heard Kragen discuss the bill once before, so she mentioned the conversations she'd heard to him. The senator had been telling someone at his dinner table that he was pulling in several markers to get the bill passed. Kragen knew that if the bill passed, it would put an end to a very lucrative scam he had going."

Mac shook his head. "You know, I swear that D.C. has more intrigue and guerilla warfare than your typical war zone."

Jonah snorted. "You got that right. Anyway, Carina had unwittingly let Kragen know that the bill would pass, but only with the senator's full backing. She later overheard a phone conversation Kragen made to one of his Russian friends, planning a hit on the senator before the bill could pass. After sneaking into Kragen's home office and taking pictures of some incriminating files, Carina brought the evidence to the FBI."

Mac whistled. "Gutsy girl. So let me guess; now the federal prosecutor needs her for her testimony in the trial against Kragen. Since Kragen would rather she was dead, she becomes your headache…or your heartache, as it turns out."

Jonah frowned at him. "Kragen has already made two attempts on her life. She says that I'm the only one she trusts, so..."

"Wait! Is this the case that you took a bullet in the shoulder for?"

"Yeah. I managed to protect her, but I got clipped."

"All the years I've spent in active duty Marines and I've never been shot," Mac claimed, his concern wrapped in humor.

"You've caught some shrapnel," Jonah argued.

"Shrapnel's different. So, how does it feel to get shot?"

"It hurts like hell," Jonah answered dryly.

"Bet," Mac agreed and swiped a last muffin crumb before Jonah spotted it. He licked it off his fingers. "And now you're protecting her before the trial begins?"

"We had her stashed in Arizona, but she ran. She says that she was being followed and barely escaped. There was another attempt on her life while she was on the run several weeks ago. I didn't know where she was until she showed up in my apartment a few days ago."

"How did they track her when you couldn't?"

"That's the mystery. I really don't know."

Mac listened as his friend told him about the second attempt on Carina's life while she was hiding in Tennessee.

"Why do I get the feeling that this little holiday at the beach is not a sanctioned trip?" Mac asked when Jonah finished updating him.

"She's paranoid, and with good reason. She believes that there's a leak in my office. I don't know that she's right, but I can't say for certain that she's wrong. So, I came up with the idea of coming down here."

"How can I help?" Mac asked.

"I wouldn't mind having you watch my back again. I don't have any evidence that we've been followed, but I just keep feeling that something isn't right."

Mac nodded. "You've got it. Anything I can do."

"Let's get my car into the garage before daylight and then we can get some sleep," Jonah suggested. They went out and shifted the Waverunner so that they could pull Jonah's car in next to Mac's. They patrolled around the beach house looking for signs of any trespassers, but saw nothing unusual. They headed back in, satisfied that they had done what they could to ensure Carina's safety.

"I took the master and Carina's in the big guestroom, but I can move," Jonah offered.

"Don't bother. I've been living in a tent. I can handle anything after that. I'll take the room on the street side so that I can hear anyone approaching from that direction."

"Okay, good plan. Let's get some sleep."

Mac nodded, but reached out to halt his friend before he could head back upstairs. "If you don't stake a claim on that woman, and soon, I will."

Jonah glared at him. "I haven't felt I have the right to stake a claim while she is under my protection, but as soon as that changes, I'll make my move. You better not be in my way."

Mac grinned and slapped his friend on the back. "You're sunk, my friend."

Chapter 7

Carina had the gym to herself for her morning workout. She guessed the men had had a late night and were sleeping in. She fixed a hearty breakfast for all, and after wolfing down hers, left the rest safely warm.

She decided to raid the bookshelf and make herself scarce the rest of the morning so the two friends could catch up on each other's lives. Between pages she'd lift her head and listen, enjoying overhearing the sound of their voices; the clack of balls and a few casual insults over a game of pool.

After lunch, she went for a walk with them on the beach. The sky was turning gray as a storm rolled in, so she really enjoyed this last chance to be outdoors. Afterward, they returned to the strip of beach in front of the house and tossed a Frisbee around. Carina laughed more than she had in months as the gusts of wind would send the well-aimed Frisbee flying in the wrong direction.

Jonah and Mac had already played a number of games of "rock, paper, scissors" to determine who should go after the Frisbee when it landed in the ocean. She was glad to see that the physical exertion and camaraderie seemed to help shake off any cabin fever.

The rain finally struck and Carina made a mad dash back to the shelter of the beach house while Mac and Jonah detoured to help their neighbor, the fisherman. He'd been standing on the beach casting his fly into the surf until the rain hit. She enjoyed watching the two friends helping gather the gear and take it to the fisherman's door.

"You know, the crazy fisherman next door has me craving fish for dinner. Something fresh. You didn't happen to see if he'd actually caught anything, did you?"

"The only thing on his line was seaweed," Jonah said.

"Hey, why don't I head into town and see if I can pick us up some fresh fish. Is there anything else you need while I'm out?" Mac asked.

"Why don't I just go with you?" Carina suggested.

"I don't think that's a good idea," Jonah disagreed. "We need to be cautious."

She frowned at him. "But we went out yesterday. You said you thought it was safe."

"I just don't want to take any more chances than necessary. Mac isn't related to the case at all, so he should have no problem shopping locally, but the fewer people who see you, the better."

She stared at Jonah and wondered what he wasn't telling her. She watched the men share a look and determined that she would get it out of Jonah after Mac left.

"Fine, I'll write a list of ingredients we'll need. I know that we don't have any lemons or dill." While she found paper and pen, she listened to the men discuss which car Mac should take.

"Jonah, I think I'll take your car. It's heavier and should be safer on the wet roads, especially now that the wind has come up."

"You should have thought of that when you bought that expensive toy out there," Jonah told him.

"A man doesn't think about things like the weather when he's plunking down a major portion of his life savings on a Maserati," Mac answered with a devilish grin.

After Mac left, Carina pinned Jonah with a look. "Spill it. Why are you suddenly worried about me being seen?"

Jonah shrugged. "I wish I could tell you something specific, but it's just a gut thing."

"A gut thing?" she questioned.

"Look, earlier when we were playing Frisbee, I got this tingle between my shoulder blades."

"What does that have to do with your gut?" she asked, suspiciously.

"When you've done this job for as long as I have, you learn to listen to your gut. I got a tingle, and that translates to a gut feeling that we should be more careful."

"Is this like your Spidey-senses or something?"

"I don't claim to be Spiderman. Hell, I hate spiders. If I see one, I'll yell for you to come kill it."

"I wouldn't kill a spider for you. I'd relocate it outdoors, but I wouldn't kill it."

Jonah rolled his eyes. "Fine, I'd call you to relocate… How the hell did we get off on this ridiculous tangent?"

"You were telling me about your gut. So, there's nothing that's happened, but you have a feeling."

"Yes, I have a feeling. And, I just went you to be safe. Okay?"

She looked at him and then stepped closer to slide her hands around his waist and link them behind his back. "Okay," she agreed.

✳ ✳ ✳

Carina began to pace when Mac had been gone for a full hour. She picked up Mr. Darcy and cuddled him close for comfort. "I shouldn't have suggested fish. We have plenty of food here. I could have fixed something else."

"Mac is the one who latched onto the idea and wanted to go out in this weather to get it. I guess that's what happens when you spend a year and a half in a desert. You start to crave fresh seafood."

She couldn't believe Jonah was as calm as he pretended. As the time stretched on, and she saw him constantly checking the clock, she realized he was as worried as she was; he was just better at masking it. Time seemed to stretch interminably.

After another full hour, Jonah grabbed his phone and put in a call to Mac's cell. When there was no answer, it only increased his worry. He couldn't leave Carina alone and was afraid to take her out of the house. He put his shoulder holster back on and placed his gun in it. It was easier to draw from the holster than from his waistband. He went from door to window to door, checking the locks, keeping the lights off, and looking out of the upper level windows for any sign of threat.

He was on the third floor when he heard the doorbell. The main outside stairs led to a front door that opened into the second floor living area. Carina was down there alone.

"Wait for me before you open the door," he called out and charged down the stairs. She was standing in the kitchen, frozen in place.

He went to her and put a comforting arm around her shoulder as he steered her towards the hallway. "Go back to the gym. If you hear me shout, you get outside. You can hang from the deck and drop down onto the sand without hurting yourself. Then just run and hide."

He watched as Carina scooped up the cat and locked him in the bathroom that contained his litter box. She headed to the gym and closed the door, giving him one last worried glance as she did. Jonah pulled on a jacket to cover his holster before he checked the peephole, his gun drawn.

250

He slipped his gun back into his shoulder holster before opening the door.

"Officers," he said to the male and female uniformed police officers standing on the porch.

"Do you know a Colonel Thomas MacBride?" the female officer asked.

"Yes. Has something happened? He went out a couple of hours ago and we were getting worried." Jonah was trying not to appear too worried, but his stomach was knotted with fear.

"There's been an accident. The car he was driving went off the road and into a drainage ditch. It was filling with runoff from this hard rain, but he managed to pull himself out of the car and up onto the roadside. A passing motorist spotted him and called 911. He's been taken to the Outer Banks Hospital. We can give you a lift, or you can follow us over there," she answered.

"How badly was he hurt?" Jonah asked.

"He was conscious when we arrived on scene, but he was pretty banged up. I don't really have more information than that. He asked us to inform you of the accident. He said that he knew you'd be worried."

"Can I see some ID?" Jonah asked.

Both uniformed officers looked at him in surprise, but produced their badges and identification.

After a careful scrutiny of the badges and ID, he nodded at them. "Thank you, Officers. I appreciate you coming out in this rain to let us know. Can you wait for a few minutes for my friend and me to get ready? Then I'd appreciate it if we could follow you to the hospital."

"Certainly, sir," said Officer Owens, a competent-looking female.

"We'll go down to the garage from the inside stairs and meet you outside," Jonah told the officers. "We'll be in Mac's car, a silver Maserati. It's hard to miss. He was driving my car. You don't know where it is, do you?"

"It was about to be towed to the impound yard when we left the scene. You can see about getting it out and towed to a repair shop tomorrow, though your insurance adjuster will probably write it off as a total loss. It sustained a great deal of damage from the crash and then the water had filled the interior before they got it hooked up to the wrecker," Officer Owens told him.

"The car isn't important, Mac is. We'll be right behind you," Jonah said.

He carefully locked the door behind the officers and hurried down the hall to update Carina. They bundled up, Carina tucking her hair into her knit hat and wrapping the scarf around her neck so that her lower face was partially obscured.

Jonah gave her a nod of approval and then grabbed her hand. "Let's go."

"No, wait. Mr. Darcy." She shrugged off his hand.

Jonah followed her into the into the kitchen. What, she wanted to bring the cat?

But Carina only moved the cat's food and water dishes from the kitchen into the bathroom, where Mr. Darcy was locked in with his litter box.

He then hustled her down the stairs to the garage. After stabbing the remote for the garage door, he started the Maserati's powerful engine.

They followed the police escort to the hospital. The male officer offered to park for him, an offer for which Jonah was most grateful. He took Carina's arm and together they hurried through the raindrops into the Emergency entrance.

Emergency told them Mac had been taken to the Critical Care unit. But once they reached the CCU, the nurses said Mac was now in surgery, where repairs were underway on a badly broken leg. As Jonah led the way to yet another floor, he had to wonder where they might get sent next once they got there.

The waiting area on the surgical floor was empty. Just as Jonah was about to sit down next to Carina, Officers Owens and Parker caught up with them.

"That's some car," Parker said, handing back the keys.

Jonah stuffed them in his pocket and sat down again. "I suppose you have some questions."

The officers sat down. Jonah explained where Mac had been going and stated he hadn't been drinking prior to leaving the beach house.

At the same time, he asked the police questions of his own. He wasn't surprised that no one was certain as to why he went off the road. The police assumed that the weather had played a role. Jonah had his own ideas and concerns about what had caused the accident.

After the police left to file their report, Jonah found himself filling out paperwork for the hospital. Carina sat quietly next to him the entire time. When he handed his clipboard back to the hospital staffer who'd brought it to him, she reached out and took his hand.

It was a two-hour wait before the surgeon walked into the waiting room to fill them in on Mac's condition.

"You're here for Colonel MacBride?" the tall woman in scrubs asked.

Jonah stood up, bringing Carina with him. "Yes, how is he?"

"The leg looks good. There was some crushing of the soft tissue, as well as a break in both the tibia and fibula, but they've been set and the area is getting adequate blood flow. I had to do some vascular surgery to repair a torn artery, but it seems to be holding just fine. It's amazing he was able to get himself out of the car with that injury, but I understand he's a Marine."

"Yes, he's been in worse situations," Jonah confirmed.

"He's got a couple of cracked ribs and a contusion on his forehead. He doesn't believe he lost consciousness, but we will monitor him, as we would anyone with a head injury. I've moved him into ICU for the night. He was soaking wet when they brought him in, but his lungs are clear, so we don't believe his head was ever submerged underwater."

"The police said that the ditch was rapidly filling with water and that's why he had to climb out on his own."

The surgeon nodded briskly. "Yes, that's what I understood, as well. My advice is that you go home and come back tomorrow after nine. I imagine he'll be moved into a regular room by then."

"How long will he need to stay in the hospital?"

"It'll be a few days. We're going to have to keep a close eye on that leg to make certain that there is no sign of infection and that the vascular surgery I performed was successful."

"Can we please see him before we head out?" Jonah asked.

"I'll arrange for you to see him, but he won't be conscious. He's still recovering from the anesthesia."

"Thank you," Jonah said and paced the waiting area until a nurse came to lead them to the ICU.

Jonah just stood and stared down at his friend. It wasn't right, seeing him like this, still and pale, weak and defenseless. There were IV tubes and monitor leads connected to his body. His right leg was in a cast and slightly elevated. There was a large bruise on his forehead that provided the only color in his face. He stared in disbelief. His friend had managed to avoid serious injury in a war zone, but got badly hurt in a car wreck?

The warm squeeze on his hand reminded him of the woman at his side. He saw her other arm extend, her hand reach out to Mac's limp, upturned palm. As if Carina's physical connection between them completed a circuit, Jonah's sense of reality returned.

"Get better, Mac. Get better real soon," he heard her whisper, her voice thick.

He didn't let go of her hand all the way back to the parking lot. Or, maybe, it was Carina who refused to let go of him. When they separated to get into the car, his hand felt cold, but his mind was clearer.

"I think I'd like to stay closer to the hospital," he told Carina as he started the engine.

"Whatever you think is best," she said.

At the Nags Head Inn, Jonah went to the concierge, and Carina made a beeline for the ladies restroom. Good timing, he thought, because it would be easier to explain getting a single room after the fact.

255

By the time he turned from the desk with the key, she was coming toward him.

"Come on, we're upstairs."

"Adjoining rooms?"

He hesitated only a second. "No. I'm sorry, but I think it's safer for us to share. I don't want you left alone."

"It's not a problem," she told him. "We're both exhausted, let's just get some sleep so we can go back to the hospital in the morning and check on Mac."

The room was clean and spacious, and the concierge had made a point to say it had a lovely ocean view. Too bad they weren't here to enjoy it. They had more serious things to worry about.

"Are you hungry?" he asked Carina. "We never ate dinner. I guess we should have stopped and picked something up on the way here."

"I don't want anything." She tossed her scarf onto the bureau. "I'm so sorry, Jonah, I don't know if it's safe to be anywhere near me. If only I hadn't suggested fish for dinner…"

She turned away from him, but he could see her body convulse with a deep shudder.

"This isn't your fault." Jonah crossed the room and pulled her into his arms. She leaned against him, continuing to shiver with reaction, but there were no tears.

As she had held onto him in the hospital room, he held her now. He tried to offer her comfort while his mind raced, considering the possibility that Mac's accident had, in fact, been no accident.

He'd asked the police about the car, wondering if perhaps it had been tampered with. It didn't make any sense to him that Mac would have crashed, regardless of how hard the rain was coming down. One of the officers suggested that he might have swerved to miss an animal.

Jonah felt that the likelihood that Mac's accident was related to Samuel Kragen was too high to discount. He wasn't going to tell Carina that his gut feeling was the main reason he'd brought her to the Inn instead of going back to the beach house.

He felt her shivering cease, and for several more minutes he held her gently as she snuggled against his chest. Then she reached up, wrapped her arms around his neck, and kissed him. It was a light, sweet kiss. Maybe only a thank you, so Jonah held himself back at first. But it soon evolved like a banked fire bursting into flame. His mouth ravaged hers, demanding a response. His body tightened when she gave it willingly.

Jonah's mouth left hers as he explored her cheeks, and her jaw, the lobes of her ears. Her soft, throaty sounds drove him beyond control.

"We should stop this," he growled as he used her hair to pull her head back and expose her neck to his mouth.

"Why?" she panted, tugging at his jacket. "We're both unattached adults. We both want this."

He started to pull back. "You're sure?" he asked.

"Oh, I'm very sure," she answered. "Take that off," she commanded urgently, gesturing to the holster.

He complied and hung his gun and holster from a nearby chair. When he felt her pull at his sweater he grabbed her wrists, causing her to protest.

"Carina, I don't want you to make love with me because you're scared or grateful or just in need of comfort."

She pulled free, reaching up to fist his hair in her hands. Her grip forced him to look into her eyes. "I know the difference between all of those feelings and the feeling of falling in love. I'm falling in love with you, Jonah Carter. In fact, it's quite possible that I've already fallen," she declared.

"That's all I needed to hear," he said on a groan and swung her up into his arms to carry her over to the bed. "You're so beautiful. I want to take this slow, but I want you so much I don't know if I can. Give yourself to me."

"Take whatever you want," she agreed and pulled him down to her.

Chapter 8

Carina woke early the next morning to the feel of Jonah's hands on her body, driving her up to a place where thought was submerged to sensation. The tempo of their lovemaking was faster and more desperate than the night before. When they lay tangled, trying to catch their breath, she tilted her head up to look into his eyes.

"Yesterday, I was reading a romance novel while you and Mac hung out. I kept thinking that the author had a great imagination, but didn't have a handle on reality. I never thought that lovemaking could be like this except in books. It's never been like this for me. Thank you."

She wasn't surprised to see his satisfied smile at the compliment.

"Any time," he offered. "You're pretty incredible," he confessed.

Carina returned his smile and reached up to place a kiss on his chin. "Ouch, you need a shave," she complained.

"It's a good thing the Inn has a complimentary razor since we don't have anything with us."

"Yeah, the night clerk left us in no doubt about what he thought of us checking in with no luggage."

"Well, my thoughts were pure until you seduced me," Jonah claimed.

"Yeah, and it was such a challenge," she agreed.

"I tried valiantly to resist you," he said piously.

"And which one of us woke up the other for an encore this morning?" she asked with a lift of an eyebrow.

"Speaking of encores," he said and rolled over on top of her.

"There's no way you…oh," she said.

"Where there's a will, there's a way," he told her as he proceeded to make slow, leisurely love to her.

* * *

Carina wasn't sure what to expect when they arrived at the hospital just after eight the next morning. But the news was good: they were told that Mac was being transferred to a regular room and that they would be able to see him after nine. Emotions flowed through her, flushing out all the negative worries of the night before. It left behind relief… and hunger.

"Nine, huh? What do you say to breakfast?"

Did he read her mind? Carina nodded. "I'm starving. Lead the way."

Afterward, she pulled Jonah into the gift shop. They had a few more minutes to kill, and she wanted to take something in for Mac. While choosing a flower arrangement, she saw Jonah in front of a book display. She had to grin at his choice when they checked out. A spy novel, of course. A manlier gift than flowers.

She enjoyed the scent of the blossoms as they walked to Mac's room. They found him sitting up, eating his own breakfast.

"Oh Mac, you're looking so much better," Carina said, leaning over to kiss his cheek.

Mac finished chewing and swallowed. "I'd be even better if you'd go beat whomever cooked this breakfast over the head with a rolling pin and then go cook me something yourself," he joked with her.

Carina looked him over anxiously. His bruise had spread and darkened, but that was normal. Bruises always looked worse the day after. She had no doubt it was more tender today, as well. His right leg was propped on a pillow, his bare toes left exposed by the sheet. As she fussed over straightening it, he shifted, wincing.

"I was so worried, when you didn't come back last night, I just had all sorts of horrible visions running through my head." She helped him shift his position and adjusted his pillow. "I'm sorry that you were hurt, but I'm sure glad it wasn't more serious. How did it happen?"

Mac grimaced. "I went into a skid and couldn't correct it. Next thing I knew, I was in a ditch and the water was nearly to my knees. I decided it was in my best interest to get out of the car. I had to go through the window and then pull myself up the embankment, but I lucked out that someone drove by when they did."

Jonah watched his friend and knew that there was more to the story, but he wasn't going to say anything in front of Carina. She'd been under enough stress without them worrying her more.

After letting Carina dominate some idle chitchat for a solid half hour, Jonah sent his friend a signal. They needed to talk, and without Carina in the room. Mac immediately gave her a look that stopped her chatter mid-sentence.

"Carina, darling, I'm really craving some ice water. Fresh ice water. And I can use some more pain medication." He shifted and grunted again, his face screwing up in pain.

Jonah wasn't sure how much of that was real and how much was acting, but he had to admire the results. Without question or hesitation, Carina snatched up the plastic pitcher on the tray and left the room.

"That was slick." Jonah sat down and crossed his legs. "So, what really happened?"

"Someone messed with your car. Right before the skid, I heard a popping sound. Suddenly had no steering and no brakes. If you get the local police to inspect the car, I'm sure you'll find evidence of some kind of explosive device. Whether it was detonated by remote or something else triggered it, I can't say."

"It doesn't make sense that they would try to take you out while you were alone," Jonah mused.

"Maybe, maybe not, but that car was tampered with. We need to figure out if they did it while it was garaged up in Quantico or if it happened while it was parked in the street outside the beach house."

"Either way, it's a good bet that they know where we are."

"Yes, I'd say they do. It's time to call in some reinforcements," Mac said. "You can't go this alone, not when they know where you are, where she is."

"I hate to do this, but I think I'm going to have to abandon you here," Jonah apologized.

"I'm a big boy, I can take care of myself. You will call my mom though and let her know, won't you?"

"Your mother would have you up and walking by the end of the day. You really want me to call her?" Jonah teased.

"No." Mac grew serious. "I want you to take care of yourself and your lady. Take my car and get out of here. Leave straight from the hospital and just go."

Jonah reached his hand out and Mac grasped it. "I owe you, man."

"Make me best man at the wedding and we'll be even."

"Getting a little ahead of things," Jonah said, but was surprised that the idea appealed to him. "Take care of yourself, buddy. I'll see you soon."

As he went into the hall, he nearly collided with Carina, a full pitcher of ice water, and the nurse she had firmly in tow.

Jonah extracted the pitcher from her right hand and disengaged the left from the nurse's arm. Handing the pitcher to the nurse with a smile, he nudged Carina away from the door. "We need to head out now," he told her.

She looked at him questioningly. "What about Mac?"

"He's the one who suggested we leave. We're going to take his car and head straight out of here, back to D.C. Our location has been compromised."

"Wait, Jonah, wait," she pleaded, hanging back. "I can't just leave Mr. Darcy."

Jonah stopped and turned toward her, gripping both of her arms. He gave her a shake. "We're talking about your *life* here. You want to risk your life for a damn cat? All this crap you survived through, made it through, you want to throw it out for a *cat*?"

Carina's eyes flooded with tears. "I'm not asking you to risk yourself. I'll take a cab back to the beach house and get him and then I'll meet you somewhere."

"Don't be ridiculous! Let's go." He let her go abruptly and stormed down the hall, then turned to see if she had followed.

Instead, she was rooted in place, tears streaming down her face.

"Aw, crap," he muttered, going back to her. "Look, don't cry."

She'd been through more than most people could tolerate and here she was shedding tears over a damn cat. Of course she had a breaking point; he'd just found it. He pulled her into his arms. She resisted at first and then sank into his chest. His arms came around her and he just held her close, stroking her back.

"It's okay, we'll get Mr. Darcy. It's going to be okay."

She sniffled. "I can guess Mac was hurt because of me—and that it wasn't because I asked him to go and get groceries."

Jonah realized that her guilt was the root of the tears. "It could have just as easily been us," he admitted. "Yes, the car was tampered with. I don't have any details yet. It might have been done before we even came down here, I don't know. The only thing I *do* know is that we're no longer safe here. Mac's going to be okay and he doesn't blame either one of us for what happened. Don't blame yourself. You know who is at fault for all of this."

"Samuel Kragen," she whispered.

"Yeah, Samuel Kragen. He must be getting desperate by now. The trial starts in a week and he still hasn't been able to neutralize you. Between the evidence you gave to the prosecutor and your testimony, he knows he's looking at a very long time behind bars. We have to be really careful and really smart."

She nodded her head against his chest. "What do we do?"

"Well, I guess the first step is to contact the Nags Head Police Department and get some backup. I'll let them know who I am and that I need them to run some tests on my car to determine exactly what caused Mac's accident. Then, I'll contact Rodriguez back up in D.C. She can arrange for a safe house and protection for us for the rest of the week."

"Are you sure you can trust her?" Carina asked in a shaky voice.

"Yeah, I've been through doors with her and she's always had my back. I can trust her."

"Okay. I'm going to use the ladies' room while you call the police. I need a few minutes to get myself back together."

Jonah nodded and moved to the nurse's station, keeping an eye on the ladies' room door. He showed the nurse at the station his badge and asked to use her landline. The hospital didn't permit cell phone use and he had no intention of going outside and leaving Carina in order to make a call.

Jonah found that the Chief of Police had the holiday weekend off, but the Deputy Chief agreed to send two patrol officers and a K-9 unit over to the beach house and another squad car to the hospital to escort them to the beach house and out of town. There would also be an investigation of Mac's accident, including testing on the car to determine if there had been any tampering with the brake and steering systems.

264

Satisfied with the response he'd gotten, he looked up to see Carina waiting for him. "They're sending a squad car," he told her. "I told them we'd wait in here for them." He didn't want to be outside and exposed.

Ten minutes later, a uniformed officer approached them and showed his badge without being asked. "I'm Sergeant Turner, sir; ma'am. Where can we talk?"

They sat down in an empty corner of the lobby.

"I'd like to be certain that there isn't anyone at the beach house waiting to ambush us and then, after we gather our belongings, that we have police escort out of Nags Head."

"Don't forget Mr. Darcy," Carina reminded Jonah.

"Mr. Darcy?" Turner asked.

"Her cat," Jonah answered.

When Sergeant Turner said he understood completely about her cat, Jonah saw Carina's sad eyes warm. He felt a momentary jealousy that some animal-loving cop was suddenly her knight in shining armor. He shrugged. It wasn't the right time to dwell on it. Besides, he was feeling grateful himself, especially when he heard Turner arrange to have officers sweep the beach house and surrounding area to make sure it would be safe for a quick return under police escort.

✳ ❄ ✳

At the beach house, Carina found out that a female officer had been assigned to escort her, ordered to stick like glue to her side until she and Jonah were back in the car and headed out of town. Even in the bathroom? she had to wonder, then told herself that it wouldn't be for long. With help she could pack up and get out all the faster.

Officer Drake was a friendly and competent assistant. The bags were packed up in no time, and soon they were headed downstairs again, Carina carrying Mr. Darcy's carrier and paraphernalia; Drake with the luggage.

She stowed Mr. Darcy in the small back seat of the Maserati, making sure her bags and Jonah's, already stowed, would keep the carrier from moving.

Jonah and Sergeant Turner were standing just outside the garage, talking. She approached them, offering a little smile to Turner when he nodded politely at her.

"Are you sure it's safe to stand out here like this?"

"Don't you worry, Miss Woods," Turner said. "We've got you covered. Officer Drake here can definitely take care of you, and her partner, Officer Wilson, is out with Officer Chen and his K-9 partner, Klink, maintaining a perimeter."

She didn't have to fake a smile this time. "Klink? What a great name for a police dog. I'll just be another few minutes. I have to freshen up."

She turned and headed back upstairs, Drake like a shadow at her back. After a quick glance to make sure she hadn't forgotten anything, Carina stood in front of the bathroom mirror to do her hair and makeup. Wiping a smudge near one eye, she decided no amount of makeup was going to improve her looks any time soon.

She had looked better after working the non-stop, no-sleep craziness that was Inauguration week in D.C. She pinched at her cheeks, hoping to bring a bit more life to the pallor there. Oh well, she supposed being on the run wasn't the best for her beauty sleep. Then again, perhaps Jonah's stamina was more to blame for her lack of sleep.

That thought cheered her up, so she dropped her mascara back into her makeup bag and turned to open the bathroom door.

Her back and shoulders hit the porcelain tub with enough impact to knock the air out of her. At first she thought Officer Drake, who stepped back to give her some privacy, had attacked her. Then she realized the wall was gone. The entire wall, including the bathroom door, was in splinters. In a daze, she stared uncomprehending into the bedroom just beyond, watching debris fall from the ceiling, gradually becoming aware of the smell of smoke and a roaring sound.

Fire.

Faster than she could have imagined, there was heat, the bright lick of flame, and a rapidly spreading inferno consuming its way toward her. Paint, wallpaper, and flooring bubbled up into a huge charred mess in what seemed like seconds.

Gathering what remained of her wits, she pulled herself into the bathtub and turned the shower on full. Grabbing a towel, she wet it and draped it over her head.

The smoke was filling the room and the heat was unbearable. The water was coming out cold and she tried her best to shrink into the spray as much as possible, but the fire continued to eat its way closer to her.

What happened? What the hell happened? She couldn't remember an explosion. Maybe there had been—whatever blew her back against the tub robbed her of hearing it. She heard all too well now. The fire roared louder than the hard spray of the shower, the flames licking hungrily at her arm. There was another sound from the wall just beyond her head. Her heart nearly stopped as a hard blow made the wall shudder. Another explosion?

The wall behind the shower cracked. Carina shrieked in terror, fearing that the fire had surrounded her tiny bathtub oasis and she was about to perish.

Another smash. More debris.

Then she became aware that a voice was shouting her name.

Choking, she screamed back, "Here! Here! I'm here!"

The wall hadn't been exploding. There were people trying to rescue her, trying to break through the wall. Now she could see hands pulling and ripping away wallboard. The head of a small axe cleared a wider opening, knocking plaster and pieces of tile everywhere.

"Stay down! Cover your head!" a voice called as her rescuers continued to tear a hole in the wall big enough for her to get through. The dry wall was pulled away easily enough, but the studs took several blows from the axe before they buckled to allow a sufficient sized opening.

"Give me your hands," Jonah shouted through the opening.

Carina ducked under the spray one last time to get as wet as possible and then stood bent at the waist to dive through the wall. As her hands reached through the hole, she felt them grasped and pulled. Other hands helped to lift her and yank the rest of her body through the opening until she was all the way inside the smaller guest room Mac had used.

"Let's go!" a man's voice shouted.

She was hauled up dripping and tossed over Sergeant Turner's shoulder in a fireman's carry.

"Officer Drake!" Carina cried. "Where is she?"

"Here!" she heard a woman's voice respond. "I had stepped out into the hall just before..."

"Not now, keep moving, let's go!"

That was Jonah. But Carina had heard enough. She fervently thanked God that she hadn't been the cause of another innocent's death. She closed her eyes and tried to brace herself as she bounced on Turner's shoulder all the way down the stairs.

The coolness of the concrete floor on her damp back was a blessing. "Jonah," she croaked and then coughed as her smoke-filled lungs protested.

"Hush, it's okay. Just stay down," he ordered.

Just as he finished speaking, a line of bullets penetrated the garage wall and shot up the side of Mac's car in rapid succession. Everyone else hit the floor.

Carina lifted her head, wondering if there was anything she should do…could do. She just stayed down and prayed for the officers' safety as they took position.

Officer Wilson, who must have run back inside to help after the explosion, lay on his stomach facing south with his gun drawn.

Officer Drake bellied over to the car and opened the back door, pulling the cat carrier out and down onto the floor next to where Carina lay. She whispered her thanks, as Drake crawled over to take position opposite Wilson, facing north.

Carina looked over at Sergeant Turner who was busy barking orders into his two-way radio.

"What's the situation?" she heard Jonah ask the sergeant.

"I don't know what the hell they fired into the upstairs, but if they have another one, we're sitting ducks. There are at least two gunmen with automatic weapons, one on either side of the house. We're outgunned. Officer Chen and his

269

dog are pinned down behind the detached storage shed and the rest of us are all trapped here."

"How? I thought we were clear," Jonah shouted above the roar of gunfire that continued unabated into the north and south walls of the garage and the fire that continued to blaze above them.

"There was a fishing boat anchored just off shore. It seemed harmless enough until it launched some kind of missile or something into the upstairs bedroom," Officer Wilson reported.

"I was on the north side of the house and I was keeping my eye on the boat, but it didn't seem threatening. Then there was just this streaking light through the sky and the explosion."

Carina closed her eyes in horror. Missiles…they were shooting missiles! All to try and kill her.

"A smaller craft was launched and two men came on shore with some big ass guns and started firing. I ran back in here," Wilson said.

Carina couldn't blame him. Their handguns were no match against automatic weapons.

"Officer Chen reports one gunman with an assault weapon on the south side of the building using the neighbor's vehicle as cover. There's at least one more on the north side," Turner added.

"Backup?" Jonah asked.

"We've got a Coast Guard cutter en route and two helicopters flying in now. I've got additional units less than five minutes away." Turner shouted as another barrage of bullets rained down on them. "But they won't have anything with them able to go up against these weapons, either."

There was a large crashing sound above them. "There went the third floor," Turner said. "We've got to do something or the fire will get here before backup can."

"I've got an idea," Jonah shouted.

He bellied over to a storage cabinet at the front of the garage. He pulled out beer bottles from the recycling bin, grabbed some old rags, and siphoned gas out of the Waverunner's tank.

"Let's toss some Molotov cocktails their way," he said. "They'll be more effective than handguns."

Carina watched as the two police officers and Jonah began filling the beer bottles with gasoline and stuffing the rags into them.

"Primitive, but it might work," Turner agreed.

Wilson again took his position on the north wall, as Drake took the south. Jonah continued to fill bottles.

"Let me help. I need something to do." Carina took over the rag stuffing, passing the completed bottles to Turner. The Molotov cocktails, along with a few lighters someone found near Mac's barbecue supplies, were soon distributed to the officers on either side of the garage.

"Everyone stay down until I give the order," Turner said tersely.

Carina saw him signal. She wished she knew what those gestures meant, but figured it out soon enough when Jonah joined Wilson and Turner partnered with Drake.

Another round of bullets penetrated on the south wall, followed by a round on the north wall.

"Now!" Turner shouted.

She held her breath. Just don't drop them in here, she thought as the rags were lit. Her teeth bit into her lower lip as she prayed for their safety. Standing up enough to aim

271

and throw their bottles might earn one or more of them a bullet.

Carina listened as glass shattered, flames sprang to life, and a man on the north side of the garage shouted in pain. Bullets flew again and the same choreographed dance took place. A second shout of pain from the south side of the building let them know that they had wounded the second gunman on that side of the building.

But she was more concerned with sounds from above. It sounded like the ceiling was about to cave in on them, as the fire burned through all three floors of Mac's beach house.

"Everyone out!" Turner shouted.

Chapter 9

Jonah scooped Carina up and dumped her and Mr. Darcy into the back seat of Mac's mangled Maserati. "Keep down!" he ordered. He got in and started the engine. Hitting the automatic door opener, he barreled out backward as soon as there was enough space and kept going until they were clear of the building. The three police officers dove out behind them.

Just in time, as the house collapsed in on itself with a cracking, popping roar and shower of sparks and flames.

Then, all was quiet, other than the sound of the helicopters overhead. Sounds he hadn't noticed until now.

Jonah waited to hear more shooting or explosions. He sighed in relief when he heard Sergeant Turner declare the scene secure and order in fire and rescue.

When the ambulance pulled up, he carried Carina over to be treated and then took stock of the situation.

Officer Wilson had subdued the injured gunman on the south side and Officer Drake was spraying the small fires still burning from the Molotov cocktails with a fire extinguisher. She wasn't wasting her time on the house—that was a goner.

What the hell was he going to tell Mac? Running a hand through his hair, he stared morosely at the scene until he took note of the gunman who had been on the north side.

That man had been closest to the garage and must have run towards the street. However, it appeared that Klink had knocked him down, and his human partner, Officer Chen, had the gunman in restraints before he had recovered.

Jonah smiled hugely as he recognized the bastard.

Sergei Dvorkin. Kragen's chief of security. Taking him out would put a serious hole in Kragen's power base. The Feds were pretty certain that Sergei was an enforcer from the Russian mafia. With him in custody, Kragen would be lucky to make it to his own trial. His Russian friends would be none to pleased with how this operation had turned out.

He quickly checked in with Sergeant Turner regarding the safety of all the police personnel. It was a relief to hear that only minor injuries had been sustained, the worst being a gunshot that went through the fleshy part of Officer Chen's left arm.

"Anything on that boat?"

"Coast Guard boarded them," said Turner. "Still waiting for details regarding exactly what they fired at us."

Jonah wondered if he should mention that one of the charges Kragen had been arraigned on was running weapons. No, there was enough going on right now. "Going to be a hell of a debriefing," he muttered.

Turner nodded. "Damn right." He gave Jonah a nod and left him when another officer called for the sergeant's presence.

Going back to check on Carina, he found the paramedics were working on her. She had an oxygen mask on her face and her eyes were closed, but they opened when he started talking to the paramedics. She suffered second-degree burns, some cuts and abrasions, but she was alive. And that little smile she sent meant the world to him.

Satisfied for the moment, Jonah stood and looked at what was left of Mac's personal property. Fire crews came in to douse what remained of the fire, but Mac's beach house was a complete loss, and judging by the looks of Mac's car, Jonah was certain that the insurance adjusters would consider it a complete loss as well.

"Hell." Jonah shook his head. "He'll never speak to me again."

As soon as the paramedics loaded Carina into the ambulance, he hopped in beside her and rode with her to the hospital, leaving Turner to clean up the rest of mess and coordinate the remainder of the arrests.

✳ ✳ ✳

He was further reassured about Carina's condition in the hospital. After arriving at the emergency room, she'd been admitted for observation. Although none of her injuries were life threatening, she had inhaled a great deal of smoke, so the doctors wanted to monitor her breathing and blood oxygen levels.

Two police officers arrived to stand guard. Jonah felt secure enough with Carina's safety to have a quick visit with Mac. If he reacted badly to the news, well, at least both of them were already in a hospital.

Jonah found his friend flirting with a very attractive nurse who was changing his IV bag. "Looks like you're feeling a bit better," Jonah observed.

"I am. I've got Nurse Stanton here to keep my spirits up," Mac agreed cheerfully.

"I have a feeling your spirits aren't going to be quite so high after I tell you what happened," Jonah said.

"Is Carina okay?" Mac tore his eyes away from his curvy nurse, the flirty smile disappearing first into concern, then into shocked astonishment. "Hell, I haven't seen you this beat up since we got penned down for those two days over in the Gulf."

Jonah grimaced. "I think this experience was worse than that. In fact, I know it was."

"What happened?"

"Before I tell you, I gotta know. Are you insured against missiles?"

"*What?*" Mac nearly shouted.

Jonah took a breath, then told him everything. "I'm really sorry. I don't know how I'll ever make it up to you."

Mac just sat in the hospital bed stunned. "It's all gone? All of it?"

"What the missile didn't get, the fire got, and what the fire missed…" Jonah shrugged helplessly. "It looked like the fire crews were pretty much finishing off anything remotely salvageable with their water hoses and axes when I left."

"Damn!" Mac said. "I guess you'll be spending all of your weekends, for a long time to come, coming down here and helping me rebuild."

"Whatever you need, it's yours," Jonah agreed.

"I guess when I get out of here, I need to go car shopping. I was thinking that it might be time for me to turn in the testosterone-mobile for something a little more practical. I don't guess my trade in value is going to be quite as high now though, is it?"

"I guess not. You're covered though, right?"

"Yeah, I've got full coverage on the house and the car. Don't worry about it. I'll just rebuild bigger and better. After all, I've been thinking about putting in for retirement. I've got my twenty in and I'm ready to give civilian life a try. I was a little worried about being bored, but…look how it turned out for you."

"Don't use me as a gauge," he warned.

Mac smiled at him. "I was thinking of selling the beach house and looking for something to call a permanent home. Now I'll just skip the selling part and build my dream home."

After spending an hour with Mac, his guilt was somewhat eased, but he didn't think he'd ever be square with the guy. Hell, he knew he'd owe his friend forever.

Jonah headed back to check on Carina and found that she was asleep. He also found Sergeant Turner, who had come in to check on his injured officer and to touch base.

"I've got something here that ought to make Ms. Woods feel better," he said, holding up a pet carrier.

"Mr. Darcy? I guess I left him in the car," Jonah remembered.

"Yes, we salvaged your satchel and luggage too, although there are a few holes in the suitcases. The satchel made it through without a scratch, though. Christmas present?" he asked.

Jonah grinned, something he hadn't thought he'd do ever again. "Yeah, it was. Thanks. I know that Carina will be very happy to see that her cat survived with no injuries. Considering all of the gunfire and everything else that was exploding or burning around us, I'm amazed that everyone seems to be as healthy as they are."

"Yeah, well we've got the two gunmen here at the hospital for treatment and then they'll be heading over to lock up. Deputy Chief Swanson put a call into the Feds and they'll be coming down to pick them up tomorrow morning. I guess they think they might be able to get one or more of them to make a deal and give them more on this Kragen guy. The Coast Guard has three men from the boat in custody and they'll be bringing them in to lock up within the hour. It's all wrapped up, but for the paperwork."

"I had no idea what I was taking on when I agreed to protect Carina. A lone assassin maybe, but not this all-out warfare."

When he was told Carina would be discharged in the morning, Jonah arranged for transportation to a safe house in the D.C. area. Sitting down in the chair next to her bed, he let out a long sigh and tipped his head back to stare at the ceiling for a moment.

God, he was tired. It had been a long day.

✳ ❄ ✳

Carina started feeling normal again late afternoon on the second day. The doped-up haze from the painkillers had cleared. There were a few muscles that twinged if she moved a certain way, and her burns felt tight and hot, but some sunburn ointment took care of that.

She shared the safe house with Marshal Juana Rodriguez. She didn't know where Jonah was, she hadn't seen or heard from him since the hospital. She knew he'd come with her to this location but at the time, she was so cloudy from drugs she didn't recall very much.

She had to satisfy herself that he was busy wrapping up details from the incident in Nags Head. Rodriguez wasn't any help at all. She was polite enough, but getting any information out of her was impossible. Not even her famous muffins produced anything but a "Yum" and "Thanks."

✳ ❄ ✳

It was late afternoon on New Year's Eve when Jonah came to the safe house. Carina was overjoyed, but restrained herself in view of Rodriguez.

Rodriguez expressed her joy as well. "It's 'bout damn time! I thought my fine ass was going to go to waste locked up in here on New Year's Eve. I got me a hot date," she announced.

"Yeah, your cat called and said he was waiting for you to get home and clean out his litter box," Jonah agreed.

"Cat, my ass." Rodriguez grumbled.

Carina smothered a grin. Poor Rodriguez suffered from allergies to cats. Being confined to the safe house, even with allergy medication, hadn't been easy for her.

After she left, Carina sat on the couch, Mr. Darcy next to her. As happy as she was to see Jonah, she suddenly felt awkward and disconnected from him. Only a few days ago she'd awakened in his arms, feeling comfortable and safe. Now she felt that there was some type of force field around him, locking her out.

"How are you?" He nodded to her right forearm.

Carina picked at the light cotton bandage there, over the worst of her burns. She still shivered to think just how close she'd come. "I'm doing better, thanks. Yourself?" she asked politely.

"I'm good," he answered.

"And Mac? Have you heard how he's doing?"

"He's out of the hospital and staying at his parents' house for now. I talked to him this morning and he plans to stay with them until he's able to get around better on his own. He's spending his time making drawings of the new beach house he plans to build."

Carina nodded and then sighed. "Please sit down."

Jonah took the armchair that sat adjacent to the couch. "I guess we have some talking to do," he said.

"I guess we do. Have you made any headway in the case against Sam?"

"Yeah. Sergei Dvorkin isn't talking, but the others have each taken deals for lesser sentences. They'll still all spend the vast majority of their lives behind bars, but they may see daylight before they die."

"And Sergei? He was the one who killed Brian, wasn't he?" she asked.

"We may never know. He'll go down hard along with Kragen and several others. You'll still need to testify, but Kragen has been arrested and is being held without bail based on the information we got."

"How did they find us?" she asked.

"Davis," he answered abruptly.

"Who?" she asked, confused. And not due to any pain-killers, she thought.

"Arthur Davis, a veteran marshal—a disgruntled veteran marshal. Apparently, when he was passed over for promotion and I was given the supervisor's job, he decided to cash out while he had something to sell."

"I'm sorry, but I'm not following," Carina told him.

"There's a man I've worked with for the last six years in the D.C. office. I thought he was a little less than stellar in his work performance, but he wasn't a bad guy. According to him, Dvorkin approached him on behalf of Kragen, offered him a lot of money to tell them where you were. Davis knew about Arizona. You were right there. You were being followed and they would have killed you if you hadn't run."

Carina wished she felt some vindication to know she was right, but all she felt right then was exhaustion. She sighed and tuned back into what Jonah was saying.

"But he didn't know that you were in D.C. with me. I guess he got suspicious when I took vacation and dumped all of my active cases on him, but wouldn't give him a contact number. He followed up and found that I didn't go to my parents' house, as planned. Only, I didn't tell Davis where I was going. Dvorkin told him that they knew we'd been in Richmond at the mall and then Davis remembered that I had a friend with a beach house in Nags Head. Suggested we might have gone down there."

"Richmond?" Carina whispered in a strangled voice.

"Yes. How did they track us to Richmond? I've been trying to figure that out. I've gone back through all of the steps we took. How could they possibly have known we were in Richmond if they didn't know that we had changed cars? If they had followed us, they would have known where we were. So, how did they find us?"

"Allyson," Carina said, looking up and into Jonah's eyes. She felt raw.

"Allyson?" Jonah asked.

"She's a young girl I mentor. I met her when she snuck into my place of business to steal some food. She's fourteen and a foster child who had run away from her foster home. She'd only been on the street a couple of days when she broke a window and climbed into the kitchens. I was in my office working late, heard the noise, and went to investigate. I was about to call the police when I realized that it was a young girl. She'd lost her family in a house fire."

Carina shuddered as she realized she now knew what Allyson's family had gone through. She swallowed hard before continuing. "She'd been away spending the night with a friend. Her story resonated with me. We hit it off and I've been a part of her life ever since. Her aunt had been living in Africa working with a relief agency and it took her about six months to get back to the States and get custody of Allyson."

"And Samuel Kragen knew about her?"

"I never told him about her. If he knew about her…He must have tapped both our phones. He probably was spying on me while we were together."

"That would be in keeping with his character," Jonah agreed.

She nodded, staring at the floor. "Allyson has lived in Oregon with her aunt for over a year now. The last time I saw her was when I flew out to visit her at least two months before I met Sam. She's happy now and doing well, but every once in a while the grief swamps her."

Carina looked back up at Jonah. "People who have lost someone they love can relate. When Allyson feels it coming over her, she calls me and we talk. She tells me about her mom and dad and her kid sister and baby brother. She shares her memories with me. Her Aunt Sally is great with her, but every once in a while, Allyson just needs to talk to

281

someone who understands how she's feeling. I'm that person for her."

"And you've been calling her," Jonah said in a flat voice.

"Yes, I've called her about once a month just to check in. She's doing well, but she hasn't been able to call me when she needs me. I've been calling in to make sure that she knows that I haven't abandoned her. I couldn't just disappear from her life. She's lost more than any kid her age should have to lose and I won't let her lose me too."

"You'll just put your life in jeopardy. And mine. And Mac's. And Brian Marsters," Jonah said harshly.

"No, no, I didn't...I was careful. I only called when I was moving from one place to another. I only called when I was on the road. Except..."

"Except?"

The tears streaked silently down her cheeks. "I called on the anniversary of the fire that took Allyson's family. It happened the weekend before Thanksgiving. I called from Tennessee and that phone call got Brian killed."

"And Richmond?"

Carina nodded. "Yes. I went to the restroom and when I came out, I saw a pay phone. It was an impulse. I called and spoke to Sally and Allyson, but just for a couple of minutes. I wanted to let her know that I was thinking about her with Christmas coming. I hadn't been able to send a gift and I was there in the mall with the Christmas music playing and the decorations everywhere. I just called to wish her a Merry Christmas and to let her know that I would be thinking of her. Holidays are hard for kids who've lost their families. Even though she has a loving home, she still remembers what family Christmases were like."

"If we had known about this, we might have figured it out sooner. If you had trusted me enough to confide in me. Why the hell didn't you tell me?"

Carina's head whipped up. It was hard to meet the anger in Jonah's eyes, but she forced herself to do so. "I did trust you. I do trust you. I honestly never put it together. I had been calling Allyson at least once a month for the last six months. They never found me until Tennessee. I didn't put it together, because Sam didn't know about Allyson. I…I don't know how to make you understand," she said.

"I don't know that I'll ever be able to," he said coldly, then stood up. "The trial will begin as planned. Despite the new information, the federal prosecutor is determined to start the trial as soon as possible. He's got you slated to testify the following Monday or Tuesday. You'll be given protection throughout the trial and then pending the outcome, you'll be free to return to your life."

"It sounds like you won't be around," she said.

"I begin my new job on Monday. I'll assign your case to Rodriguez. She'll coordinate bodyguards for the trial and security here at the safe house."

"So, this is goodbye."

"I'm sure we'll see each other, but I won't be protecting you on a daily basis like before."

"All right. I just want to say thank you for…for everything you've done for me. I'm sorry. More sorry than I can say for all of the trouble I've caused you and Mac."

Carina searched Jonah's stony face and knew that there was nothing she could say or do to repair the damage to their relationship. She'd blown it and it was over. Now all she had to do was get away from him before she completely fell apart.

"I'm going to go lie down for awhile. I still get tired easily."

He nodded, seemed to hesitate. "I'll be leaving in an hour or so. I have another female marshal coming to stay with you. Her name is Tasha Reed. I'll let her in before I leave, you don't have to get up."

She stood up. "Thank you," she said as she scooped up Mr. Darcy. Cradling him against her, she headed back to the bedroom.

Chapter 10

It was the first week in February when Carina sat in the courtroom awaiting the verdict on Samuel Kragen.

In addition to her testimony and the computer files she had copied, the federal prosecutor had built an impressive case. The additional witnesses against Kragen added a great deal to it. They included several of the men who had been sent to kill her and Jonah down in Nags Head.

Kragen's friends in the Russian mafia had thrown him to the wolves. As far as they were concerned, he could rot in a prison cell. He had after all, failed them and exposed them to close federal scrutiny. Carina imagined that they would be the focus of an intense investigation following the Kragen trial. She could only be grateful that she would have no part in it. Samuel Kragen had kept her far away from his business dealings when she was living with him.

The verdict would simply confirm what everyone knew, Samuel Kragen was finished. He would be living out his days behind bars. Sergei Dvorkin was scheduled to stand trial in two month's time, but was remanded without bail until his trial. There was little doubt about the outcome of that trial.

Carina listened to all of the "guilty" verdicts read on a laundry list of charges and felt a sense of intense relief, but not the elation she had expected.

✳ ✳ ✳

After Kragen was led away to begin his sentence, Marshal Reed escorted her back to the safe house to collect her belongings. They then went to Rodriguez' office to complete the necessary paperwork.

As Carina sat at Rodriguez' desk, she noted that Jonah was conspicuously absent. It wasn't until her stomach dropped that she realized she had been hoping for one more look at him.

She shook the hands of both marshals to thank them for everything and wish them well. Rodriguez offered to take her home, but Carina declined. She was free now, and she was going to be able to walk out of the building and take a cab home without fear for the first time in months.

Home. It seemed like a foreign word, but at least Carina had already been able to meet with Phoebe, her business partner. She intended to go back to work the very next day. Valentine's Day was just over a week away, and Phoebe had booked several intimate meals to be catered by their firm.

Carina was ready to dive back into work. She had felt like an automaton since Jonah had left her on New Year's Eve. She didn't know if it had been her worst New Year's, but it ranked right up there. She needed to move on and find some measure of peace. And she had to put her life back together.

Jonah Carter was an unfulfilled dream and it was time to face reality.

At least, that's what she kept telling herself. Some day, she might even listen to herself. The overwhelming grief that gripped her at the thought of him told her that it would be a long time before she'd be able to move past her feelings for him—if ever.

* ❄ ❄

A week later, she was standing in the kitchen of her business when she heard a sound. She glanced up, startled. She wasn't sure how long it would be before she got over this feeling of being stalked.

But she was happy to see this stalker.

"Mac!" she said to the man standing grinning at her.

"Hi, pretty lady, can I buy you lunch?" He pulled her into a hug.

"Of course. But, you're still talking to me? I can't believe it." She stepped back from the embrace, pulling off her apron and toque.

"I don't blame you for what happened. In fact, I just may thank you," he told her as they walked out.

"Thank me?" she asked in surprise.

"Come on, I'll buy you lunch and explain," he told her.

* ❄ ❄

They went to one of Carina's favorite places, a small café with a quiet, relaxed atmosphere. Customers never had to shout to have a conversation here. And the chef was top-notch.

After ordering, Mac sat back and stared at her.

"What?" she demanded.

"You're not exactly looking happy and vibrant," he said.

"Always gallant," she complained.

"Sorry lady, I shoot straight."

"It's been hard picking up the pieces of my life. The business survived, but my partner had to do a lot of scaling back to cover all of the bases. I've been trying to make up for lost time. I gave Phoebe some much needed time off and I've been putting in sixteen hour days for the past week. It's like being back at the beginning, building the business from the ground up."

"And on the personal front?"

"Sixteen hour days. There is no 'personal front'."

"You haven't heard from Jonah?"

She lowered her eyes to hide the pain hearing his name still caused. "He made it very clear that he and I were over. I screwed up and he blames me for what happened in Nags Head. Rightly so."

"Well trust me, if you think you look bad, he looks even worse. He looks like hell. If you ask me, he'll come to terms with whatever it is he's having trouble dealing with and then he'll be back."

She looked up. "You didn't see his eyes when he left me." She shook her head. "No, I do believe it's truly over. I lost nearly a year of my life thanks to Sam Kragen. I need to put things back on track...with a few changes."

"Like what?"

"I thought we came to talk about you," she said.

"We'll get there. Tell me what your plans are."

"I plan to spend some time volunteering at a culinary school for inner-city kids. It's a program that helps teens learn a marketable skill while keeping them off the streets.

I've hired some of my assistants from there and now I plan to give them a bit of my time."

"You're not doing penance, are you?" Mac asked. "You were as much a victim in all of this as anyone."

"I don't know that I agree with you there, but I'm not doing this out of a sense of guilt or duty. I'll get more out of working with the teens than they'll get out of my teaching. Seriously though, what have you been up to?"

"Well, I've hired an architect to design my new house in Nags Head. And I've met a woman who's been helping me decide what I want."

"You met a woman and you're already designing a house together? That was fast!"

"Not really. She was one of my nurses in the hospital in Nags Head. Terri and I flirted while I was there and after I got off those damn crutches, I went back and asked her out. We're taking it slow, but…she's amazing. I put in my retirement papers. I should be out in about six months and I've been researching some jobs that would allow me to home base in Nags Head. There are several firms in North Carolina and Virginia that have government contracts and that need people with my particular skills and experience."

"Wow, that's a lot of change in a short time."

"That's not all. I bought a car. An SUV."

"No!" she said in mock astonishment.

He chuckled. "You kicked my complacent butt and made me realize that I wanted more out of life than what I had. I'm looking forward to being a civilian."

She angled her head in confusion. "I'm glad, but I don't know what I did, except get shot at a lot."

"It was seeing you and Jonah together. Seeing what you two had between you. I wanted it too."

"Careful what you wish for," she said in a near whisper.

"Jonah came down last weekend to help clean up the property. The demolition crew came in and knocked down what was left of the beach house and carted away the debris. They'll start pouring the foundation for the new house, as soon as I get the permits signed."

"I'm glad, Mac. I hope you get everything you want. I really do."

"I know you do. And I hope that you get everything you want too. You've had a rough year. You made a few mistakes…"

"You mean like getting involved with a man with no morals who thought that gun running, racketeering, and murder were acceptable means of getting what he wanted? Or were you referring to the fact that I ran from the Witness Protection Program, called a friend, and put other people's lives in jeopardy? Or were you referring to the fact that I didn't tell Jonah what I was doing that allowed Kragen to track me, kill an innocent man, seriously injure you, and end up getting your house burned down and your car shot up?"

"You got involved with the wrong guy. It happens. When you found out what he was doing, you tried to do the right thing by going to the feds. People were trying to kill you, including one of the marshals right there in Jonah's office. Frankly, I think that's what has got him so upset. Knowing that it was one of his men giving information to Kragen that nearly got you killed. You're here blaming yourself and he's wherever he is blaming himself. You two could go a little easier on yourselves. You know?"

Carina enjoyed the time with Mac, but it was bittersweet. As much as she liked Mac, he was Jonah's friend, not hers.

And Jonah had broken her heart. Everything that had to do with him had to be put firmly in her past, she decided as she finished pouring the chocolate sauce over the miniature chocolate soufflés. She was serving them as dessert for the intimate Valentine's Day dinner for one of the richest men in the U.S. and his equally powerful wife, one of the President's cabinet members.

As her clients enjoyed the final course, Carina began the clean-up. The meal had been prepared and served in their home and she knew that they wanted her to leave quietly while they enjoyed the dessert.

Her two assistants had cleaned up the dishes from the previous courses and carted them out to the van. She turned off all of the appliances and gathered her remaining items before quietly letting herself out.

It had been a very long day and this was the fifth meal she had prepared. The first had been breakfast in bed for another wealthy client. The second had been a brunch for a club for seniors. Then she had prepared multiple romantic picnic basket lunches for a variety of clients who were either crazy enough to brave the unpredictable February weather in Washington, D.C. or who planned to lay out their picnic blankets indoors. Then she had served a high tea to a group of women who defied the fact that they were single with their annual Valentine's Day Tea. And finally, she had cooked and served this late supper.

Carina decided that all she wanted for Valentine's Day was a long soak in a tub followed by a foot massage. Unfortunately, her reality was a load of dirty dishes that needed to be placed in the industrial dishwasher back at her place of business and then maybe a glass of wine with Mr. Darcy at home.

When she finally dragged herself to the door of her townhouse, she was beyond tired. She thought she'd be lucky to make it to her couch, where she planned to fall down face first.

"You're on your own, Mr. Darcy," she mumbled softly as she put her key in the lock. Opening the door, she froze. She had a feeling that she couldn't put words to, but she knew that she wasn't alone. She was about to run until she saw Jonah step into the lighted foyer.

"What...what are you doing here?"

"I needed to talk to you, to apologize. I needed to ask you to give me, to give us, another chance."

She took a step into the foyer, far enough to close the door behind her. She felt numb and disconnected from her body. She wasn't sure if it was the fatigue or the shock that was causing the feeling. She glanced down when she felt Mr. Darcy ribbon through her legs, at least she was able to feel him, so she wasn't completely numb.

"You...you want to apologize to *me?*" Her voice rose on the last word.

"Yes, I do. I...damn!" He strode to her and pulled her into his arms, pressing her tightly against him. "God, Carina, I missed you," he declared roughly, his warm breath sending a few straggling locks of hair back to tickle her ear.

The sensation was soon lost as his hands traveled over her back, up her arms, and up until his fingers tangled in her hair. He pulled her head back and looked deep into her eyes.

"I love you." He claimed her lips.

Carina's head was spinning and all she could do was respond. When he finally let her up for air, she sucked in a breath and choked out, "I love you. I thought…I thought you didn't want me. I thought that you…"

"No! I was hurt and angry and guilty and all of those emotions were mixed up, but I always wanted you. I'll always want you." His fingers combed through her hair, stroked her cheek, her jaw. "I was an idiot. Can you ever forgive me? I was devastated when I found out that Davis had sold the information about where we were and I knew that you were right, that there was a mole right in my own office. Then… oh hell, it doesn't matter."

Carina squealed in surprise and locked her arms more tightly around his neck as he scooped her into his arms. She was carried into the living room.

"Oh my God," she gasped.

Candles, masses of them. Bouquets of long-stemmed roses seemed to grow from every surface, every corner.

"Jonah, what—"

He silenced her with a kiss, then set her down on the couch and then slid to one knee at her feet.

Carina's breath caught in her throat. She sat stiff, unable to move.

Jonah placed a hand softly on her knee. "I know that we need to clear the air and to discuss a lot of things, but I need to say that I love you. I've been in love with you for a long time, maybe from the first time I looked into your amazing eyes. I knew on Christmas Eve that you were the one I wanted to spend my life with. I'm sorry that I blamed you for calling Allyson."

"I…" Carina tried to interrupt, but he placed a finger to her lips to silence her.

"You could no more abandon Allyson than you could leave Mr. Darcy behind at the beach house. When you give your heart, it's forever. You're loyal and you're brave, and I hope to hell that you're forgiving. Please say that you'll forgive me for what I've put you through…for what I put us both through these last weeks."

"Yes, I forgive you. But do you really forgive me?"

"There's nothing to forgive."

Tears sprang to her eyes when he pulled out a small black box from his jacket pocket. He opened it to show her the diamond ring inside.

"Will you marry me? Will you make a family with me?"

"Yes, I'll marry you. I want to be your wife and one day to have kids with you, but you're all I need for now. I want to be your family," she told him as he placed the ring on her finger and rose to sit next to her on the couch.

It was the day after Valentine's Day before they did any more talking.

The End

About Lelani Dixon

Lelani Dixon was born in California, but moved every three years due to her father's naval career. She returned to California to attend college at U.C. Davis, where she earned a degree in Animal Science. Her career eventually led her to a job as a farm manager and animal care instructor working with adults with developmental and intellectual disabilities. She continues working in administration at the same agency and writes in her spare time.

About...

Zapstone New Voices

Zapstone Productions hopes to continue the New Voices program. Check our website and blog for announcements of upcoming anthologies.

Zapstone Productions LLC

Publishers of unique, quality voices in fiction
A small independent publisher headquartered in the lovely Tualatin Valley of Oregon. Visit **www.zapstone.com** for more information, sneak previews, and upcoming titles.

Please write with any comments, concerns, or questions.

To contact, please email:
publisher@zapstone.com

Visit
www.zapstone.com
for the latest releases, updates, sneak previews, and more!